Dragonfly

Jari Moate

ⓐ Tangent Books

This edition published 2018 by Tangent Books

Tangent Books
Unit 5.16 Paintworks
Bristol
BS4 3EH
0117 972 0645
www.tangentbooks.co.uk
www.jarimoate.com

ISBN 978-1-910089-79-8

Copyright Jari Moate. All rights reserved.
Publisher: Richard Jones (richard@tangentbooks.co.uk)
Cover Design: Joe Burt (joe@wildsparkdesign.co.uk)

Jari Moate has asserted his right under the Copyright, Designs and Patents Act of 1988 to be identified as the author of this work.

This book may not be reproduced or transmitted in any form or in any means without the prior written consent of the publisher, except by a reviewer who wishes to quote brief passages in connection with a review written in a newspaper or magazine or broadcast on television, radio or on the internet.

A CIP catalogue record for this book is available from the British Library.

Printed on paper from a sustainable source.

DRAGONFLY

Rakkaudella muistaen.
In loving memory of
Eija Anneli Moate
1941-2017.

Contents

Part 1: Love Ha!   07

Part 2: Elements of an Insurgency   14

Part 3: Victory Cocoa   37

Part 4: Higher Ground   105

Part 5: Asymmetric   174

Part 6: Heartland   271

Opening music:
Johnny Cash, *Hurt*

More music:
Pan Sonic, *Aaltopiiri* (album)
Rufus Wainwright, *Agnus Dei*
Massive Attack, *Protection; Teardrop*
Alt-J, *Left Hand Free*
Juhani Einovaara, *Cantus Arcticus, Op. 61*

Closing music:
The Edwin Hawkins Singers, *Oh Happy Day*

No soul worth saving ever comes through here.
- Dante, *Inferno*

Part 1: Love! Ha!

The investigators are on the stairs. They creak and whisper on the steps I jemmied, thinking I can't hear them.

I carefully put down my Airborne Stew – the supper we eat behind enemy lines – and I am not afraid, anymore, my love. What's done in the dark will be brought to the light, and I have run on, for a very long time.

So I wipe my mouth and pick up my phone, scroll to the file and start uploading, releasing my weapon, confession, my fire and soul.

I am not their soldier anymore, my love.

I was never just their soldier.

01: Day Zero Minus Six Months: 'Inch High'

I am shaking in a ditch in Syria. I have a loaded rifle in my arms and my eyeballs float on the stolen morphine I took just to stop her words from killing me, praying the sun won't rise today.

All I wanted was to be a good man. The sort who's hard to find, who brings his tools and fixes stuff and sleeps at night because tomorrow he'll do the right thing. Ha! Look at me now, all blood and tattoos and drugs and pain, facing this job with her words in my head. I'm a no-good man and no good comes of being near me.

Don't come home, she said. *Ever again.*

Sweat fills my helmet, my armour and gloves. My rifle won't hold still. But I have to get a grip, and do it fast, or bad things will happen here.

Two Section are in the trench beside me: Privates Mawson, Okonkwo and Jones 270, Spooks the Sniper, Mohammed 13, Medic

Sands and Sapper 'Lucky' Jonas. Even Padre Blackwood and the kid Lieutenant are here because of me. I have to get them through this, so I tell them to stay down while I get up, slip, go again, hoist my weapon over the top and pull myself up with it.

Don't come home.

The land blurs. I breathe and fight it, shutting off her words by using my scope to scan the nearby mountains where sunrise has started colouring the tips and turning the sky to steel. I take my time to track the light as it bleeds across the rocks and soaks into a grill on a cliff that I remember suddenly is a monastery, looking to my drugged mind like a knight's visor, lost and battered, gazing back at our war in the plain. But her words keep coming, again and again, punching me in the gut. And I deserve it all. Whatever comes. I'll pay the price.

So I lower my scope until it sharpens. There! The compound where the hostages are held, in a village gathered from a field of rocks that the enemy has packed with guns and madmen and spiked with a flag as black as any slaughtered crow.

Don't come home.

I grind my weapon into my shoulder. Two Section are waiting for my report. People safe in British beds need me to act. Even the locals want it. But I'm so fragged and exhausted. So sick to my stomach. I regret it all. Everything I am. I drift off and see the green hills I knew as a kid, the places I ran when the shit hit the fan…

Don't come.

I check my weapon for the fiftieth time and my brain slithers on painkiller. Two Section want answers but her dealer, the toe-rag she met because of me is on my sofa, drinking my beer, shoving his junk up her nose.

A missile unzips the dawn.

Home.

It thwacks the village. Thunder rolls and my earpiece chatters with the first big hit of the day, while a drone, high above, gives eyes to a laptop in Wiltshire where The Brass watch our progress from the safety of strip lights and apple trees.

-We'll take the fight to the enemy, I told Two Section last night.

-We'll kill bad men in there, maybe even some from the UK, and when we've extracted the hostages, the airstrike will kill even more. We are Advisors. Cut-Price Special Forces. British Ghosts. Deniable. And we are here to bring you justice!

Two Section cheered.

But I regret it all.

Tuk-tuk go the guns in the hills – the Peshmerga thumping chunks out of the village from an overwatch position. *Tat-tat* go the small-arms, answering back. Ha! No one overwatched my mess at home. They left that disaster to me.

Don't.

So morphine is my only friend. Last night the Padre caught me stealing autojabs. Yes, me, a thirty-something Royal Marine Sergeant who's supposed to be a guiding light to the lads and lasses and their kid Lieutenant. He wanted to know what the hell was up, so I let him have it.

Perfect love casts out all fear, he said, as if it would help. He gave me chocolate that I threw away and a poem on my phone he called 2SAM22 because he knew I read those Army poets, you know, the Wilfred Owens and ones from Afghan, but his eyes were cold:

All fear.

Okay. So maybe he stopped me doing something stupid, just for a moment. But the drugs do work, except now I can't get their voices out of my head.

Perfect love.

Sweat pours into my kit like an alcoholic's panic and I gaze at this country that wants me dead and I'm thinking okay, I'll stand up and let fifty AK's turn my way and the problem will be solved. Me.

The problem. I will be solved.

But Two Section need me. Alive. They haven't screwed it up yet or sat here watching missiles, hating what's behind me more than what's in front.

Love.

A contact by the Shiites crackles into life on the far side of the village. I get a hairline on it and beyond that, the monastery, held by a handful of Kurds with the last surviving monks and orphans of those who were murdered down here.

Perfect.

I have a Bergen packed with sixty pounds of rage on my back and an SA80-A2 in my hands. I have a pound in my pocket to remind me who I am. I narrow my gaze. This is the moment. A hit like no other. No booze, no coke, no E, no brown, no sex can get you this. It all makes sense when it's lit up by death and the firefight.

I need to shut off the Padre's words. Okay, his intel brought us here, confirmed by locals, and it's my chance to make a difference, maybe even disobey. But if I lose my focus now, I'm browner or my unit gets whacked, and no help will come for us.

Fear.

But I need a drink. Real drink. Cold Stella with a Jaeger bomb. Or maybe just the bomb. A line of coke. I slow my breathing... In... Out... Intel and consolation. What a combo. I rise on morphine and scan the village. All attention's on the Pesh and Shiites. Nothing moves on our side of Habiballah. We'll grab the hostages and be back at the RV by oh-eight-hundred, brewing up while the locals tear each other to bits. I speak into my mouth-mic:

-Eyes on me... Attack at state red... Five-four. Three-two...

I sprint from the ditch.

Perfect love drives--

Wrath erupts from the ground and punches me in the chest.

The world spins.

....

I'm watching vapour trails in the sky... A grain of sand blows across my shades... Tinnitus... It's taken a bomb to make me stop... *colder*... I see Kats, red-eyed and yelling at our last disaster, and me yelling back that it was her I wanted, not the skag we were doing in epic amounts. Love! Ha! Love is a place you guard with your life, skin-thin and busted by the nearest needle. Love didn't make me good. It made me drag her down.

I watch Mum smelling of booze while kissing my knee when I was nine, her little soldier, been in the wars, not like the other kids on the estate by the green hills, spitting and fighting: "Reading all them books. You'll be a knight in armour, one day." "Then I'll rescue you first, Mum." I see my Army photo on her wall, Catterick rigid. Then fire in the desert. Girls in clubs. Doors kicked in. Basra. I see the skulls of men we turned to charcoal and the first kiss with Kats on the night I can't remember ending because when we touch, I feel dead lips. I wash it off with more alcohol. Sex. Armoured assault. Legs in the air. Heads in ditches. Iron boxes. Tour after tour. Tattoos of beasts and regimental markings. Ketamine. My skin gets inked with swirls and warnings. Kats doesn't hear me. I tell her how a farmer brings me his boy in a wheelbarrow and I pay him for his loss with a fistful of dollars. I reach under the sheet and she shrieks: A kid? With you, P.? No way! Then she has the abortion and my heart explodes. Now I'm here, on my back, and she's there, on hers. I'm an old dog who's killed too many others and I'm on my way to hell.

Perfect love casts out all...

Peace! I hope, not beautiful missiles. It's only thing that scares me: 'peace', stuck on a rat-wheel of sex and money, never full, never finished. See, when we've done all this filthy work, done all this killing and suppressing, what then? Go shopping? Get drunk? Get debt? Ha! The Brass said I'm the best man for this job: urban insertion,

speed, surprise and violence of action, breaking new officers in. But I can't do this on empty. Not now. There's a shadow growing in me.
Home.
I'm shaking at the memory of all I've touched and broken.
And the sun hits me in the face like an oven.
I twitch my fingers and toes, check tongue's not bitten off, hear the buzz on the radio now and the lads in the ditch yelling: -Psycho!
I haven't paid the price. I will go back to work. I will break into that compound and extract the hostages before ISIS can behead the male on You Tube and sell the female for sex. He's a poet, a jihadi praising their holy war but he wants out, according to the Padre, and we've come a long way to find him and rescue his girl. Instead of a bullet in his head, today, we'll fly him to Qatar where they'll fix him up, with his fiancé, and he'll recite his ceasefires on the Arabic platforms. Thousands will listen to this not-dead Sunni poet, according to the Padre's crazy plan: *Perfect love...?* Soft power.
Gimme one more chance and I promise...
Bullets crack and whip so I go firm, crawling on my buckle, desperate for cover to shoot from but there's only this field of rocks and the enemy angling their AK's and I'm pork unless we get them first, so I drag my rifle up but it's jammed. I won't even die like a soldier. I'll go out like a sick dog, begging.
Home.
I scrape the gravel toward my face, screaming for suppressing fire but the dirt only comes up to my chin so I push my eyelids into it, don't care if they hear me on the radio now, old Psycho losing his grip. I wanna go to places I've lost. I want this mouthful of Syrian grit to be my sweetest household bricks... Come on...!
I see him, then. Death with his orange-juice beard, black turban and verses, kit on his shoulder, striding this way. He knows me and I know him. I want to be toy-soldier small and hide inside my gravel house, put a lamp on that pebble, a telly and a sofa there. I'll ask Kats

over and we'll drink and make love on the sand, eat pizza, shut the world out. I take the pound coin out of my pocket and shove it into the earth, like a vow, a sign of what I'm leaving behind. But Death has other plans and a howl shoots out of me, praying for a whole empire of dirt, not a wall that's inch high when Death comes, teeth snapping.

 -Don't cry, mate, he says. -It's nothing personal. Just business. As usual.

 And flames rip across the back of my head: -Home…! Jesus..!

 All the hurt. I regret it all.

Part 2: Elements of an Insurgency

Here's a ghazal that I keep on my phone. Listen:

May Allah the Merciful
rid us of invaders,
grant gardens beneath which rivers flow,
planted with grains that swell in their casements
and roots that drink deep on the knee-joints and hips
of the sons of Britain
that the Hidden One fixed in his sleep.

These are my field notes, scribbled when I find a quiet corner and a torch. If you're reading them, it means They got me, and you're my judge and jury. Or it means I'm vapour. Or maybe we're winning, after all. But know this:
    Everything I was, and everything I am, I always looked for new life to come.
    So join us, if you understand me.
    And together we can save the world.
    Or we can go back to business as usual, as empty as when we came here.
    It's nothing personal.
    But those are the options.
    Am I crystal?
    Am I..?

02: Day Zero: 'Assessment'

I'm kneeling by a streetlight in England, sweating with a Bergen on my back while my breath pumps out in orange clouds, facing a wall that soars into the night and marches away on either side. I'm not sure how long I've been here or if I'm dead or alive. It's like I've been running forever.

This is my country, but something's wrong. It feels thirsty and trampled, defeated and lost. I spot a few kids Trick-or-Treating while the population shelter in their terraced houses. I can see them through their curtains, self-medicating, waiting for Halloween on their screens.

This wall is vast, with broken windows starting eight feet up. I reach out to touch it, and it reacts. It actually moves. I snatch my hand back as the brickwork ripples, supple and lithe like a beast. A noise begins somewhere inside it, low like the wind across a bottle, growing to a sigh that rises to a howl of agony...

Then silence.

Freaked, I jump away and collapse into an alley back across the street where weeds and trash provide good cover and from where I can assess my target.

Derelict. Historic. And very, very weird. That's the technical word for it.

I ease my Bergen off, aching all over, open a can of Lightning and drink it in three swallows. The sourness cuts me, and I want another one.

I've got everything I own here: two hundred in cash and a Bergen packed with alcohol and emergencies. No missus, no kids, no work, no home – just a head filled with horrors and chances, so any mission will do right now, as long as it keeps the fear locked down, the one that says: peace, brother, you're a mistake and can't be fixed.

I see one window that doesn't move, and I reckon it could be reached. Getting up there's going to hurt, though, with all the injury and running that's rotted my soul, but this is it. Loyalty. A second chance. Maybe I'll pay the price this time.

All I know is that my future is in there.

I push adrenalin through my fatigue and make a move, forcing my legs to sprint between parked cars and pools of orange light until I slam into the wall and press my face against it, smelling the dampness in the bricks.

I reach for the sill. Bird shit and grit drop into my eyes but I grab the concrete, climb up and nearly lose my balance when I come face to face with a skull that shows its teeth at me, but it's just my reflection glaring back in knives of glass that'll slice a vein clean open. I look like the Defeated. But I'm not. I'm still here, still fighting, and this time, disobeying.

A breeze blows out like the breath of a tomb, crunching in my mouth as I try to make an assessment, when headlights appear along the wall to my right. I drop to the pavement and duck back into the alley as the vehicle arrives, sounding like the cab my dad used to drive, before he left us. I risk a look.

The van halts and a security guard gets out, goes to the sill and runs a finger along it. I know that action. I'm not going back, no matter what. I will not re-join the Defeated.

A second door opens and a dog barks inside. I look away and think of weapons to tackle it but both doors slam and the animal is muffled, the engine ticks and headlights slide across the bricks as the van moves on.

Now or never. I balance the Bergen on my shoulders and stride to the wall, place the pack down, step on it, reach the window, wriggle my fingers into the frame and it opens easily, meaning I'm not the first.

I get down and tip the pack through, hear it thud on the other side, grab the sill and start heaving.

I'm risking everything on a voice I thought was dead, to break into a building that screams in pain. But my options have narrowed to zero.

The van stops.

The guards and their dog start pelting toward me.

I pull myself up, so shattered, now.

03: Day Zero Minus Three: 'Unrest'

Scroll back three nights and I'm in a tent in central London when the phone goes. I've been roughing it after running from Army hospital to Kats' place, where I lost my grip because I found her with her new man, the guy I brought into our life.

Listen. I've known the greatest high a man can get, the one that comes from taking the fight to the enemy, hitting the asshole who's blown your lads to bits, pure and uncut, in your guts and in your senses. How do I come down from that? How do I kill an ISIS butcher one day and stand in a queue at Tesco's the next? You tell me. The Army Way is to drink – 'decompression' – and boy, Kats could 'decompress'. So look. I ain't no TV hero. I'm the other one. I'm a streak of sinew and madness held together by tattoos and alcohol. But I still need hope. A chance of being admired, even if it's Rizla-thin, even if it's by the wrong person. It keeps me focussed in the field and I can work harder and kill harder if I know a sweet kiss is waiting for me when I get back home. But the kiss gets colder if I see the enemy in every face, and the mess gets all over the floors and walls, and peace makes everything echo, so I need a high, and the drugs get harder and harder, and that's how Kats and me became poison to each other. I was too fragged to know when to stop, with no plan and no overwatch – all the ingredients for a royal shit-storm – then she made my world shatter. She got rid of our kid. The one who could've made us normal, or mean something. How can I fix that? How can I fix any of this now..?

I keep a few pictures on my phone: good times on the London Eye and dark ones of our feet in ashtrays because we strayed, yes we did, but we always found each other in the end, in the smoke and alcohol.

Until she did that. And told me not to come home.

A silent phone is what I deserve. For what I led her into.

So the Army tried calling me a few times, but they'd slam me back in the mental ward because of what I might say, and anyway listen: hurt a man, live with it. But pump him full of drugs so he spills his guts and he will love you and keep quiet after. It cuts the cost in blood and treasure, in these defeated times, to sack twenty thousand squaddies but make them feel good before they claim damages or top themselves. With me, The Brass see their own black hearts in what we did in the field, and I've signed papers that will put me in jail for what I'm going to say. That's the risk they took. That's why I tore out the tubes and made a break for it, to Kats' – despite her text – and she screams at me, says they're getting out of London and heading west once they've "got sorted". Makes me sick to the stomach. Things get broken and I leave him with a little souvenir... Don't come home. I should've listened.

I remember the streets next, and drinking, and ketamine, and waking up in doorways with blood on my clothes, cleaning up at hostels, reading books and thinking: "I don't need this" but starting all over again because hell is sweet, even when it's eating you up.

And nice British people sleep in their beds.

I saw the Protests on a hostel TV. I'm not fooled – 'The News' is Their story – but the next day I'm stood in front of a cathedral with a brew from the vicar, this tent-city all around me and Protestors saying it's real, this time: workers, soldiers, hippies, migrants, anyone who can't afford to live while the fat cats are back in business. Many good lads died for this 'way of life', and this is what we get: go shopping. The enemy must think they've won. The Protestors knew it and threw a party because only a tyrant would break up a party, especially one that's on Facebook and Twitter – it would show them up for who they are.

So I lay there in my tent hoping something would crop up, hearing the Protests, trying to get some shut-eye, fighting off the pictures in my head. A lot of people get them, not just troops on the run and it doesn't mean we're the Defeated. What we do about it does, and Lightning helps, when peace comes crashing down.

A phone call put an end to that.

The call of a dead man.

I shove the empty cans aside and stare at a number that makes no sense. No-one makes calls these days. Update your status, fool!

I hit the button and a voice says words only I would understand.

Panic starts. Am I that drunk or stupid? I thought I'd switched the damn thing off.

It breathes, like one of those broadcasts that orbit the Earth long after they're made – impossible, but I've seen things that defy the odds.

-Darling God, it gasps.

And whoosh! I'm upright, head in the canvas, fire in my chest.

There's no code-word between the quick and the dead, nothing in the manual for this. The deceased is protecting himself but quoting a name I never thought I'd hear outside of a court martial.

-Hidden One... I croak in reply.

There's coughing on the other end and my head spins.

I do not call him by name. Operational safety takes precedence. He on the other hand never saw the need. He stood outside of it and he put us all at risk.

-Marine P, he says, breaking up, -...pen...

I pat my pockets, find a biro and stab my thigh like an autojab. I need to know that I'm not dreaming.

The dead voice gives me coordinates, so I guess he's had time to study a map since he was killed. 'Killed'? I saw him engulfed in flames! I wedge the phone against my ear and write the numbers on my arm, pressing into my skin to get some wakey-wakey pain, using the blank space below the tattoos of beasts and regimental marks that swirl up my body under the shirt line.

The voice breathes: -Three.

And the line is cut.

I lie back, chest tight. All my kit is ready in the Bergen: first-aid, clothes, rations, headtorch, a multi-tool that was a present from her, a bomb-proof Nokia, a poncho, stolen GPS, twenty cans of Lightning and a memory stick with encrypted folders on it called Confidential this and Herrick that, plus 2SAM22 on a smart phone. I open it, and read again a warrior's poem, an ancient one that unlocks everything I once thought impossible, and the only thing I fear.

With you, I can scale a wall... With you, I can bend a bow of bronze...

I reach for a drink.

By 0700 hours, vehicles are thick on the road outside. I study the alpha-numerics on my skin, evidence of a call that should not have happened, pull on dry socks and boots, and unzip the tent.

The place is like a festival the morning after. Flabby balloons, pallets in a path, armchairs and builders' materials, all gone a wartime khaki, and above it all the cathedral crouches, hackles raised, pointing at the sky, tapering to a cock and lightning rod.

-Stevieee... growls a guy in a Guy Fawkes mask, using the name I've given.

-Troy... I reply, using his.

He dumps cans into sacks labelled 'Recycling'.

-Mate, I say. -It breaks my heart.

It's the only truth I can tell them: that my heart is broken.

-When the Protests go down, Fam, he says in urban patter, -I'm goin' for the squats, innit. Some nice fat houses on a hill, feel me?

He's right. The State will end this unrest with quarantine and jabs, so I copy the numbers from my skin into my field notes, because I have a choice now, and it feels like oxygen.

I've seen defeat, and it's here. They know I carry death with me and when I say it breaks my heart, I mean it. I'm only running tactically, seeking the elements of an insurgency. My weapon is my story and I need to follow it.

04: Day Zero Minus One: 'The Importance of Time'

The Police form up with that look of the Defeated obeying orders because their kids are trapped in schools and their balls are gripped in mortgages. They're just doing their job. I know.

And so will I, if I can find out what it is.

So I pull on a poncho, slice the back of my tent open and exit with the Bergen against my chest, staying low, moving away.

I cross the road between commuters with cappuccinos shaking their heads because a Protest's about to make them late. It's a bad location, all symbolics and no dominance of the ground; hearts and minds based on victim status when hearts and minds are late for the office. So the Cops march in, banging shields and crushing tents, breaking the circle of hands linking hippies, trade unionists, anarchists, Muslim leaders, army vets, the unemployed, the vicar, making arrests in the muck.

I spot Troy with a phone, videoing – most people are, like shooting, for civvies – and a Copper points a helmet-camera back at him in a Mexican stand-off, pixels drawn, until a TV crew brings in the big guns...

I disengage down Ave Maria Lane to Creed Lane, and at Pilgrim, I turn to see if I'm being followed but Coppers in full gear don't favour running. Even their bird, chugging above us, is only filming.

I move on to Black Friars, with images flashing. The war has come home. And everything about it is lost already.

I cross the Thames with the crowds, descend to the river and throw up behind a pillar, needing a drink and a piss, and once my mouth is swilled with Lightning, one thing is crystal – there's no turning back.

I study the GPS I squirreled from standard issue and the numbers show a location in the city of Bristol. The RV is obscured, but it gives me an aim.

I swap my coat and head to Temple, change clothes on the Tube before jumping off at Paddington, backpack on my chest and an I-♥-London cap on my head, spend cash on a ticket and by 1100 hours I'm in a shirt-and-collar, reading the Metro, smelling of anarchy but pulling through London, heading west.

The capital, the countryside, the towns that follow, all seems drained, held up by hoardings advertising ways to ignore the Defeat. Passengers consume whatever offers R&R, and only a kid seems okay, talking in a stream of questions like: Do snails have bums? while her mum reads a magazine with the in-between time that the Defeated hate weighing on her face. I do that trick where your thumb comes apart, to amuse the kid, but the mother looks at me like I'm a paedo so I stare out of the window, keep shallow breaths, fight off nightmares and focus on planning.

When the train pulls into Bristol beside an eyeless crate of a building, I'm ready. Coat slung over my Bergen, I use the thickest part of the crowd, letting its hunger be my cover.

There's a car-free path from the station to the target – a godsend, so I take it, sticking to the verges, avoiding eye contact with the lycra'd cyclists and earphoned walkers, noting CCTV and tower blocks – measures that I've taught my covert teams for years.

The Defeat is here. It's a despair that makes people reach for anything that might stop it. Call it 'guilt', call it 'hunger', adverts along the track promise help, in ways that'll only make it worse. I see faces lost in fever for more stuff, even on kids, and people frantic to be elsewhere, terrified they'll not consume enough.

After two miles of houses, the land drops away to allotments and signs of remedy – crops that remain free, safe to eat. Tabbing a mile further on, though, the damage intensifies with an estate of new homes standing empty where the population have been driven out or too few are left to occupy them, all in weeds and plastic, with wonky fences, windows with factory stickers in them, signs of the illness that's overrun the country I've woken up in. Further along is an area scarred by trenches and abandoned material, an off-road vehicle sitting motionless beyond a house with fading banners and a flag, limp on a pole. Placards show blondies gone blue in the daylight, smiling around barbecues and swing-ball. This is a mistake. This is a place with dead eyes. Exhaustion crashes over me.

But the far end of the estate is blocked by an older building. A huge, silent mass of Victorian redbrick that rises twenty storeys high to a stack of roofs that stagger off into a horizon of their own making. Glass, brick, tile, concrete extensions, industrial shanties, ironwork, funnels, arched windows parading across every wall, smashed or blocked up, fuzzy with weeds, this is nothing like the crate at the railway station; the place pulsates. Each time I look, it moves away or butts forward, like there's too much junk for the eye to see. Defeat itself radiates from it, like a ground zero of guilt and apathy, penetrating England, me, Kats, and her dealer, all of us.

But the GPS says this is it.

I fight off the sensation of faces in windows, guns on roofs, of kids on bikes with the wrong colour kites. The Defeat is invading my guts and wanting me to leave, go to a warm hostel, not into that compound that won't stand still.

Perfect love casts out all... Sod it.

Every tattoo on my skin crawls like it wants to get inside there. I can't go back, I have to step forward.

I spend the hour before nightfall walking, notebook in hand. I write down gaps in fences, rubbish in drifts, slopes of shrubs, fly tipping, broken tarmac with hatching for parking, corroded skips and railings balanced on warning signs. I could fill my book and never get my head around this place. It blends with the streets then muscles out into fresh air, each block hiding another one half a click away. And for every chunk I survey, the only sign of life is the wind flapping a tin sheet here, fluttering a vent there, slapping a cable. As dusk falls, the monster sinks into the night, breathing through thousands of bits of glass that twinkle in the city lights with a violent magic that wants me to stare at it, like at a ruined, dictator's palace…

Now or never. I could stand here like a mental case or find the mission, so I tab through the streets, avoiding Trick-or-Treaters, seeing my breath in clouds and sweating until the target bursts into view and I collapse into an alley.

And a noise, a moan, swells from its openings, starts dripping down its walls, rising to a howl, screaming, trapped, left behind, crying for those it lost and the crazy who remain… then it stops.

Not an echo.

My breath is stuck.

Whatever the hell that was, my mission is in there.

05: Day Zero Minus Half: 'Melee'

We had dogs on the estate I grew up on. Angry mutts that gasped on leashes, yappy critters in tartan trolleys, Labradors that out-of-breath painters and decorators huffed and puffed up the green hills around the estate.

Now I'm snorting cave-rot and glass in a broken window while a dog clatters into the bricks below, catching my boot. There's nothing left out here, nothing at all. Wherever I go, the same rage chases me.

So I tip myself into the building, falling deeper than I expected, smack onto my pack but before I can get my breath, a snake lunges at me from the darkness. I dive aside in panic but it curls onto the wall. Jungles of pythons and warriors writhe in a patch of reflected streetlight. I laugh out loud. Graffiti. That's all it is! Beasts and leaves are scrawled all over the place, every inch covered in a mutiny. It's like I've fallen inside my own tattoos.

I crouch and let my eyes get used to things, listening. I'm in a corridor beneath the only window – blocked now by the silhouette of a female guard who coughs. I camouflage myself against the monsters, with my pack, when a violent yell, deep in the darkness, makes me freeze. The guard in the window swears and her dog goes crazy while in the murk, there's more shrieking, closer, then silence.

I step out, making the guard cry and nearly fall in, get across the corridor and tuck myself behind a pillar of brickwork jutting from the inner wall. The guard tries to pick me out with a torch so I signal with a finger on my lips and point to a figure taking shape down in the corridor to my right, its footsteps staggering this way. The guard shines her spotlight on it and it screams as if she's burnt it but keeps on coming until it dives past, panting hard. It's a guy in a business suit who trips up twenty metres further on and sprawls, groaning, unable to get up.

I consider helping – and getting some intel – but a siren and blue lights screech up to the window outside and the guard vanishes. I spot a recess to my left and I whisper to the guy on the floor: *Nothing personal*, duck into it and press my back against a second doorway so I can see, but stay out of sight.

A Copper's head appears in the window, framed by the blue behind him and he calls out, waving a spotlight. As my system crashes from the last Lightning fading, I think of handing myself in, of getting the hell out and escaping from custody later, so exhausted I am now, and I'm about to do it when there's a woman's cry in the direction that the runner came from, like the wail of despair this building made before. It repeats, closer, and the Copper's attention swings to it.

It's an approaching group of five or six, calling for help, waving torches, with hi-viz and construction helmets. I pull myself into cover as four breathless men and a woman arrive, she in a black jacket and beanie carrying a daypack. They clatter into each other and yell at the Copper to get them out of here. Now!

There's a bellow, deep in the building, and lights appear in the murk where these people came from – a dozen sparks or more down there, whooping and heading along the jungle walls, giving chase.

The construction guys try hoisting each other up to the window but it's too high. The men argue while the woman in black tells the Copper in a Bristol accent to find a ladder. But there's no time. The catcalls are loud and hungry with all the lust of a hunting pack, and there's no doubt that the construction guys are the target, screeching at the Copper that one of their pals has already been torn to bits. Three of the men panic and leg it past the business suit who's dragged himself onward a few yards. The last man urges the woman to run with him.

I make an assessment. Going deeper into the corridor won't help and if the pursuers land on them, I reckon these guys have had it. So I step out. The woman shrieks and her torch dazzles me. The approaching mob roars and glitters.

We have ten seconds.

There's no way these two can climb out without my help but that would leave one of us standing, and there's no time. So while the Copper shouts pointless instructions, I hiss at them all to follow me.

The woman blinds me again, so I swear and head to the alcove, kick the door in and take a position, holding it open.

The male hurtles off but the woman hesitates. I step out and grab her, my fingernails stinging as I pull her in, kill the torch in her hand, shut the door and hold her tight in the pitch black, hand over her mouth, bracing my back with the extra weight of my Bergen against the sealed entrance.

She screams into my fingers, squirming her daypack into my chest, pleasant and wrong as I squeeze, telling her to shut up and maybe we'll both make it.

The noise arrives, hooting and baying, taunting the Copper, smashing and shrieking outside our hiding place. It makes my skin prickle and the woman moan. Fingernails scrape the door, just an inch of board between my Bergen and the melee outside reaching fever pitch with the noise of eating, getting stoned, laughing, swearing, shouting "Trick or treat" until, in time, the scraping stops and the noise moves away. When it's died to an echo, I relax my grip.

The woman bursts out of my arms and faces me, torch on, wild as a trapped cat. I could drop her in one move and be out of here, but there's a code. No matter what some may say. Only assholes on crack or ten cans a day. And right now I'm sick of all that.

She stings my ear, swings away, then shrieks and backs into me. I saw it, too – a figure at a desk, watching us. She waves her torch and the ghost reappears, its face in tatters, eyes shut against her dazzle, smart phone on the desk, opening one eye, then the other, grey-blue under its straw-for-hair, more scars than I remember, the side of its face like sellotape.

Outside in the distance, sirens are approaching. Deep in the derelict building, a violin plays up and down. There's a massive peal of laughter and the place begins to howl.

And my ghost is thick with static when he says:

-Welcome to this Sanctuary... Marine P... Take shelter...

06: Day Zero: 'First Contact'

My head spins. I can't tell what's real. My phantom scratches the desktop, then points at my neck, at a wound only one man would know the cause of. I'm seeing Hajis, Tally, ISIS, dead lads, beheadings...

-It seems we have been... 'occupied', he says.

A ringtone blares with Beyoncé doing the song about all the single girls, and the woman attacks her pockets, blathering. I grab her torch and point it at her; she's in her thirties, lightly built, dressed in what I can see now is a biker's jacket.

I tell her to make the phone stop.

She gets her phone out and the screen bathes her face in blue. Care is etched into her forehead and her eyes have shadows but she's fine-featured – beautiful, actually. What a dumb thing to cross my mind...

She stops Beyoncé and asks the phone: -Are you all right..? as if someone else is in bigger trouble, and her accent is strong now. Stressed.

My ghost watches.

She adds: -Good-good and Mister Green is on the other line.

But she's a long, long way from being good, and 'Mister Green' will be her codeword for it. I flicker my fingers, c'mon, c'mon.

-I have a child, she clutches the handset. -Please...

Ancient begging that I've heard from those who thought it would make a difference.

My ghost has a sharp intake of breath and unscrews a bottle.

-Marine P, he gasps. -Let her make the call.

He's in pain when he lifts his arm to drink, and his fingers are claws. Pills go between his lips as the woman has a low argument on her phone, and not with a kid. I step forward but he grabs my sleeve, his hand gnarled and stiff, as real as she is, and she hangs up.

-Thank you, she stammers, stuffing the phone into her coat.

I need to focus. I need to know what I'm dealing with. I start with my ghost: -If you are what you look like, Padre James Blackwood, Chaplain to 42 Commando... I turn to her: -Who are you?

But she's transfixed – by him – like he's suddenly off the cover of Gracia or something so I ask her again, sharper.

-My name's Zoë Palmer, she says. -I'm a...

-Yes..?

I see a dozen faces including Kats when I study this woman hugging herself, keeping things hidden. I feel a shock of warmth and I wish she wasn't here. Perfect love. Good God. I need a drink.

-Who do you work for, "Zoë Palmer"? I say.

She blinks. -... I'm... just a surveyor... and I want to go home. Please?

-A surveyor..?

-Yes and I'm... lost... she coughs.

-Names... says my ghost, -get broken in here. And homes change.

I crash onto his desk, and the light flickers.

-Who are the freaks out there? And why're they in this madhouse..?

The two of them exchange glances.

-Squatters..? she murmurs. -Illegals? People who got lost...?

Lost...? I open the door. The Copper has left the window, no doubt to fetch reinforcements, while the blue light flashes. There's only the first runner, now lying ten yards away. He may know the way out – and he'll be needing treatment – so I slip out and approach him, crunching debris, to where a graffiti oak tree loaded with mythical birds arches over him. Half naked now, his limbs are bent at nasty angles and silvery sweets have burst from every orifice. He reeks of old booze, even to me, with a bottle of clear spirits smothered beneath him. His face bleeds into a puddle, eyeballs glazing. Crack. Smack. Fully Defeated. Across a golden splodge on his forehead, in marker pen, it says: *Trick or treat.*

I search his body, find nothing, and draw the bottle out from under him, aching for a taste. He shudders and vomit growls out of him. His limbs go into a violent shake, head drumming the concrete, then limp. I put a finger to his neck. Nothing. I check for other signs. Nada. I sigh and ditch the bottle and leave him, wiping my hands on my combats, nauseous, remembering others who've lain at my feet. It seems wherever I go, it's business as usual.

Back in the room with the desk, she looks up, wide-eyed.

I plant my feet down in defence. -What's going on?

She starts to tell me but Blackwood cuts her off.

-I told her you're a hero, P.

I tighten, take fetid breaths of air, pull a can of Lightning from my pack and spray it open as it travels to my lips. Gas belches into the space between us and I'm on the lawn again, shouting at the flats, defending myself. I know all about this.

-I told her you're here to save us, he says.

She's a statue.

I cough. -You what..?

There's a crackle in his lungs, and half a grin on his mangled face.

I wipe my mouth. This 'Chaplain', who should've been blown to pieces, is back with his words, trying to put more craziness in my head. I drain the can and toss it away, more grounded with fizz in my belly, and shrug myself into my kit. Is that why I'm here? To be his idiot? Re-live the bad old days..? But she mustn't stay; that much I do know.

-Let's get out of here, I tell her.

Blackwood pales. -Where to, Pilgrim..?

And he gives the torch to Zoë Palmer, who watches me like Kats did, back in the day, wondering what's next. It makes my stomach churn, but she looks to Blackwood, like he means something to her. -...James..?

I open the door and suck in a breath. Blue lights strobe the window and a uniform drops to the floor, calling for Zoë Palmer. It points a lamp at the body, then at us.

-Police! it yells. -Come out!

More Coppers appear at the window.

Electrified, I turn back and glare at this woman who makes me see my past, and this man I've walked through fire for... and I know it, they've set me up. I'll have to take my chances with the mob. At least it looks like they've got some alcohol. So I exit, striding away from the Copper shouting 'Stop!', past the dead guy, off in the direction that the builders ran.

Behind me, Blackwood's voice cries: -No!

I turn and he's thinner than I remember, lost inside an old Army greatcoat stripped of rank insignia, standing in the corridor with Zoë Palmer beside him. He rasps: -I mean it, Soldier. This way.

And a booming cry like a football crowd goes up behind me, in the direction I was heading, dropping ice down my collar, the mob approaching through a breach in the darkness and they're on a high, trick or treating. The Coppers back off, aiming torches over my shoulder as the corridor behind me erupts. I don't look. Zoë Palmer's hand flies to her mouth, telling me all I need to know. She edges toward the Coppers but they won't make it out in time as the riot bursts into our space. She grabs the Padre by the sleeve of his greatcoat, her features bright with horror and he pulls her back into the alcove. I tab toward them, the Copper's Taser missing my leg and I join Blackwood at a second entrance, this time covered with plastic strips and facing deeper into the building.

I cling to the alcove as the crowd thrash past waving torches and screens and hurling themselves on the first Copper, who's buried in cracks and yelps, while the ones in the window scream.

I turn to Blackwood but a shudder in my spine makes me look back. A man in a white suit is standing there, framed by the ruckus behind him, facing us, grinning with fang-white teeth, raising a finger.

My choice is made. I turn and see three things in front of me.

The entrance has a sign above it with a blond boy eating chocolate and smiling: Welcome to Victory Cocoa! while across the plastic strips, in red graffiti it says: Learn your lesson, ye who enter. And Zoë Palmer is standing there bright with hope and scared to death at the same time.

But it's my sleeve she grips as we enter the shadows together.

> **For just as fire**
> **Moves upward, as a form that's born to climb**
> **To where it most thrives, so, into desire**
> **The mind thus seized must enter.**
> - Dante, *Purgatorio*

Part 3: Victory Cocoa

07: Dark Zero: 'Foot Patrol'

I don't know how he navigates the darkness, since our torches have died. All I see is tinnitus, like looking at the back of my brain. Enemies lunge, even though they're not real. I trip on invisible crap and my pack unbalances me. All I can do is follow his wheeze, the scrape of his boot and the thud of something he keeps throwing into the blackness ahead. The mob's noise varies, close up, then in a vault, never shaken off, and Zoë Palmer digs her nails into my arm. The pain is good, it feels like action, and when I slip and crash onto something wet, she tugs my sleeve, telling Padre Blackwood: -Good, good, all good – as if I'm the prisoner, here.

We reach what feel like iron stairs that twist upward into silence, or down where the noise is stronger. He throws an object that clangs on a step, and begins to climb.

I'll whack him, as soon as we get some light. I'll find out what he told her when they were alone, because it sure as hell wasn't what he said it was.

-How come you didn't die? I call out.

No reply.

-God finally saved you, eh, Padre..?

His boots halt on the ironwork: -No, P. I don't know any god who would rescue me. None at all. And don't call me that, anymore.

And it puts a strange, sudden pain in my heart. I feel like a guy I saw by an Afghan road once with a girder sticking out of his chest, the surprise and disappointment on his face. That's me. I should be grinning. I have the weapon to hit this priest with. But I can't think of a reply, just the weight of my pack, this unexpected pain, and a fresh, raging thirst.

-I want to go home... repeats Zoë Palmer.

And I'm thinking yeah. Even a hostel. But the noise is growing – the mob calling up through the hole down which the stairwell dives.

Blackwood clangs upward, keeping a measured step, followed by Zoë Palmer, less controlled, the voices rising, and I accidentally brush the back of her leg with my hand. She squeals but my whole arm zings at her warmth. What a mess.

Blackwood halts. We have reached the top and with noises echoing below us, he scrapes a door open, revealing gloom, takes a rag and a stone from his pocket, making a cosh, slings it through and listens to it thud. When satisfied, he steps in to retrieve it and we follow.

Zoë Palmer gasps.

Ranks of lockers march down the left hand side of a vast hall. On the right, frosted windows print arches of moonlight onto the floor, which for as far as the eye can see is strewn with thousands of pieces of silver that glitter like stars, in a dense, disordered universe of twinkle-twinkle.

I pick one up. It's a sweet in a shiny wrapper, like those surrounding the body in the corridor. Light as a sparrow's egg, it smells of medicine and cocoa. For a moment, I'm a child at the store where if they were on the floor, you could take them – a Saturday perk for a kid off the estate. But I remember these from elsewhere, too. The Padre gave me one on the night he caught me injecting morphine against Kats and the war. I'd thrown that one away.

-Eat, he says. -These don't go out of date.

And because to chuck it away seems wrong here, I pocket it. Beside me, Zoë Palmer is quiet, but with a crinkle, she opens and eats one, sighing as she does so.

She gets up and approaches the vast row of lockers. I follow as she brushes each one with a finger as we go, reading the nameplates: Halley, Smith, Payne, Patel, Hapgood, Adams... There's no order to them, and Blackwood ignores them, slinging his cosh ahead like a comet, through shadow to moonlight, limping to wherever it lands, sweeping for IEDs across this milky way.

She stops. Her hand trembles. A noise escapes her throat.

"Palmer", says the nameplate.

I want to send Blackwood back to where his lunacy belongs – he's even stirring stuff up in this woman he's only just met. I'm embarrassed that I lost myself to the smell of these sweets.

-Hey..! I bellow. -Padre..?

Twenty metres off in the greyscale, his coat sweeps around him as he stoops to collect his marker. -Let's go, he says. -The people who did this are not that tidy...

-Blackwood!

He carries on, crushing stars beneath his boots while Zoë Palmer scrubs her eyes and unwraps a second sweet, pops it in, cheek bulging like a child fighting off tears. She zips her biker's jacket tight up under her chin, puts her head down and chases Blackwood.

I hoist my Bergen higher. I see IED's and a poet abducted for his verses. I feel a lover's hand slip out of mine while she bleeds to death in a sacred corner. I tread on chocolate. The only way is to move, and if you stop moving, to drink.

Blackwood pauses.

I put out a hand, maybe to finish him off but he pulls away and leans on the wall, sinking into blackness.

Zoë Palmer dives after him and I'm alone in never-ending sparkle. I should turn back. But I can't leave a woman to her fate, not again. I dragged her into this. I glance at the field of stars then follow her into complete, cramped darkness.

There's a knock on metal and a rod of light appears at Blackwood's feet. My fists get ready as bolts are drawn and light floods in from a blinding hallway.

-Two, says Blackwood, entering, one hand on the wall for balance. A wiry figure stands aside. Zoë Palmer goes next, then me, past the skinny guy, who shuts the plated door, sliding locks into place. There's a torn-up look about him, as my eyes normalise, just a teenager in a tracksuit and baseball cap, with a way of walking that I've seen many times before. Ahead, we enter a spacious, well-lit room where a woman in an oversized jumper and a London Paralympics cap sits at a table with an anglepoise lamp, sketching in a pad. Her face is full, but pale, like she's recovering from illness and she watches us in a way that feels like triage. I sense for other occupants down a further passageway, but get nothing.

There's three battered sofas and a table, four or five jars of those sweets, a kettle, cups, plates, plastic chairs, an unfinished mural of a jungle and a shelf of books with a spider plant. Blackwood flops onto a sofa, breathing heavily, and his eyes close. In this light I can see he needs a hospital. The teenager sways beside the woman, who scrapes her chair back. There's a swell in her belly and breasts.

-So, she says. -Shall I be mum?

07: Dark Zero Plus: 'Brew'

She peers out from under her Paralympics cap and it's obvious now: she's pregnant. The teenager swings when he walks and his trousers are hollow from the knees down.

-You lazy oik, she shoves him toward the kettle. -Get the brews on.

He grins, insignia tattooed on his neck.

-Rifles? I ask, but he reaches for powdered milk, ignoring me.

The woman stares at me. -You don't remember...?

Blackwood groans and the woman moves with sureness to prop him, take his pulse, examine his eyes.

-Good... she says, but he's blotchy and unfocussed, in pain.

Zoë Palmer by contrast to us, is healthy. She's taken off her beanie in a way that seems polite but she twists it in her hands while fiddling with her phone. Her dark hair is pulled back into a bun, with studs in her ears and her cheeks smeared with dirt. She has black nail varnish and a sports watch. Her biker jacket has a tailored fit with a slight pouchiness around her middle. She keeps her daypack on and goes to help with the mugs.

Blackwood is waxy. Air escapes from his teeth. Maybe I won't have to finish him off after all. Paralympics crouches beside him.

-I'm "P.", I tell her.

The Teenager drops cutlery.

Paralympics doesn't take her eyes off Blackwood, just points me to a corner where I shrug out of the Bergen and feel the ache in my neck and shoulders, freed from the weight they'll pick up again, soon enough.

I ask her: -So are you and the Padre… an item..?

The kettle lowers to a gargle.

-They call me Miss Morphine, she says. -And I'm nobody's item, Marine P. How's yours?

The floor tilts. I feel heat go round my neck. Corporal Sands "Miss Morphine" the Medic. She was there. And she knows about Kats. I thought chaplains were supposed to…

She puts a hand on his head. On instinct, I step in and pull up his sleeve, see the track marks and sigh. Zoë Palmer clatters a cup.

Miss Morphine elbows me aside. -It's the jabs…

It's torn him to pieces. When his lips part, it's a shadow of the grin I remember, where the burn scars let it. I feel a surge of pity, but I have to lock it down or it'll boil out of me too fast and pull everything else out with it, so I drag a can out of my Bergen, and open that, instead.

-That's quite a scar, she says, -on your neck… Sarge.

I shiver. I should tattoo over it but in compliance with the manual, all my beasts and letters swirl beneath my shirt-line. Besides, that scar is fresh, and I deserve it.

The Teenager sways, handing out supermarket sandwiches and I recognise him, now, so different out of context. "Work Experience" we called him, from here in Bristol, but he had his legs back then, and what was his real name..? He puts down a mug of tea near my hand, and I'm shaking. Everyone can see it. The liquid dances in muddy circles, under shellfire, so I leave it while the room rotates and it's an effort to scrape my fingers across my skull…

Mum always made the best cuppa – big, sugary teas that she brought to us bored kids sat on the wall of the large, mown garden we had on the council estate – my half-brothers, half-sister and me, since Dad ran off to London with his floozy, and we'd throw stones at gnomes until the neighbour came yelling and we'd dream of what we were gonna be. Firemen, boxers, singers. I was the spaceman. Good tea.

I can't touch it now. I need hooch, not memories, like the first time I met Blackwood. It was in Helmand... over tea. That day, our section had just cleared a Tally compound; hard, dirty work, without air support, so we sat down to catch our breath and make our brews. What does drop in from the sky is two, clean-cut officers: one from our battalion and one US Major. They stride off their Chinook fresh from Lashkar Gah – "Lash Vegas" to us – with creases in their combats and crosses on their lapels. Our platoon Lieutenant – a northern, public school lad a decade younger than me with a rugby obsession, called Walters – raises an eyebrow.

-The Padre's in from Vegas...

-Yup, I mutter, -with a Yank 'to meet the guys'...

The American shouts Howdy Doody at the lads who sprawl around, sweating and putting hex-stoves on to boil. We're in our armour due to risk of further contact, not least from their helo attracting attention, crowding into any shade we can.

-You Brits! he bawls, -My Gaahd, I love you guys!

He smiles like he's up for election, his face a net of lines sliced-in from years of meet-and-greet, built of pure T-bone from somewhere with rolling wheat, and he pumps our hands like we're the ones who've just arrived.

-You Brits are crazy..! Y'all set down in the middle of a firefight and light your biddy fires and your kettle goes on..! Man you love your tea and I love y'all!

He lets go of Lieutenant Walters. The Padre beside him, all cheekbones, cricket and hair like straw is grinning like a blue-eyed agent bringing us a buyer.

-It's *like* tea, he tells the Yank, -but it's not. It's Brew. It's a bit of home wherever we go.

Walters: -A Brew with nine sugars turns a foxhole into a Commando's living room. Sir.

The American blinks. -All riiight..! The Englishmen builds his castle wherever he goes... The ol' Empire keeps stewin', huh...?

-We only got rid of what's lost its flavour. Sah, I say. I can't help myself.

The Yank howls with laughter like we're in Wyoming. -Coz all we got to show for kickin' out you Redcoats is our Tootsie Rolls...! I love you guys!

Walters glares at me through barely-repressed tears: -Sergeant haven't you got a child or something you should be snatching from certain death?

It's Signalman Finchie who saves the day with two extra mugs. His battledress is shredded by thorns and blood has mixed with muck around his face. The tea jitters in his hands. He's done some nasty business today.

I gesture to the Major, who accepts it like fine wine. -With pleasure, "mite".

Signalman Finchie twitches at the Dick Van Dyke, but I give him a stern look. The thing about Finchie, is, he was tea mad – had a massive collection – and he even liked the green bathwater full of twigs that the locals served up at shuras.

-Here's to hearts and minds, declares Lieutenant Walters. -Or shock and awe if Finchie's brewed it.

The Major sips, and the sun rises in his face. -Gahddamn, he bawls. -that's fiiine..! You're gonna have t' teach me this!

The Padre catches my eye.

So they do a round of spiritual succour: handing out chocolates to the lads – Tootsie Rolls and Yorkie bars branded "Not for civvies". When they've gone, Lieutenant Walters cries with laughter.

A week later, Finchie's in a WMIK when it hits an IED. There's a firefight but the enemy melts away and when we scrape his body out of the wreck, his head is missing. It's in a ditch twenty yards away. The lads are in a state. I've puked, but I can't let them know how bad it is, how I see wraiths every day and Tally behind every tree – nor what I'll do to the shits who butchered my Signalman or to the politicos and fat cats who sent us to this hell-hole to look after their interests in the first place. I'm sick of it but I'm a pro. I hold it down and look for angles.

Two days later, the chaplains sweep in again from Lash. The Yank brings a box of Lipton's, some stoves and mess tins, puts them on to boil, in silence. The lads watch, cleaning their weapons, waiting for him to get it wrong, but he gets it right, even the tinned milk and massive sugars. He serves it up in china cups from a casket with his initials on it. Beside him, the British Padre watches us.

The American stands and raises his Brew:

-Here's to home, he says. -And Signalman Finch who got there first, is all.

Lieutenant Walters breaks down. The British Padre stands aside.

And that's when I knew I'd never drink tea again. I hope to God Finchie's on a cloud somewhere, where none of it matters, with his kettle and his Tetley and his PG Tips, his Typhoo, Miles, his Yorkshire and Supermarket Own Brand, Darjeeling, Assam, Earl Grey, Fair Trade, Welsh Brew and his Finest sodding Afghan Chai. Twigs and all.

A week later, the British Padre contacts me. Says he's gutted about Finchie. Says he wants to go on patrol with 'the guys'.

Well, that's not in the manual, I say, and I'm only the platoon Sarge.

But I do a little background, and it turns out he's got a degree in Arabic – not a massive use in Afghan, but still – and he's known for completing his Commando physical. So in some ways he's earned his beret, and he's blogged about it and that makes me wonder.

-There's a shura next week, I tell him the next time he calls. -You could discuss paradise with the village imam.

He ignores my tone. -You'll let me know?

I need to be crystal. My lads come first. They are mine, and no-one can take that pain away.

-I'll think about it.

-Exactly, he says. -We need to think again about this whole war, Sergeant P.

So Blackwood had my attention.

09: Dark Zero Plus More: 'Safe Haven'

Now when I see him, all mashed up, I wonder what's left in that head of his. He was ready for something new, back then, but neither of us saw what it was, and when it came, it took the form of a shitstorm in Syria.

So I leave the brew and everything it means while Zoë Palmer watches Blackwood like there's something she, too, wants from him.

But there's no time to analyse - there's a rattle at the main door.

Miss Morphine jumps and Work Experience falls off the sofa, thumbs still playing a DS, but he gets his pins beneath him and swings down the hallway.

I withdraw into a corner. Zoe Palmer copies me. There's knocks and bolts removed; muffled words and five people in sports gear and combats stride into the room with plastic bags. I pull myself deeper into shade, and prise open my multi-tool.

A British Jamaican heaves his cargo onto the table. -Bare vex out there, fam. Feds all over…

I recognise him, and shudder.

The second guy is angular and pockmarked with a black moustache, and he sees me and drops his bags, cursing in Arabic.

The Jamaican eyeballs Zoë Palmer, Blackwood, then me, and sucks his teeth: -…Psycho…

Sapper "Lucky" Jonas.

He's frizzed out his hair and put on timber. Last time I saw him, he was a nervy streak of muscle barely able to hold a rifle, shivering in forty degrees of heat until our kid Lieutenant had the balls to threaten him. Nothing else moved him.

Humza Mohammed, aka Mo 13, on the other hand, was all kahunas: an atheist Marxist lecturer in agriculture at a Mosul college, he'd attacked a rogue Iraqi checkpoint with his bare hands for touching his kid sister, nearly got himself killed. He came to us for a Terp's job, and collected death threats like Top Trumps while his country tore itself apart even before ISIS. I've no bad word for him.

I clock the others. Luke 'Spooks', my sniper who killed more men in a month than most soldiers do in a war, and from so far off that those standing next to his victims never heard the shot. He'd lost it and popped some renegade greens, against the Rules of Engagement. With him is a male, civvie contractor, plus a female crap-hat – a community liaison called Filey who'd always been film-crew liaison, to me.

I turn to Blackwood. What. A frikking. Surprise.

They regard me with hostility and even Zoë Palmer inches to the Padre.

That hurts.

Mo 13 barks sarcastically and Lucky Jonas steps into my face, his chin jutting, eyes yellow, his breath clotted and shitty, and I'm ready for this to get messy, but Blackwood tells them to cool it, in a voice like broken gears, and to my surprise they do, to brews, sandwiches, sweets from the jars and that sugary, medicinal smell.

I turn away from Blackwood.

He says I should try one. -It's a syrup of herbs and spices. All natural.

-So is deadly nightshade, I say, but they're calmer now, laughing even.

Zoë Palmer unwraps one and pops it in, which warms me unexpectedly. I push those useless feelings away and she blows fumes.

So Blackwood has held off this pack of wolves. I rip open a can of

Lightning while he knocks back pills all the colours of the rainbow, coughs and calls the room to pay attention, like survivors in a post-apocalyptic movie. They settle.

I sense a ritual about to begin…

-We're safe in here, he says.

A drop of water hits the floor, followed by two more from the ceiling. Work Experience shunts a bucket with his Nikes. Droplets thunk into the plastic.

-Raining again, says Blackwood. -Somewhere.

There's a couple of chuckles at how deep we are, how far from the weather. Mo 13 watches Miss Morphine; Lucky Jonas watches me, and when Miss Morphine gazes at Padre Blackwood, I know the word for this but I won't say; the pressure in my throat knows I miss it. Besides, they look Defeated. They consume as if it's their last chance. But it's not that. I watch Zoë Palmer nibble a sandwich, eyes down.

The light flickers.

-Shall we give the newcomers shelter..? says Blackwood.

Lucky Jonas sucks his teeth at me.

It's like were in an episode of the A-Team, with Blackwood getting the old platoon together, forming ex-army crazies into a maverick team… except that here, there ain't no good looking one and we're all fragged in the head.

-So what's the mission? I ask.

They regard me like a pillar of shit in a shit museum.

-"The mission"? frowns Blackwood. -Marine P, we're going to hide out here because there's nothing left in the outside world… So we take shelter.

-Shelter…?

-Yes, he says. -We're on our own.

There's a tense silence.

-Okay, he sighs. -I'll start: My name is James Blackwood and I was a Marine chaplain. I'm here because I can't live with that.

And he tells them how back in ancient times, if the "bible" can be believed, the Hebrews had cities of sanctuary that anyone accused of murder could run to, and be safe from feuds. They'd wait for their case to be heard.

-So we wait.

I wonder what he means but I remember the Protests and the empty houses, and the Defeat in people's faces when the only idea is to consume and breed more consumers. Business as usual – quiet and commuting, or raving like the mob.

-They ain't never gonna stop hunting us, says Spooks, -till they make us into, like, model citizens, yeah, till they make us build our own houses for a f'ckin' Army charity or put us in jail. I ain't got nothin' out there. Never gonna fit that, man...

A chair scrapes and the civvie agrees. He's been kicked out of house and home, redundant, nowhere to go.

Water thwacks the bucket, beginning to splash.

-So, croaks Blackwood, -there are people out there who say we did bad stuff. And they'd be right...

I think of the bolted door and the corridors beyond, the factory walls and its brick defences against the world. He's set up a safe house in a cave-system of dereliction – but it's crawling with gangs and that white suited guy. I have a bad feeling about this.

Zoë Palmer chews a black-varnished nail. On my estate, she'd've been chased until she had three kids by the age of eighteen. And a dealer. I glance away when she catches my eye.

-So we take shelter, shrugs Blackwood, -like in a temple.

Jonas murmurs but Blackwood says it's okay, the temple was a fortified building. It meant the accused were kept aside. 'Holy'.

-...if they could get past the guards, murmurs Mo 13 the Terp.

Blackwood bows: -The Christians took it and built their chapels, then bishops bought peace from emperors and it all became a whip in the hands of the powerful, so there was no refuge left for the poor sods who needed it. "God" did not care to keep the idea going.

Miss Morphine chips in: -But maybe it changes? It sounds like a red cross on a building... or a red crescent... She glances at Mo 13, who flushes, and mutters:

-Until some god-loving A-hole fires a rocket at it.

Blackwood agrees, but Jonas has a problem in his face.

-Hey, Blackwood says. -We're on our own, Jonas. Remember that.

The Sapper drops his gaze – they've had this argument before.

And I remember in Helmand before Blackwood's first shura, him standing there on Remembrance Day in our FOB with a wooden cross on sand-bags next to him and he's stopped mid-script, arms by his sides, robe white down to his knees, then brown with blood and the dust we're standing on. He's staring at a space in our platoon, supposed to be reciting words before we go out for the second time that day because this war's gone to hell and we need to hold the Tally off our trucks and defend the school we built – and at his feet is the blood-soaked stretcher we carried Lieutenant Walters' body back on – or what we could find of it – and Blackwood takes a minute, two minutes, three, and someone coughs, radio in the background, terps running, till the Base Commander has had enough of this chaplain starting to doubt – on this, the holiest day of a soldier's year. He dismisses us and gives Blackwood a piece of his mind while the Padre stands, hands rigid, with the stretcher that shouldn't have been shown. Walters had been gooning around with a rugby ball that morning. It was Jonas who found the guy's legs in a tree.

-So this time, says Blackwood, -we stay safe and we stay inside.

Jonas spits: -I got nothin' but troubles out there, fam. The rich is gettin' richer.

The Teenager rolls up his trousers and shows us his metal legs, with Nikes on the end like comedy golf clubs. -See me Oscars,

Sarge..? he says in his Bristol twang, stronger than Zoë Palmer's. -... Sarge..?

That's me. I'm to blame, that's what he means. He wanted to be a Police dog handler. Now his head's in pieces and his legs are Pistorius blades.

Spooks spins a knife in his fingers. -What about you, Psycho?

Jonas pipes up. -Yeah, come on, Psycho P..!

Names, names. -I went on holiday.

-Well you look like shit for it.

-It was nowhere sunny.

And Zoë Palmer's biting her lip. I wonder what she makes of this. She sleeps safe at night because of what we do, but no-one interrogates her about every mistake, every little dropped brick. Or maybe they do. She watches the Teenager cover his legs, Miss Morphine wiping her eyes, Mo 13 choking, saying that if he's sent back, the militias will kill him or his family whom he misses. Liaison Filey says her nightmares happen in the daytime now. So apart from Zoë Palmer, we all were there – even the civvie was driving a truck in the background. What must this lost surveyor think of us? What can she care?

I feel the rage, and the drink in my hand turns evil: -You all knew the risks. Why d'you losers join up in the first place, eh, Padre..?

He's picking his thoughts off the floor where they've smashed, while a weather system of memories crosses his half-face: -I lost someone special, he whispers, -in a car crash. She was everything to me, my first and last one. She was being driven home by the guy she'd spent the night with. He was drunk and hit a tree. He walked away. What can I say, P...? Helmand put meaning back in my life. What about you...?

My rage has nowhere to go. My self-pity doesn't belong with these guys, so I suck it up, and ask instead: -How long have you been here?

-Three months..?
Six weeks, say others.
Two.

I bang my Lightning on the floor making Zoë Palmer yelp, turning her into the centre of attention and she fires out nervy questions: -So how do you live? Do you have any money..? Benefits..? Food Banks..? Is there even a toilet..?

-Oh yes, says Miss Morphine brightly. -And you'll want showers, too, right?

Blackwood flares: -Guys! We'll turn this place around! We'll get water, heat, light, whatever: bathrooms, feather beds, duvets, a piano, a balcony, a garden, art – lots of art – and music...

-Chandeliers..? says the Medic, leaning against the half-finished mural, and I sense a familiar game.

-And a table that's polished every day, with fruit, and walls of books...

-And Wi-Fi... says Work Experience.

-Ahh but do you want to let the Outside in..?

-Xbox! he pleads.

-And big windows... the Medic cheers.

-But not to let the Outside in...!

-And sunsets..?

-Rooftop gardens.

-A swimming pool...!

-An' a kitchen, says Lucky Jonas, into a silence; his cooking was so bad we could've dropped it on the Tally: -For chicken, innit.

-Family quarters, says Mo 13, turning his cup slowly, and others agree. Family quarters. Kids.

And Zoë Palmer calls it, straight at Blackwood: -How're you going to pay for all that..? Plus squatting is illegal unless you...

She laughs nervously and back-tracks; she's offended him: -Ok, if I'm honest, there's times I could've used a "panic room"...

-Well, you're welcome here, says Blackwood, but she wasn't joking – the blood has left her face, even with her edgy smile, and he holds her gaze until it drops, then to me: -So why are you here..?

I'm blown backwards. What? Is he crazy? Of all the things I could say, while Zoë Palmer sits there close to tears: "Because you called", "Because I thought there was a mission", "Because it's cold outside"? I see my childhood on the green hills rising to meet the sky and me imagining what lay beyond... before I see Kats shrieking and the incandescent murder I became. I buried five lads in a day, once, and for what? I shot men in the head who deserved it. I poured death on civilians who didn't. I led Kats into something she couldn't get out of and the fuel, alcohol and ammo I've consumed is monumental. I am a man with much to fix. So sod this talk of hiding and panic rooms, the accused and all that: I see a man lying dead at my feet with his brains shot out – the peak of the universe, a human mind that knew loved ones, had pictures of them inside it – splashed on the road like weekend vomit when it could've been taught to go home to those it loved, before I broke it with my bullet. God. Dammit. Me. Him. All of us. To Hell.

I scour my skull, filled with blood and images, I deserve it all. Unless...

-Do we get a second chance, then, Padre..? Forgiveness and all that?

-What's done is done, he growls. -We hide.

-Until we pay the price?

He lowers his eyes.

-I'm cool with that, I tell the room.

But I am not cool with that. Not cool at all. I see ghosts and I know them all. I want to fix stuff. I want the ghosts to see me do it. Miss Morphine says Zoë Palmer should inspect their showers and sleeping quarters... My head spins. The lost surveyor's caught off-guard, too.

-I just want to go home, she pleads. -Can we do that?

And her word is the punchline. Home. I've destroyed so many. I smell like a burning car and the scar on my neck is livid. I kick my chair away and there's one thing I will fix, if there's no other mission: I will get this woman out of here. But first:

-What do you remember..? I turn to the Padre. -From Darling God..?

He stiffens. -A catastrophe, he murmurs, -that's all.

And I see it, now. The core of him has burnt away, destroyed by guilt. Well, he must be right, because looking at his red eyes now, the one thing that will bring me to tears more than alcohol or horror is the knowledge that something much, much bigger than us died at Darling God, if he rejects it. I plant a finger on his chest and quote:

-*With you I can bend a bow of bronze… With you I can scale a wall…*

-We did what we did, he sighs, -and we were alone.

-Then you've become ordinary. That is the catastrophe, "Padre".

10: Dark Zero Plus Lost Hours: 'Host Nation'

I have to get out of here. I have to find a hostel, face Defeat. This could've been something, this meeting of the dead, but his soul has gone. He, of all people! I needed him to believe in things for me, but he's lost in dreams of chandeliers. See, we squaddies keep it simple: fight for the guy on your right and the guy on your left. Motivate the soldier with that buddy-buddy crap and when he's told to 'pacify' an area, he doesn't think, he does it for his mates because the war aim is generals with jumpers for goalposts doing what the politicians and their business bosses want. It's their pantomime and we're the arse of its horse. So I need someone to stand outside of it all. I need someone to bring me loopholes for my badness and all the pointless crap. I know many guys who agree but they don't hope for it, beyond what their mums and WAGS think of them, but we need someone to be our attorney against the Big Man, our side-bet against being plain wrong and nasty. "Marine P is paid up, If-You're-There-God-Sir; he had six ounces of good in him to balance his sixty pounds of shit." Spiritual succour might only be the bottle of malt the Padre brings but he needs to bring it for a reason, because if not, then this really is just Call Of Duty and nothing fucking matters. If even the Padre who buries our dead doesn't believe in something higher, then what's the point? He's a clown doing tricks while time and death carry on. But we need more than a clown. I see it in the others, too. I'm just up front about it, like the man with the girder sticking out of his chest because he went first, surprised and sad, on display, moving his arms. That's me, if Blackwood won't stand up and be counted. But dammit. Seriously. Why should I care..?

Because if nothing else, this wreck was my friend. That's why I'm here, sweating in the arse of the horse. Buddy-buddy crap.

The guys make brews and share out sandwiches so I grab something with ham, to combat fatigue and frustration, and spot Zoë Palmer staring into Miss Morphine's sketchbook, although the Medic's not around. I go across to see. It's open at a page where the Medic's drawn a game of Tetris, with labels and arrows. I swallow hard and ask Zoë Palmer if she's okay.

-It's a map ... she brushes her fingers across the paper, -of the building.

I put down my food and lean closer. Most of it is blank and the perimeter is unfinished. On the left is a place marked 'Out' which could be the window I came through. She plants a finger on the centre. -This must be the room we're standing in...

I grab a pen and scrawl 'Yer be monsters'.

She chuckles and the sound goes through me. Behind us, the Medic coughs, reaches in and grabs her sketchbook, grips it over her bump and leaves. Zoë Palmer watches her, biting a nail.

-Tomorrow, I say. -I'll get you out and back with your kid.

She smiles weakly, turns to go to her room and I want to stop and hold her, but it's a delusion. I'd be told to eff off, and rightly.

I glance down the hallway to the main door and its bolts. Two nights ago, I had nothing but canvas between me and my troubles. I could do with the break. So I head to my billet – a windowless office with a camp bed – dump my Bergen and grab a shower from a watering can in a side room where the smell of soap is like fireworks. I towel myself and pull my clothes back on, put batteries into my head torch and listen. The only noise is Blackwood's gang talking in the staff room, so I go to my billet, jam the foot of my bed against the door, boots off, and stare at the wall while three cans of Lightning go down my gullet, hearing Zoë Palmer sobbing in the next room.

My thoughts drift into deserts and riots, a hollowness in my gut, morphing into Kats and other women, villagers, soldiers, children, and a man chased by fire who falls in a heap when it catches him. It'll fade in time. Just gimme more time and more Lightning until time catches up.

But a man needs more than just the crap that happens to him. I get up and piss into the empty cans with hands that won't warm up, wipe fingers on my combats and crash back onto the bed.

Now all I can see is Zoë Palmer, burning in the road, her body rising into the air with cash pouring out of her eyes, and cars and buses rising with her, separating out in the blast, the road lifting up in chunks.

I roll off the bed and take my torch to the staff room. It's deserted now, apart from the wreckage of dinner and Blackwood snoring on the couch, slack-faced, a blanket sliding off him, his feet like innocent peaks. I search his greatcoat, find a manila envelope stuffed with papers that make no sense: Embassy of Ghana and suchlike, and put them back. I run a finger along the bookshelf, seeing what I snag on. They must be his: Kierkegaard; Greene; Dahl; Jon McGregor; Dante - as if anyone reads it; an illegal copy of the *British Army Counter Insurgency Field Manual*; a *Lord of the Flies*; a crisp Koran and a Bible looking like a convoy's run over it. There's a history of the Quakers; an *Architects' & Builders' Price Book* and a wedge of Wilbur Smiths and Andy McNabs. I choose *Snow's Industry & Architecture* - a maroon hardback that weighs very little and I'm guessing it's 1940s.

I walk out, slipping it into my combat pocket.

I pause by Zoë Palmer's door - quiet now - and carry on down the passage to a door at the end. It's a cupboard with mops and the smell of detergent. I tap its walls, and the back one is hollow, with a latch, opening into a vault. I hop down into the space beyond, and crunch across to an iron door, firmly locked.

Closing everything behind me, I head back to my billet. I pull out the book, *Industry & Architecture*. There's a scrap of paper inside, torn from a child's diary by the look of it, describing eczema on a summer's day. I use it as a bookmark and carry on, while nightmares trawl by, getting up for a piss, losing myself in reading, trying to forget. The book describes houses with gardens for workers to grow food, has drawings of apples and factories with roads called Co-operation and Gratitude... and The Congress for Modern Architecture 1933... its opening page denouncing: Ignorance, Repetitiousness and Gravity... I drink and carry on. The closing chapters have dreams of machines, and elsewhere a Universal Christ.

I scrawl in my notebook, trying to remember days under trees reading adventures with sunlight on the pages... Oblivion comes, with scrapes and hoots in the walls, materials dragged and footsteps in the ceiling. There's laughter and the pish of smashing glass, and a hum that rises from the floor.

A shudder hits my bed.
-Salaam aleikum, Crusader!
I scramble. So this is how it begins.
But the face is Blackwood's.
-P, he says. -I'll be your psychopomp, your guide, and you can see for yourself.
Bloody words. I ache all over, every muscle.

My phone says 0800 hours and everything smells of toast and medicine. I splash cold water over my skull and go into the staff room, where Lucky Jonas is mashing eggs.

Zoë Palmer sits beside Miss Morphine and the Crap Hats. She clasps a mug of hot chocolate printed with a picture of the boy in a sailor suit who was in the poster above the entrance, with the slogan: Satisfaction… It's Victory Cocoa!

The place is so homely, it makes me unsettled. It's warm, with hot scram, and chatter. Miss Morphine goes to her corner, starts sketching. The Teenager gets his thumbs on a DS and Jonas sets up a speaker to run off his i-Pod. It's UK rap, but it'll do. They chat, planning what they'll "trade sweets for" – whatever that means – listing things to make the dream come true, before Blackwood stands and makes an announcement.

Apparently, today is Work Experience's eighteenth birthday. There's a low cheer, and a bunch of soldier-songs that the boy shrugs away.

Miss Morphine says she'll find cake, and Lucky Jonas promises chicken like Nando's. Spooks says there'll be fireworks. The Medic asks where he thinks he'll let them off..? The reply involves the Teenager's pants.

I watch the boy squirm. He was born in this city, as far as he ever let on, and joined up even younger than I did. He rarely said much. It seemed like he'd already been worked harder than the Army ever could, and known enough fights to pick up a gun and use it. But he always did a bit less than he was told and had to be reminded what came next. So we called the lad Work Experience. Pretty soon, we'd almost forgotten his proper name, and he wouldn't say. On a good day, he would talk about dogs – his only passion apart from X-Box. On a bad day, he would shut off and live inside video games full of murder and ghosts.

11: Day 1: 'Human Terrain'

In the hall of stars, the aroma takes me to the Mongol steppe where herbs in the grass crush under your boot, and horses produce sweet milk. I could let it drug me but Blackwood throws his marker forward and the gang moves on.

He's formed them into a patrol, heading away from the Sanctuary and they follow him without question, through inky spaces where torches show girders and rubble, crates, sheeting, and rags like collapsed skins. A clang of metal rings out and a breeze blows in, full of decay. I don't remember coming this way.

He veers into a room that's ruled by an oval table and a dozen, high-backed chairs, puts a lantern on it, and splits us into two groups. Sending the others onward in a direction they seem to know, he asks Zoë Palmer and me to wait here. I'm impatient to get to the window and get her out of here somehow. But as the main group head off with Sapper "Lucky" Jonas on point, Blackwood tosses his stone through a second door, where his torch shows cabinets bursting with files.

I'm ok to stay at the table with Zoë Palmer, I realise. Maybe I can find out who she is – better than losing her to the outside world without a second glance. So while Blackwood crumples papers next door, I take out two cans of Lighting, pish them open and slide one across to her.

I take a big pull on mine. She considers hers, picks it up like a glass of wine, sips it, then takes a thirsty glug. This is interesting. There's hidden stuff. She dabs at her phone uneasily, her face bathed in its glow.

-No network, she mutters.

Heat rises. Her phone will carry a tracker but I'm trusting all this brick and steel to block it. My heat isn't about that.

She wipes her mouth: -I hate war, Marine P. No offence. I prefer business.

I cough. Lightning makes things very straightforward.

I tell her to just call me "P", and a guy explodes on my left, making me twitch and grab her phone. She reacts, too late.

-Tell me something about you, I say. -After all, a good story forms the basis of all business. Right?

She watches nervously as I poke at the network settings, glances into the other room, turns to me and whispers: -James says you're here to save us.

I choke into my can.

-He told me you did it before - saved someone's life?

-I'm a criminal. A psycho. Stick to that.

-It was him, wasn't it…? Him you saved…

Fire licks across my skin and a boy lies in a wheelbarrow… Villagers… Haji… First guy I shot to my certain knowledge… She only knows what she sees on the News.

-What's that scar? she asks. -On your neck? It looks sore.

-It's from someone I didn't save…

So I take a risk. I'll give her a story, gain some trust and see if it draws some from her. I begin with how I come from a council estate she wouldn't want her own kid growing up on. Every day, we knew how small our world was and how it was always going to be that way. Nobody starved - it was bloated and poor at the same time - just petty. Petty crimes, petty reasons for big crimes, petty jobs and benefits, petty arguments flying out of control. There was a street with charity shops a mile away where rich people left good books behind. One day, I went and nicked one: it had an action cover like a film poster. Before I got home, I was reading it, and I went back for more. If the other kids found out, I'd be dead meat, for getting above myself. "Gay" would be their word for it. So I beat up other kids, got beaten up, burnt cars, did all that stuff so I could get respect and read in secret. But books don't put out fires and books don't stop crack-heads with knives. Teachers wanted me to stay in school for more tests when they caught me reading, so books don't set you free, either.

I take a breath.

There was good stuff, too, like a summer's evening with underage cider behind the garden wall or lying back on the green hills watching the clouds, but we lived small and no-one could afford to make it bigger except with TV or video games. Even going to Marbella was the same but hotter with more booze. So I jacked a car – Renault, dead easy – did handbrake turns in the school field and got expelled. I played pool with hippy social workers who figured out that if I was reading, I was doing their job for them, right?

-I guess. She glances at her phone, still under my hand.

I tell her how Day of the Jackal led to Catch 22, and a crazy one called In Parenthesis. No-one's ever heard of it, but it made me think of sacrifice for the first time. And from these I built myself an arsenal of words. The hippy-dippies panicked when I told them I wanted to join the Army, but it meant I'd get off the estate and I didn't need them caring how I did it. Maybe one day I'd come back and sort the place out. Rich folks who needed to know the truth would see how the poor live. Given time, and weapons, I'd sort them out, too. I was full of ideals. If the adventures in books went bad… well, I would do better. So at seventeen I walked into the Army careers office with a copy of War and Peace in my pack, I kid you not. They didn't know it. You do, now.

-He knows some of this, I say, -because on my phone is a warrior's poem he sent me in Afghan when my ex finished with me. It's ancient but those words hold firm. They do not tell you to fuck off and die. They tell you to scale a wall. They do not change their mind.

She closes her eyes.

-So do I sound like a hero..? Stealing from charity shops to learn the art of war?

She apologises. -But you did escape... You worked hard and did something about it..? You bettered yourself, in a way?

In a way...

She bites a nail, regrets it, and a tear wells up: -P, I have to get out of here. I miss my little boy... Can I have my phone..?

I swallow my feelings. I should examine her phone for pictures and work emails – verification of her life outside and an answer to a problem that worries me about her. But I don't want to make her feel worse, or she will clam up and I will be plain nasty again so I spin the phone back to her and she catches it, with a gasp of thanks.

-You knew this building was unsafe when you came here, I say. -What about your boy then?

She clasps her fists, wringing her fingers, checking her phone for answers, glancing at me, deciding something. Finally, she speaks.

-I didn't have a choice... she sighs. -I work short contracts for the developer who wants this place and... I grew up round here and I've known this building all my life, or I thought I did... But I'm stuck, P. I don't know what to do. I have this nightmare every night where I'm running from a cliff-edge but it's pulling me back, okay? I'm up to my eyes in debt. I don't have the power to look after my own life, even... But everything changes if I find a deal...

She wipes her eyes. -I hate this place, P. I was told to come in and map it but we got lost... it goes on forever and that mob is... animals... Then I found James because you pulled me into that room so I guess I owe you and he's-

-What? You don't owe me anything.

-...I have to go home to Tyler...

I drink and wait.

-He's seven. His dad's a shit. He's supposed to be looking after him but he's unemployed, acting like a caged animal…

Ah, I'm thinking, the "panic room"…

-Have you got kids? she asks.

And the question pours through me. I feel the ache like a knife-wound… But I also see Zoë Palmer's problem. Whoever the guy is, he frightens her.

A tear escapes her onto the table. -So this is how I live, she says, -like I'm waking up and finding I'm chained up, and I've got no choices, and I have to do whatever they tell me, even if it's stupid. With a kid, and a house. I have to pay my way, P, and if I don't he'll… you know…

I take a drink, and yes, I can imagine it. With a kid to fight for and come home to, I would've paid my way. I would've been calm for it. But it's gone, now, and that pain drives me under. Being a soldier was supposed to make me free. Being professional was supposed to make Zoë Palmer free.

-Why do you stick around with him?

She looks at her phone for answers.

-Why do any of us, she says, -keep doing things we regret..?

Blackwood is quiet in the other room.

She whispers in a Lightning-hushed conspiracy. -You know what? It's even worse if you can still have dreams. And this building still makes me dream… There's magic in it.

-Magic?

-Yeah. It could be flattened and some nice, tidy houses put up instead, with the older bits made into lofts? They'd sell for a bomb! If I can just find the deal… she glances into the other room.

Bomb…

She brightens. -People will recover.

She produces an envelope and peels out some twenties: -Prices

are coming up again. Here.
  I shake my head. -What for..?
  -For food, for whatever you're trying to do here. I signed for it...
  I stand, my weariness huge. -I'm not trying to do anything here.
  She sniffs. -But money gives you choices.
  I empty my can. This room needs a bin.
  She leans forward, tucks the money into my breast pocket, finger pressed on me, then she spreads her hands on the table, glowing: -P, she says, -I hope you find your forgiveness. Kids. And a home.
  I'm punched. Nobody says simple, kind stuff like this. Not to me. And make it sound like "goodbye, get lost".
  Blackwood is in the doorway.

  When we go, I leave the door ajar. This is where we spoke like two human beings, without fighting or promising. It feels wrong to shut it.

  We halt inside the plastic entrance. Beyond it, the corridor with the window is lit up like a football pitch. Police are scratching around. Crime scene. Voices. Radios. Amongst them is Zoë Palmer's pal, the one who ran away, pointing at the walls like a frightened boy. Others scramble to get out of the window, but none of them are making it. A detective is swearing about evidence but the Police won't go beyond their cordon.
  Zoë Palmer touches Blackwood's arm.
  -We'll hand you over, here... he says.
  She hisses. -Wait. I want to help you get what's yours.
  Blackwood winces.
  -Let me bring, she says, -a contract, a couple of guys and bigger equipment..?

She'll get the place surveyed with a team, she says. If we can bodyguard her, she can finish Kerry's sketchbook.

Blackwood shuffles.

-I have a budget, she says, giving me a glance. -I want to do this.

Blackwood shrugs: -What about your colleagues? And child? And what about the Others in here..?

She straightens her beanie: -I can take care of work and Tyler, she says. -If you'll be our guide, James. You can help my team avoid the Others. We can stay under everyone's radar, she nods at the Police.

She's not being straight with us, but I don't want her to walk away.

Blackwood watches a detective poke the dirt with a ballpoint pen.

-I tell you what, he says. -Come with your kit. Alone. We will be your team—

I laugh and the Cops yelp at the sound. Some try harder to leave.

Zoë Palmer twists her torch like a flannel, chewing her lip. There's a gap in what she and Blackwood are saying to each other.

-I can pay you three hundred a day, she says.

Blackwood's eyebrows soar.

-Okay four hundred.

He holds up a claw. -It's not about money.

-Five, she hisses. -In five days that'll be two and a half grand and you get a map. She brightens. -You can put it towards your Sanctuary...

A Copper has come to the edge of the cordon, peering into our darkness.

Blackwood rubs the side of his head and says, low: -You have my offer. Come alone. Swap phone numbers, he waves at us.

Zoë Palmer hesitates but swaps her number with me, getting ready to walk through the plastic.

She freezes.

The guy in the white suit and white teeth is there, wearing a white construction helmet, grinning at the Police with a mini-skirted girl beside him, also in a hard hat. His hand is on her backside and her hat is tipped back, showing a gold patch on her forehead. He whispers something and she giggles. A thug in black leather stands beside them, hands crossed over his balls.

-Shit-shit-shit, Zoë Palmer panics and slips in the grime. I pull her back on her feet while shushing her cry. She's shaking and wild-eyed. She needs to be moved, or she'll bust our cover so I hand her over to Blackwood to guide her back into the shadows where she won't be seen or heard, and she does not resist.

I check the situation. It's 11:50 hours on my phone, with her contacts on it, held in the palm of my hand. Hell of a way to get a girl's number.

But I'm still filthy, I'm still free. And I do not deserve it.

White Suit laughs at the Copper who jumped away from the sound of Zoë Palmer, and who's now moaning that they can't get out.

None of them can.

White Suit drops the girl, takes an aerosol from his inside pocket and sprays gold onto the Copper's forehead, making the policeman reel.

I see the window, and a streetlight outside, before it slides, the brickwork moving like scales over muscle as graffiti curls around the sill in pale green, spelling out:

Who dares to leave while still Alive?

-Blackwood, I murmur, retreating. -Nice touch, you freak...

12: Day 1 Plus: 'The Importance of Unit Strength'

Having put distance between us and the Police cordon, we enter a room where my lamp shows banks of washing machines covered in silt, their doors like port-holes to nowhere. We pull up some crates and sit down, heavily.

Zoë Palmer's in pieces, asking for another way out. I remember White Suit's teeth and it makes me want a gun.

-He's your boss, I tell her, -isn't he? The one who gives you no choice?

She sobs, like a roof collapsing after an explosion, telling me what I guessed from her, so I turn to Blackwood and spell out my question in sharp shots:

-So why exactly are we here in this, particular, outstanding, shithole, Padre?

And I remember Troy's "fat house on a posh hill". -You could've hidden out somewhere nice, for pity's sake.

He slumps, studies his fingers, then us both. It's as if we carry equal weight. Now I've been through fire and hell with him and whatever I think about the pretty woman sat next to me with stuff hidden out of reach, I've earnt the right to hear it first from him. Come on!

So when his words soak forward and the walls flex, I don't think I hear him. I hear Zoë Palmer gasp, though.

He repeats it for my sake: -I own it. This place.

I laugh, but Blackwood doesn't make many jokes. -You..?

-I think so...

-"Think so"..?

The walls pause in their movements and he reaches into his coat, draws out the manila I saw last night and tips its contents into his lap. It's scruffy papers, the stash of a madman, but Zoë Palmer grabs them, wipes her eyes angrily and reads.

He holds his head. -They came to me when I was in hospital …

The floor vibrates, and Zoë Palmer holds the top sheet up for me to see. It's 'Embassy of Ghana' like I saw in the night, and a bunch of words that say 'to whom', 'demise uncertain' and 'a room he will remember.'

Zoë Palmer lowers it and sighs: -The Title Deeds are missing. But otherwise, it says you are the owner. My God.

But it's not his deeds that are missing, it's his marbles. This is a crumpled guy in a crumpled building, holding a crumpled African scam.

-So call the Police and chuck everyone out, I say, getting up. -You coming, Zoë Palmer?

-Sell it! she says. -Look! I'll negotiate the deal, you'll be rich!

His face is brittle, shaking his head.

-Why not..?

-Because..! he bellows. -I don't know who I am, or what to do, or who I've been… He thumps a knee: -But I know this place!

She drops her daypack.

Blackwood raves: -It's got no beginning and no end, it doesn't even stand still… and… it's a beast..! It's our lives and our legacy..!

I tell him to calm down.

-But they can't touch me while I'm in here, P. You saw them! They're more scared than we are! So until I find out what's going on, we can shelter a few others in here with us and isn't that enough for you..?

No, it isn't. -How come it's yours but you're not sure?

Zoë Palmer's tears sparkle: -Finding those Deeds would prove it…

He scrubs his face. -There's a missing page. I kept one in a book at the Sanctuary and I have to find the other... Now the book's gone missing...

Crazy priest. It's that child's writing I saw. I kick my crate back and go to the doorway. Zoë Palmer follows. She's beautiful, and frantic: -What next?

I don't have an answer.

Blackwood shakes a fist: -But we've got Marine P, he declares. -And he's the best there is. He'll save us..!

I'm livid. I'm desperate for something but this isn't it. This nutcase who's lost his faith in God can do the deal with Zoë Palmer, for all I care. Her boss will stitch him up, but never mind, he'll get hard cash and can stop the dreaming. I'll do my bit and extract her to the outside. But that's it. Game over. Part of me is alive to this simple stuff: a woman needs my help, and no, she wouldn't touch me with a bargepole, so that keeps it even clearer. But the big, banging problem, the rat wheel that I'm on, is that my only choice is to suck it up and be Marine P., yet again, the Commando smacking metal into people's heads and protecting someone else's wealth and investments. Nothing changes.

Zoë Palmer lays her pack on the ground and draws out a pistol. I jump back as she plants a red, laser dot on the floor. She does the same at the walls and ceiling, past the washing machines. She takes out a tablet, swipes an icon, points the pistol at it, fires, and a 3D shape unfolds on the screen.

-This, she plants her feet, clearing her voice, -is mapping.

She's a geography teacher on acid, I'm thinking, before the screen glitches to a snapshot of a dark-haired boy looking out at us, holding a Transformer. In the background is a man in a track suit lifting a can of lager. Zoë Palmer scrubs the tablet blank, biting a lip because that was her soul we saw.

-So you can map anyway..? I murmur, making no other

acknowledgement.
 -I don't know, her voice cracks again, -But we can try, right?
 -We can use it to find our way out.
 -It won't let you out until you learn it first, says Blackwood.
-Victory Cocoa. That's what I've been trying to tell you.
 -Like the words you've been spraying on the walls…
 He shakes his head. -It's not me doing that, P.
 -Then who?
 -The building does it.
 -Then you are properly fragged, mate.
 Ignoring any graffiti that tells me what to do, I hoist my gear, itching to get out. But this time, Zoë Palmer clings to Blackwood. And as we walk, she targets the floors, walls and ceilings with ruby dots and halos, slicing the factory with her laser light, stopping now and again to check the tablet, seeing boxes grow on the screen.
 When all we know is where we've come from, even that can strengthen the unit…

13: Day 1 Plus Hours: 'Operating Within A Sovereign Nation'

The building puts my nerves on edge. Turmoil echoes down the corridors – violins, voices – and a growl in the structure. The mob could screech around the corner any moment, so Blackwood throws his marker quickly, picking up the pace until he finds a roller-shutter and rattles the gate up. Zoë Palmer fires a red dot as we squeeze beneath, and a howl bursts from the shadows inside, making Zoë Palmer shriek.

-You scaring us to death! cries a voice, and Mo 13 shuffles into view: -Why you not knock first..?

The patrol. They're here, laughing and swearing at Blackwood. In a store-room filled with cartons, on pallets stacked twenty foot high, there's Lucky Jonas, Work Experience, Miss Morphine, Spooks, the Crap Hats and the Civvie, filling carrier bags with silver sweets. It smells like they've been eating their fill, too. They climb down to meet Blackwood.

-What's this? I catch my breath. -Candyman the sequel..?

Jonas sucks his teeth, and I could plant a fist in his beardy mush. Blackwood sighs. -It's our currency. Our 'rent'.

-And here's me thinking we'd stay out of trouble, on a sugar-high sleepover...

Mo 13 ignores me and runs through a checklist of who's going where, with whom, in a buddy system of routes around the parts of the building they've come to know, taking sweets to places and people who'll swap them for the things they need. Jonas knows of a shop that backs into the factory; Spooks says he'll place his sweets and see what gets left in exchange.

-So you're trading with the mob..? I blink in disbelief but Blackwood appears not to hear me. Mo 13 rolls up the shutter and the gang creep into the corridor with their loads. Blackwood suddenly turns: -What choice do we have?

I need sleep, not a fight. It seems such a long way out, and colder outside anyway, with too much unfinished business. Zoë Palmer is rooted to the spot, too.

I do have her number. I do have that. I imagine her tucked up with a mug of cocoa…

I unhitch my kit and slide down to rest with my back against the wall. -So 'currency', Padre… and this love of money that you seem to have…

His eyes widen.

-I can't save you, I tell him, -you know that.

He's staring at the bricks above my head. I look up and see graffiti swirling, curling into teeth out of which come words: *Learn & I will open.*

My tattoos itch and burn.

-This will be a big night, Blackwood frowns. -For them. They've invested a lot.

14: Note A: 'Blood and Treasure'

Invested.

The word takes me to a day in Helmand in the shade of our FOB, watching the guys play cricket with the Kandaks, and the BBC burbling in my ear about riots in the UK while Jonas sacrificed a chicken. It was three weeks since we'd lost Walters and I couldn't get anything down in my notebook that made sense. I was desperate to straighten my head out with some facts, or a new angle. Maybe the News would help. A lieutenant sat on the dirt beside me and listened in. He'd joined up from the City, a trader called Fosse seeking thrills in Afghan instead of in banks. After the riots, the next News item was the Government issuing bonds. He sighed and said:

-Investment is enjoyment delayed...

He looked around to check no-one was listening, and added:

-The West is in Defeat, my friend.

I raised my eyebrows: -Come again..?

He frowned: -Where the West makes mistakes, Sergeant P, investors see market corrections and put their faith in predicted behaviours. It's a good time to buy.

-Buy? Buy what?

-Trust.

-Have you been on the poppy-juice?

He pulled a face. -The Government are saying "Your money is safe with us because we have taxpayers. Trust us: if they don't cough up, we jail them. If they riot, we crush them. If they're bombed, we kill the bombers."

-OK...

-All cash is built on Government trust. Whose face is on the notes anyway?
-Darwin..? I quipped.
-And what do they want from us?
-I dunno. What?
-Lives.
-Lives?
-Investments are the lives of working people gathered up and concentrated, packed for transport. Those lives should not go to waste, P. Not in my view.
-So what's a life worth, then? To the Government..?
-Say 2-3% return? On a good day? But the timeframe is for generations.

And while the BBC burbled, he drew in the sand, a diagram like a layer cake, showing investments building up, slab by slab, each one adding new percentages, with Government trust at the bottom.

He scraped away like that until chicken arrived – the bits that Lucky Jonas saved from his charcoal – and that night I wrote like a madman:

The Tale of Threat Equity.

Money is built in layers.

Layer One: The Government pacifies those who stand in its way. Invest and get 2% on Threat to Life, for a lifetime.

Two: Bricks and mortar, mortgages and rent. 'Mort-gage' is Death-grip. Most people are three paycheques from the street. That's 5% on Threat to Shelter, for long enough to raise a kid.

Three: Stocks and shares. Depends on firms and workers. Shares go up and down, jobs are lost. That's 8% return on Threat to Livelihood, for as long as a job.

Top Layer: Dragons. Angels. High growth. Hedge funds. Investing in entrepreneurs staying up all night, risking coronaries and divorces. No upper limit on Threat to Dreams, lasting until they stop having dreams.

And so underpinning all investment – your pensions, insurance, savings, mortgages – for all that shit you need a soldier, somewhere, to keep order and kill for you. Hopefully we kill more than we get killed. That's a soldier's unsecured risk.

Say hello to Threat Equity.

The dead, the wounded and the mad are its cost.

Stop paying, disobey, riot until the cops can't handle it, and who they gonna call to protect their investments..? Who comes for you next..?

We do.

We are your market correction.

On my next UK leave, I went into the basement of a tattoo shop, lay face down and told him to do me a dragonfly with its jaws on the base of my neck and its tail on my belt-line, wings across my shoulder-blades, in red, green and black. The pain of the needle was like release. The blood-loss was me changing, breaking out of my chrysalis, knowing something new, not knowing what it was going to be, or how many days I'd live once I got airborne with it.

15: The Hidden One, Phase 1: 'Shura'

Heading away from the sweet-store by torchlight, toward whatever 'big night' he's predicted, Blackwood throws pills into his mouth, crunching them as we walk. I toss empty Lightning cans into rooms where the gloom thickens like caves and Zoë Palmer's laser hits no back wall.

But it's not the dark, his pills, or his wounds that bother me most. It's this man I listened to, who I once came to life for, and went off-manual for, because he gave me hope. *Perfect love... A bow of bronze...* Something that wasn't business as usual. The idea wouldn't let me go. And now, he's dead in the eyes.

I grit my teeth. This bag of bones should be in hospital watching Cash In The Attic, not leading me and Zoë Palmer around this wreck. I feel the girder sticking out of my chest.

-What happened, "Padre"..? I squint. -To your soul and all that..?

He steadies himself where graffiti churns and he jabs his torch into my face like I'm the one who's nuts:

-My "soul", Marine P, didn't work out... You saw what happened.

-You mean the Poet's lover? She came back to life in your arms..! Humour me, Blackwood. Do it for all the faces. Tell me it was worth it..!

He scratches his cheek and blood surprises him on his nails.

I saw a different Blackwood in Helmand, a few weeks after Remembrance Day, when the sun blazed over a village we'd cleared of Tally and we waited to go in and join their shura.

A new guy, Lieutenant Bolson, had been flown in from the Welsh Guards to replace Fosse, who'd been transferred – sold on like a sub-prime. Anyway, Bolson went into the village first, looking nervy, 'salaamed' the old men under the trees and took his place. Our Afghan Terp went next, with his complicated Pashtun greetings, followed by me and the Padre to a sheltered spot by the walls, and a carpet that had seen generations. I laid my weapon down.

The elders had the wetness of age in their eyes, wearing dusty turbans and robes folded in from the fields. Younger men with pill-box caps crowded in behind them. Some were curious and others were watching for errors. One or two would be spies, 'Ten dollar Tally' – the wage they'd get for a day's killing, outstripping anything a farmer would make. Outside our men-only zone, Miss Morphine – who was also new to the unit – was holding a clinic in a nearby shelter. She'd report back any injuries that looked suspicious but it was only the women and children she'd see. Whoever any of us were, we were all just blips in the life of the mountains around us and the elders, at least, knew this. We ducked inside our bubble.

Bolson spread out packets of Peek Freen biscuits and sacks of gram flour, and the elders acknowledged them. Tea had been made by invisible women, and we sat in the odour of lamb fat and farmers' sweat, blowing across our cups and ignoring the heat crawling over us like spiders.

Their chief spoke first, and the Terp relayed a litany of what had been smashed – by whom, only Allah knew – houses, poppies, sons, sheep.

I spread out the map and Bolson outlined where we'd found IED's, clearing pathways for the farmers. Hearts and minds. Provincial reconstruction. Not a popular job with the lads, who'd established a perimeter, expecting attack any second while I watched for 'tells' amongst the committee, to see who reacted if Bolson's finger hovered over a spot on the map where Terry might set a trap. This was the game, and Bolson drew dollars from his combats and laid them out, note by note, as compensation for their losses.

Padre Blackwood was wedged between the imam and a younger guy who kept his counsel. They exchanged pleasantries via the Terp, while the rest of us studied the map's pinch points.

Certain voices in any group can silence the others with a whisper. The younger guy beside Blackwood was one of these. The shura went quiet when out of the blue, he started reciting a ghazal – a poem with Persian roots, apparently – in a low, poker-faced voice that grew and grew. The lyrics, relayed by our Terp, swerved from blasting the British in the nineteenth century, to peace in our times, and suddenly a verse made the elders shudder and the young men watch like Western kids staring at X Factor. His ghazal had called the Taliban into question.

He went quiet with a modest, downward gaze, announcing his pen-name: The Hidden One. There was a shift amongst the locals and my fingers twitched toward my rifle. The chief laughed, loud and forcibly, and offered up more tea, while the Terp whispered to Bolson and me how weird it was to have singing at a council meeting. Welsh Bolson told him with a smile that even in Swansea, singing in meetings was rare but maybe he could book the Hidden One, sometime.

The shura was over. We'd got as much as we were going to get, which was typically little, when the Padre took me aside. The poet, he said, was a foreign fighter, an Iraqi Sunni. Normally that was enough to detain him and we should have. But there was more. The Hidden One was a jihadi commander whose lyrics were the soundtracks to videos inviting others to join the murder. No wonder he got the locals' attention.

Blackwood then told me to calm down and listen. The Hidden One had asked for a girl to be made safe. I spat. Blackwood shook his head. Listen: not safe from us, safe from the jihadis. Could we do that? In return, The Hidden One could ease a few situations, bring peace to certain parts. In fact, said the Padre, it may be safe to say The Hidden One had enough influence and was sick enough of all the relentless death and was looking for a new way forward. He could convince a lot of jihadis to agree; especially the Ten Dollar guys and many foreign fighters who were having second thoughts. Okay, I said. So what's the intel? Where's this girl? Baghdad, he replied. Oh. Well that's just great. Let's just jump on a plane and go there, then. It was so stupid it was most likely a trap. I called the Pashtun Terp over, who shrugged: the Padre and poet had spoken Arabic. I slapped myself for forgetting this about Blackwood, but a plan formed in my mind; one I put to Bolson, that night.

I wanted more intel, beginning with more shuras. I wanted this poet to prove his worth to us. So for each shura, I flew the Padre in. He'd arrive with a bottle of scotch up his sleeve, which spiritual succour I shared with the lads – off-manual, you understand – and heard about his Cambridge past, his degree in languages and a hint that he was running away from bad news back home. I bent his ear about growing up on the estate with bully-boys and cut-price drugs, and how Kats was different, to begin with, and he fell silent. Each shura, though, The Hidden One was there, the Padre beside him with a new Terp who covertly knew Arabic while the Medic did her clinic and the rest of us played the game of maps.

Blackwood and the poet struck up a line of communication. They exchanged verses about nature and the mountains, even about love. When the Padre briefed me afterwards he would go soft about 'Abu' and how the girl in Baghdad secretly inspired his best-known works. I had to take Blackwood to task: let's not forget this 'poet' was a jihadi whose disciples had killed Finchie, Walters and others. His IED's were the ones Sapper "Lucky" Jonas defused every day – the nightmare job that gave him his nickname. This so-called poet's words simply attracted more psychopaths to their cause. I wanted top-level names, locations of IED's and bomb factories. But each shura ended with The Hidden One reciting classics, which the farmers respected, and ghazals which left them nervous, because they knew that MP3's of these new, unsettling verses would be in the markets of Kandahar next week, with people asking questions. It was time to act, and take the poet into custody.

At each shura, a kid had arrived on a moped, flying a kite. On the fifth occasion, he flew the wrong colour for comfort, and The Hidden One didn't show. Days later, The Hidden One's hymns appeared on new, Sunni extremist websites, remixed with even more slaughter than before; no mention of ceasefires.

He'd gone.

We'd missed our chance, if it was true, and I didn't see the Padre in Helmand again.

16: Dark 1, Midnight: 'Know Your Ground'

Blackwood stands in the entrance to a space that's filled with the noise of water, concentrating hard on whatever signal he gets until finally, we step into a void that takes my breath away. Zoë Palmer's jaw drops: -Oh... my... days.

We stand at the edge of a moonlit canyon, several storeys deep. It has a vast, glass roof above us. The Padre tosses a cosh onto a rusting balcony and we inch onto the rim of the chasm. Grey cliffs of brick turn to blood in my torchlight. Birds flutter below us. The bottom of the ravine is scored with railway tracks, and a wrought-iron bridge spans it, like an outsized Victorian city station. The roof is stained, with missing panes and scraps of night sky poking through. The sky!

Blackwood nudges us to a point where far below, the source of the noise is visible: water spewing from a pipe in the wall. It spreads into a waterfall and drops into a churning pool with tide marks and weeds, shrubs and bricks encrusted in minerals. A parrot could fly out any second.

Zoë Palmer fires her laser, in a trance.

Blackwood speaks like a tour guide over the hiss of water: -The people who built this factory, he says, -invented the first chocolate bar... and they paid for this hall with the first Easter egg...

It seems unlikely, in this place where nature muscles in, but patches of whitewash tell us what it once looked like. Clumps of guano sit on chopped-off cables like barnacles on giant anemones. Vegetation hangs over archways set into blood-soaked walls. The balcony we're on is worn so thin in places that the water glitters below, like a rope-bridge in a jungle. Blackwood takes out a handful of sweets and makes a pyramid on the ledge. I could lie down here, and sleep at last.

Zoë Palmer, however, is gunning structures, pointing out features of interest, such as ironwork curled into branches. Now, actual ferns pour from brickwork and surround soft pools spiked with metal. It's Chernobyl, or Eden, and I'm lost in it, like Zoë Palmer said: there's magic in this place. Even my Bergen feels less heavy. From a rusted beam, rock pigeons rise and melt into ledges high above, where words painted ten feet high in the silver light declare:

Victory Cocoa: Knowledge! Novelty! Lightness!

Maybe this ain't so bad, after all. Blackwood lets Zoë Palmer lead the way with her tablet. The spinning boxes on her screen bolt together as we find new halls and corners. There are rumbles in the distance, but the building seems to hold them off, and although the darkness brings me dead men rising in flames, insurgents and prisoners and lads scraped out of vehicles, I know it's only my cortex adjusting to its visual tinnitus. These hours become the best I've known in a long time, wandering through a warren of lost offices as the Surveyor blips the structure in a sort of calm. It starts to feel purposeful, while Blackwood tries every door we come across. I guess finding that second page is on his mind.

We rest in a spot where dawn filters in from roof lights over rampant shrubs and more pools. I share sandwiches from the Sanctuary with Zoë Palmer and she tells me of the scams contractors get up to, of her son Tyler, his football team and his craze for Transformers, until she chokes up, so I distract her with the antics the lads got up to like parading in drag or spiking an NCO's mess tin. I do not ask about the guy in the tablet photo. It would break the magic.

I wake up on the ledge where we've camped, wash painkillers down with Lightning and feel almost free, like on a yomp in the green hills I knew as a kid. When Zoë Palmer has rubbed the sleep out of her eyes and destroyed a pack of biscuits, I shrug into my Bergen and we walk again with Blackwood through glass-houses, in daylight sectors, laser-cutting our way through shadows, holding a railing in place for her as we cross a cavern, catching her as she drops from a ledge, avoiding unstable floors and opening doors for Blackwood to search, and it all feels... okay.

In time, noises and sightings of people from the mob increase. But they're like flies in a summer room, accumulating, to be dealt with later. I even offer to shake hands with Blackwood, who nods: -See? Sanctuary is working.

We pause at a bridge, taking in the view.

The scene is silent. My skin prickles. Before I can think, there's a slam and a moan, off to the right. I motion to the others and I drop to one knee, senses zipping, every pain suppressed. There's a louder clatter in the depths, like chains dragging, but the shadows give nothing away. Blackwood indicates a doorway on the other side, and we clang onto the bridge. Instinct makes me look back, spotting a face that blooms in an upper window. I push us forward and we stumble into a hall of pillars.

Fifty metres further on, a huddled group of figures turn toward us. I keep a grip on Zoë Palmer as I feel her panic. One of the figures calls to Blackwood, who howls in reply. Two more stand and confer. There's a dozen altogether.

I assess our options and query Blackwood.

He points at an exit, beyond the unit of mob. I pinch my eyes. We'll have to pass them. I push us forward.

The figures watch us approach and I remember the guy in the corridor. We mustn't look like victims. They are the Defeated, after all.

Some rise, others hunker, amongst them the lost construction workers in grubby hi-viz holding flames under teaspoons, sucking sweet smoke through tubes. I feel a pinch of appetite. Zoë Palmer sinks her grip into my forearm.

The biggest figure grunts: -Chew lookin' at?

Blackwood pauses as if he knows him, so I push the Padre and Zoë Palmer toward the exit and turn my torch on the grunter. Puffed in layers of coat, he curses, closing in, leering at the Surveyor. Eyes bloodshot and lost in pouches of yellow, he sniffs, tasting my presence. I step toward him. He falters. Zoë Palmer squeals a name at a shaven-headed business suit who rises, covered in sores, twitching a bottle. I'm delaying his fix, which makes him a problem. Shadows rise, pull him back, take his bottle, and bark.

They'll be the ones who come for us, once they've fed. We're insults to their fucking pride; I've seen it at corrupt checkpoints and outside hostels... I pull Zoë Palmer to the exit, fast, as an empty bottle shatters above us.

Blackwood takes us onto some stairs. I hurl a pair of bricks down them to make a clatter and we duck through a different door, closing it quietly. We hear the Defeated crashing onto the staircase and down, the crack-heads for fun and the lushers for dignity, while Blackwood limps past a fifty foot drop that I would've run straight into, and through a double door that opens onto a canyon.

We shudder to a halt.

Zoë Palmer stifles a cry.

On the broad floor of the hall below us, in a patch of light from a circle of lamps on tripods, a fat guy hovers in a dark business suit. A murmur fills the air, like an audience waiting.

Sweat trickles and my Bergen bites. Zoë Palmer struggles for breath. I need to think. I want Lightning but I cannot move, at risk of giving us away, and six new figures still in Halloween costumes enter the halogen, circling the businessman. But what stops my breath is the horde in the shadows, surrounding the light like poppies in a breeze, wavering, spread across the whole arena.

-This was an export hall once, mutters Blackwood. -Thousands of tins of hard cocoa went to British troops in the Boer War – brown sticks, like explosives... their families used the tins to store the photos of their dead...

I stare at him. Now? A chant takes shape in the air – the half-hidden horde getting up to speed. We need to stay in cover.

-...They bricked up the windows when it swallowed up the fields... Can you see..?

-...Blackwood...

The crowd sways, and a mist descends. Zoë Palmer backs into Blackwood.

-... they got rich on the Somme, too, when they sent out "waxy stuff, just a little tastier than a potato"...

His eyes flash and scars glow. The crowd bellows, making the Surveyor flinch and the building ripple in reply.

-And they got even richer in the Depression... Did you know? And on D-Day every soldier had a piece of this place in his pack. Can you believe that..? All that chocolate at the bottom of the sea and on the beaches...

The mob swells like a bladder and he seems barely to notice.

-Why're you telling us this? asks Zoë Palmer.

-Because the Owners were pacifists, very religious, he shrugs. -Maybe I like the betrayal... Those bricks over there are orange in the light, like toffee...

The dark-suited guy announces something. He reminds me of the "ethical" banker on the News who was done for fraud and drugs.

Blackwood turns away: -... I was the system's bitch, Zoë Palmer.

I put the self-same chocolate in men's mouths before they went out to kill. I did what was expected...

Zoë Palmer is getting pale. I need to calm Blackwood down.

-You did okay, mate, I hiss. -We were in Shitsville on roller skates and you did okay.

-For what?

-Put a lid on it, Blackwood.

I'm in a derelict heap, pursued by freaks who want my claret, with a civilian in my care, and this man I thought was dead who is about to go operationally blind on me. I need something better!

A roar goes up from the crowd, who press in, because the six have approached the banker and one of them has hit him, hard, with a rod. He drops to his knees. A second blow follows and he flails. It's becoming a Roman circus, a show that makes the crowd cheer with every punishment as the six rhythmically beat their victim so savagely that he's losing his shape.

The mob howls. I pull Zoë Palmer and Blackwood into an alcove, sit her down and slam him against the wall.

-Get us out of here, I tell him. -Get your head clear. Now.

-Will you help me? he stutters.

-I'll carry you both if I have to, but...

-No, I mean...

My stomach lurches and I grasp his shoulders. He's going to tell me the mission. I can feel it. I drop him, unhitch my pack, pull out a can and open it with no regard to the noise. My breath chuffs out in clouds.

-I want you to make it safe in here, he says.

The cavern booms. Grit trickles from above, the balconies heave and the building rolls like a tanker heading for a special peninsula of Hell.

Pay! Pay! Pay your way!

I sprawl to see, and blood spreads out from the banker's body and what cuts me most is the female shrieks of delight in the crowd. One of the six raises both arms, glorying, and I can see the whites of his smiling teeth.

We have witnessed a public execution. Across the walls, a shadow rises, a new shade, growing.

This is mission failure already, Padre.

And it's time to move.

17: Note B: 'Correspondence'

I found a letter in Blackwood's papers, after the events, addressed to The Times, July, 1914. It seems right to insert it here:

Sirs
I do consider it most carefully that the will of Universal Spirit - that is of Christ - is to forego the entry into war, however popularly welcomed. It is clear that all which Unifies the Human Spirit with Greater Spirit is cast aside when Men release the energies of murder. Even to take office in the uniform of the State is a form of drunkenness as manifest in khaki as it is in the pomp of Kings and Kaisers. It is therefore more Vanity than Honour, to uphold Vain treaties with use of marching men and fanfares. Thus the true enemy is revealed! Should the men of this country return in Vanity, having vanquished their chosen adversary, they might imagine they have attained a position in the World which for its credit is as passing as the noon, because in such and such a way one Nation did overwhelm another; until such time as the overwhelmed should rise again to restore their own Vanity. All wit and industry is thus employed, and machines primed once again, for men to parade in the cause of Pomp. For what is war but excellent Trade for the mongers of tobacco, hard drink, arms and usury, gaining profits to wage yet more Vanity. True industry and True profit choke on "honour" whilst debt and disease triumph. For these reasons alone, I count my enemies not Hun, nor Turk, nor Boer, nor Hindoo, nor Mahdi, but the Three upon whom I declare most desperate war are: Ignorance, Repetitiousness and Gravity.

Your servant
J F Snow esq., Prop., Victory Cocoa Ltd.

A handwritten scrawl at the bottom says it's quoted in the author's will, disinheriting Joseph Snow, Jnr, who enlisted in the next war, and that the words appear again in the preamble to J. F. Snow's *Industry & Architecture*, New York, 1948.
"These three are my mortal enemies:
Ignorance.
Repetitiousness.
Gravity."
I know that book.

18: Dark 1 Plus: 'Resources'

We withdraw through the building with extreme caution, through inky traps and sharper cold, taking our time with Zoë Palmer's tablet picking up the way we came. Without warning, a hundred yards away in the blackness, a piece of wall erupts into an oblong of light, illuminating a cluster of tables set for dinner. We drop to a huddle as five figures step through the light like astronauts onto the moon, a steamy glare behind them revealing the huge space we're in. Where they've come from is a busy, metallic kitchen, and deeper still, a restaurant.

-I know that place, Zoë Palmer sweeps her tablet. -We can get out!

She jumps up but the door slams shut, plunging us into blindness. A cry goes up in the shadows to our right. The newbies shriek. I reach out and get hold of Zoë Palmer by the scruff of her jacket, pull her down, slap her tablet shut and knock the torches from our hands just as a mob burst into the hall, flashing their lights. They veer toward the newcomers, whooping: *Pay! Pay! Pay for it now!*

Zoë Palmer resists but I drag her and Blackwood out of there, tripping, allowing one torch, limping down one passageway after another until a floor collapses into thunder in front of us and we're forced to skirt around its broken teeth like flies on its lips. But it gives Blackwood time to think, and from there, he gets us to the plastic entrance opposite the window.

No Po-Po and no White Suit.

I collect the crime scene tape – you never know – look up at the window, which has moved again so that no streetlight shows – and

Blackwood takes us into the office where the others are waiting like refugees, all except Spooks.

The room is groaning with groceries, lit by a flicker from the Teenager's DS in his hands. Lucky Jonas has his own bags under his chair, shivering:

-Where you been to, crackers?

He's putting on a face; something's disturbed him badly. He talks rapidly about the back of a shop he's traded with, as Zoë Palmer hunkers down, shuddering.

I take out my phone, shaken too. There's no network so I lean on the door, trying to think, trying to get the beaten man out of my head. Jonas gibbers on, covering up his frayed nerves. He's talking now about people he recognises in here – cousins, mates. People he didn't think were dead. Whatever that means.

Lucky Jonas. I used to talk him down from days on Barma, shaking like a leaf, getting him to tell me stuff from home like carnival with garden sheds full of peacock feathers and tissue paper stored up all year; things his Jamaican family did, like every female being in church on Sunday while every male above sixteen – if they could be found – was sleeping with a girl or dusting off their football boots, back in time for lunch cooked by the church-going women. He started burning Sunday chickens because his mum would come home in her flowery hats looking like the Lord hisself had brung down punishments and it took a bit of home-made brimstone off him if there was that cooking smell in the house – before the smoke alarm. I'm not surprised he saw people everywhere. We all do. I had to take him off Barma in the end because he was getting too angry; they called him 'Lucky' when he found secondary IEDs where others had just gone off. He turned bitter and got into punch-ups so I thought it would do him good to attack, for once. I put him in the front row of an assault unit where he could blow holes through walls. He still burnt chickens at the FOB but then his head fragged in a trench and he didn't attack when ordered. I tore a strip off him for that and he seemed okay, so two years later, I picked him for Darling God, in Syria. Since then I'm not surprised he'd want to kill me. Probably with a bar-mine, Sapper fashion.

A clatter in the corridor makes me jump. It's Spooks, sniggering, stinking of a full night's booze. -Yo!... She tol' you, yet, eh, Psycho..?

-What, you prick?

-Faces..! Everywhere..! And you can't get out..!

He laughs and staggers into a corner with, unbelievably, a bag of fireworks.

I'm fazed by my lack of kip, the labyrinth and these fools. This place, for all its magic, has taken a life, maybe two that I've seen so far, and if this is hell or a second chance, I will lead her out, no matter what.

-Happy birthday, I turn to the Teenager, ignoring Spooks. Come on. The lad should not have to do deal with all our shit.

-Where's that cake anyway? I announce. -I need a sugar rush!

Miss Morphine says: -Oh, yes. Good point.

19: Dark 1 Plus Hours: 'CasEvac!'

They get into the spirit, and the office becomes a scene of banter with the Teenager about his coming of age. He pesters Zoë Palmer, waving a bottle of pink fizz from his bag in her face, while she wants to go back to the restaurant. There's a part of me that doesn't want to lose her, but I promise to try again later. She groans as we move away from any exits and head for the Sanctuary, but I'm relieved to be putting the danger behind us and I joke about the damage Work Experience can do, now that he's legal. This feels good; it feels like the start of belonging...

We reach the hall of stars when a clang, dead ahead, stops everyone in their tracks. I advance to find the Sanctuary open and pouring with light and I'm angry for losing focus. I scout for weapons, see a strip of steel on the floor about five feet long, pick it up, fold it in half and grip the ends in my fist. I feel my face tighten.

I go back to the group with battle-sickness in my belly. Zoë Palmer looks clammy and thin as I shove a piece of wood into Blackwood's good hand. He puts an arm out to stop me leaving but I tell him to stay with her, Miss Morphine, the Crap Hats and Spooks, who's still hammered. Meanwhile, Lucky Jonas, Mo 13 and Work Experience have found sticks and bits of pipe. The past stands between us like a wall and my hatred of being the soldier again, my sadness that it follows me around like a stink, makes me hesitate, but Lucky Jonas gives me the nod, and the old familiar hit flows in my veins. I grab a string of bangers from Spooks, and the others take a squib each. Jonas has a lighter and together we inch toward the doorway. There's movement and grunting beyond. My adrenaline surges, the drug in my blood again. Yes!

I repeat the mantra: -Speed, surprise and violence of action, lads. On my say-so.

We light our fireworks. -At state red... Go.

I rush the door, spot yellow graffiti, glance inside, sense Jonas behind me, step into the passageway, rubbish everywhere – thumping, grunting. I stride into the middle room and six hoodies look up from a body they are beating on the floor. The fireworks burst from our hands, rainbows exploding over the intruders who scream as we penetrate, yelling with full intent. I swing my steel at the nearest one and contact with his head, chop him down like firewood until I see his blood, slam a boot in his chest, turn and ram my steel into the throat of a second one who has risen up, feel his cartilage pop within my wrist and I roar in exultation, slicing dirty metal into his nose so he staggers back, erupting with claret. Lucky Jonas thuds a length of pipe into another hoodie and the fireworks drive them into our attack. One of them's stupid enough to stand and fight me, fancying some ninja crap – a boot to his knee corrects his attitude with a crack and I rain steel onto his head as he falls, thinking how physically hard it is sometimes to kill a man, swallowing my nausea, wishing he hadn't stood against me and I fill the room with my rage at everything I have to be, thick with smoke, blood-iron, armpits and the fumes of Roman Candles. I yell again, from my stomach, while the Terp and Teenager thwack two remaining hoodies like cricket practice, out of the Sanctuary, bawling.

The intruders' victim crabs across the motionless bodies with trousers round his knees, whimpering. Lucky Jonas hits him, I don't know why. I bark at Mo 13 and the Teenager to check the back rooms, kicking the doors in, but they are empty so we drag the casualties into them and slam the doors. Work Experience jiggers, breathing hard. I steady my fists against my hips to hide my afterburn and tell him between my own breaths:

-Good job, mate... like smacking Mexican party donkeys... what d'you call 'em..?

But he just stares. Food is splashed around, furniture upside down. Miss Morphine's art is graffitied over and books are tossed, pot plants crushed, lamps broken. Sanctuary is trashed.

Lucky Jonas is inflamed with sweat. He straightens things up as quick as he can and I make a note never to rag him again about not fighting. It was another world, as we say, though it never is, and the vomit in my throat proves it, and insurgent faces in every corner...

-Cool, I say, my body shaking. -Well done guys.

The victim shivers. His face is sore but I've seen worse and I've seen this one before. From the protests. The one who filmed it.

Troy. Staring at me like a bad trip, blabbing: -This squat, though. It's on Twitter, bro, I swear down...

Spooks blearily leads the others in. Zoë Palmer hangs onto Blackwood and my soldier's brain finds a quip: -Shit for house prices...?

She doesn't blink. Work Experience finds his cake covered in pot plant earth, and Spooks waves at the smoke, snarling. -Happy birthday, Squirt.

Miss Morphine needs attention. Mo 13 puts an arm around her shoulder. I feel the pull, too, but my body is screaming as adrenalin burns off.

-She shouldn't be here, says Zoë Palmer, -not pregnant.

I agree.

I grab Troy by the scruff of his neck. -Talk.

-Freaks was after me innit. I ain't lyin', he pants: -They bust this place up, I swear.

Blackwood swallows medication, saying someone should put the kettle on.

I tell him not to bother, indicating Troy. -Position is compromised. There are hundreds of them out there, mad as hell, and they'll be back. Pack only what you can carry.

Zoë Palmer's eyes redden and I feel my anger rise again. I drain a can, toss it into the bucket and go to the corner where Troy cowers. Lucky Jonas pulls an armchair across so it hides us and he offers me a wet cloth, without a flicker.

I study the prisoner for a moment, the injured face and how this rag will go straight over it. Bloodshot. Clots. Bruises and swelling. Breath sour. His eyes roll, pupils coming down from acid. He's wearing a suit, ripped at the shoulders and filthy. On his forehead is a splodge, like a once-golden thumbprint.

I crouch and rummage in his pockets, finding London travel tickets, a condom, empty wraps, and a photo of him in sunnier days with two little girls in princess dresses. I shove the photo back. He tries to scuttle.

I quip to Jonas: -This place hasn't made this one look too healthy, has it, Corporal?

-No, he clicks back, satisfyingly. -Ain't no posh spa for the lady, Sarge.

Troy has a rawness. -I got cash... he slurs, fumbling his pockets. -Corporal, a brew?

Jonas turns away, knowing, and I show Troy the cloth: -So he's the good cop, muthafucker...

But Troy reaches past me, to Blackwood, who's breathing heavily and offering a sweet. -Hullo...?

I go to the toilet and throw up, trying to visualise the green hills and a stream with dragonflies, trying to catch them as a kid, each one slipping above my head, and Kats walks across my vision. I swallow a can to wash away my sickness.

The guys pick up their personal effects while Zoë Palmer sits with her bag on her lap, fists pressed into her temple so that a red mark stays there when she looks at me. She's a tree on a hill, after a storm.

I cough, a pain in my chest: -I'll get you out.

She sweeps invisible crap off her bag. -But...

I roll my neck. -But what?

It's the way she looks at Blackwood slumped at the table where sweet wrappers spin from his breath. She believes his crazy story with the African scam. He runs a finger across the bookshelf and I think of *Industry & Architecture* buried in my pack as he fishes for pills in his coat.

Troy's on a chair, less injured than he looks. The Crap Hats and the Civvie gape at him. Miss Morphine inhales at something internal. Zoe Palmer flickers between Blackwood and the onetime protestor in a wrecked suit, who's coming to earth pretty fast now.

I swig my can and bang it down.

-Tell them what's going on.

Troy wheedles and adjusts his suit. He nods at the jar. -Man get a taste, yeah..?

-No! snaps Blackwood. -Speak!

Troy crumples. He tells us in his white-boy, fake-urban patter how he's like a "decoy" and he's like "Bring it...!" The customers have to find him.

-'Customers..'? says Blackwood.

-Innit, man in criss white suit and teeth is selling tickets...

Zoë Palmer groans.

Troy taps his chest. -They got taste though...

I remember the guy in the corridor. -What d'you mean "decoy"?

Troy shrugs.

I scrape my chair back and he talks quicker. -I never followed you, swear down, bro. It's on Twitter, innit. Britain's biggest squat, though!

I lean in, and he stammers, glancing at the silver sweets, and in a rush he explains that the mob have built a game. They choose a "banker", or a "politician", someone they blame for the mess they're in, fill their pockets with coke and spice then hunt them down. Men and women. This whole place is dedicated to it, like Alton Towers built for a manhunt, a girl-hunt. If they catch a "decoy" they're like, oh shit, this ain't the one...

-Why? says Jonas.

Troy's eyes roll. -Coz they hate mans in suits. Coz there's booze an' bitches an' smokes an' no Feds? And sweets, he winks, -Try it, blud. Live a lickle.

Jonas sucks his teeth.

Troy gloats: -You're blind, cuz! They know you! They listen through your walls, savin' you up, like turkeys. They're gonna have a carnival..!

I see the horror in their faces. Blackwood rubs his eyes. -Why us, Troy?

-Innit, I come here for sanctuary, he whines. -Turn the other cheek, Padre! Ain't that your way?

-Piss off, spits Blackwood. -You know my 'way'...?. Go!

And it's not his words that shock me but Troy, slouching upright, doing as he's told.

-You're the ones who're gonna run, tho', he grins with finger movements. -Because they know how to party, and they want you.

I jump into his face and he breathes sourness: -You are gonna play with Mister Whistler, old guy.

He wipes drool from his chin and turns to Zoë Palmer. -Come, bitch...

Enough. I grab him off his feet, sink my fingers into his bony flesh and haul him effing and blinding out of the room, to the main entrance. I throw him headlong into the darkness, where he laughs. There's a roar and a cheer further out. I bolt the door and run back to the others who have barely stirred.

-'Mister Whistler'? What's that about? I ask, hoisting my Bergen.
-His penis?
Zoë Palmer looks at me with terror. White suit.. teeth... the penny drops.
-Back door! I bark at them. -Now!
Blackwood remains: -We need to talk about the future.
-The fuh..?!
-Yes! Sanctuary is finished. I think that's all there is to it...?
Whatever. I reach for Zoë Palmer but she sticks to Blackwood. There's no time for the thump of failure that it gives me. It's just another thing that makes me scream inside like Kats did. Business as usual. I will never be the man who's good.

Jonas however, rushes Miss Morphine to the cupboard of mops and marigolds, shoves the panel into darkness, going with it.

Blackwood rises and follows with Zoë Palmer, into where Lucky Jonas kneels, examining the secret room and its further, metal door.

-You've never rehearsed this..? I ask, behind them.

Blackwood indicates the iron fastness. -We need a key.

Lucky Jonas mutters: -If I had a bar-mine. Jesus...

Blackwood grunts.

Jonas reacts: -I'm just saying we could blow the bloody doors off...

-I know, sighs Blackwood.

Anger sweeps me. PTSD. Call it what you want. Man-management with gasoline. I slam Blackwood against the wall – there could've been nails, anything, and fuel sneaks through my lips: -*You are my stronghold, my refuge, from violent people you rescue me. With you I can scale a wall...* Remember, Blackwood? Focus!

There's madness in my gut and his eyes know it. He throws himself in frustration at the metal door as if his weight could shift it. The others hover in the cupboard entrance with their baggage, craning to see what's up. I order them, Zoë Palmer included, to close it, and fix its back wall. -Wake up! I yell at the Padre.

He scrapes around, looking for something, and I spot a cabinet the size of a book set into the brickwork, with a rusted padlock. Blackwood flicks it helplessly until I crowbar it open with my steel. He laughs, hooks out a key like child would draw and rattles it into the door.

Nothing.

I call Zoë Palmer over.

-Seen one of these before..?

She hesitates, says it's a prison cell: -Do we really want to go in there..?

Mo 13 says things are getting louder.

Jonas, by way of answer, takes the steel from my fist and wedges it into the loop of the key, making a crank, and all four of us, hand over hand, skin on skin, claw it in its lock. Nothing. Blackwood steps back, listening like a safe breaker.

He pulls the key halfway out. -Now, he says, and the four of us grip, elbows brushing, in unison, and there's no need for strength this time; our touch, our closeness, the door itself wants to feel this, and I'm not sure what has awoken in it, or in us, but the door relaxes and swings apart like a mouth. Wet air pours in.

Jonas shines his beam not into a cell but into a passageway, and at the far end are steps leading upward. Blackwood retrieves the key and stands aside to let Miss Morphine, Zoë Palmer, Mo 13 and Spooks go first after Jonas.

-And the others..?

The Sniper shrugs. The Crap-Hats and Civvie have made their choice. I drag Blackwood in and close the door. This time the key turns smoothly in his hand. He buries it in a pocket and we follow Lucky Jonas to the steps, and up, carrying luggage, torches bouncing, and I'm torn by knowing that Zoë Palmer is still here and needs me, while Blackwood is the prize she reaches for.

DRAGONFLY

Looking behind me, the darkness is so thick that it's flat in my face. I turn away and it reaches down my spine.
I wonder what stalks us from those shadows.

Along the edge, my Master often said
"Watch out, for what I warn is truly meant."
- Dante, *Purgatorio*

Part 4: Higher Ground

When I was a kid, our school was so bad that a wing was closed down, a 'super-head' was helicoptered in and a Pupil Referral Unit built ten miles away. Every day, someone kicked off, and we never saw them again. The open world was a mad and dangerous place. The stories from "the unit" only came out later.

So one night we broke into the empty wing. The streetlights shone in, and the others started smashing things and lighting a fire, scared of what happens when you stand in the dark with your thoughts. Me, I went at my own pace, hood up, with the swagger and bum-fluff of a kid who thinks he's figured out the game where adults in shell-suits are ruled by others with their names on lanyards, who in turn are ruled by others in business suits with i-Pads. And uniforms rule them all. So when Coppers arrived and chased us through the building, I stood in the shadows and they never saw me – they nicked the kids who didn't get out. Firemen came next, trailing kit, to put out a melted chair. When they left, I walked through walls and doors, out onto my streets, and slouched to the park below the dark, green hills where kids sat on swings. Escaping the Po-Po without breaking a sweat put me one notch up – and marked me out.

I'd rather have been a Copper right then, though, with a stab vest and radio, walking up to blaze them. It was the moment I first thought, I'm outta here, I'm gonna get my exams, get weapons, get a mission.

I wanna be better than this. I wanna stand for something.

20: Dark 1, Zero Thirty: 'Uncertainties'

It's like we're at the top of a mountain, on this landing. The air is fresh, and distant rooflights let a shaving of moon in. The magic is here. There's a door to the stairwell. I swing it shut and lean against it, letting the weight of my Bergen do the work while the post-fight sickness rolls through me, lactic, edgy and fading.

The guys sit, heavily. Mo 13 tells Work Experience what a "man's" birthday he's just had, reliving the fight while Lucky Jonas comforts Miss Morphine.

Zoë Palmer's biting her nails, crouched beside Blackwood. She whispers 'good-good, all good' when I ask how she is and powers up her phone but there's no network. This is a hallway in an unknown part of the factory. I suggest we keep moving. A wave of fatigue washes through the team, with general agreement to carry on, although where to, none of us can say.

In response, Zoë Palmer produces a red dot on the wall, and I feel a flow of comfort because in the darkness what else would you do? Shrink away or stand with your weapon? Run or make fear run from you? Her gun bleeps. I draw my makeshift sword, feel warmth pour from inside me towards her... and I need to focus. Perfect love drives out all fear, I hear in my head as Jonas takes point with a lantern. *With you I can scale a wall.* Blackwood staggers upright with a cheerful oath, and even Spooks picks up enough baggage for three. Mo 13 and Birthday Boy keep their fighting sticks in hand and help the Medic onto her feet and I know it again, for the first time in a long time, that perfect love isn't about the pleasure, when everything goes your way. It's when you walk, side by side, into each other's

terror, weapons drawn.
 Perhaps she is my mission, after all. My blood goes electric but I push the feeling down; my job is to be a good man, this time, not that.

 Okonkwo takes a shot to the neck and I hit the ground while Tally blaze over my head.
 Someone kicks me in the ribs: -Get up! and I scramble to my feet, unbalanced by the Bergen I slept in.
 The scene makes my heart miss a beat.
 There's sofas, armchairs, a dining table, a bookcase, sideboard, log burner, a sink and a cooking stove, all in a space like an old common room, lit by thin, yellow curtains letting in a brassy dawn.
 Work Experience springs across floorboards and Zoë Palmer whistles at Victorian plasterwork. Miss Morphine eases herself into a wing-back chair. Mo 13 tugs the curtains open, and stares at frosted glass. Blackwood opens a door between them. It shows a balcony, where the Surveyor runs to join him as fresh air blows in.
 I stay by the door we entered by, wondering, listening. They move about, touching furniture, plates, cups, knives, forks, linen in drawers. Lucky Jonas examines the kitchen and Spooks wipes a finger across things, narrowing his eyes.
 Work Experience calls out from round a corner: -Beds! Sheets!
 Mo 13 unhooks a musket off the wall. -Antiquities…
 I suggest we secure the perimeter. Spooks agrees and Zoë Palmer watches horrified as the guys help me drag vintage chairs, tables and a sofa that weighs a tonne down the stairs into the passageway we arrived by, where we wedge them into a barricade that can only be dismantled from our side.
 -Don't think, says Jonas, puffing on the way back up, -that we're good now, Psycho. You pushed me too far, once, an' I will murk you

if you try it again. You ain't in charge no more. Get me?

I drill a finger into his chest. -Just when we were falling in love again, Sapper.

He sucks his teeth at me and I rest my back on the wall, wanting Lightning to wash away his venom and my past, while he storms off, flicking dead electric switches. Without really thinking about it, I run a finger along the skirting board beside me and it comes up clean. Spooks watches me, rubbing the tips of his fingers, too. I get up and test a shelf. Clean. I go to a sideboard and fling open the lower doors, pushing Jonas aside. He protests but I call Blackwood over.

Detergents. Jay cloths. Baked beans.

These are no 'antiquities'...

I sink to my knees.

We are not alone.

21: Day 2: 'Clear-Hold-Build'.

I join Zoë Palmer on the balcony. She smiles faintly – there's no view from here, surrounded by solid roofs. She points to the right, where the balcony becomes a walkway along the base of an enormous wall, with more tiles at the end. To our left is a large, flat valley enclosed by massive slopes that rise into the clouds. Mo 13 follows us as we explore that way, noting pools of water on the surface and the clouds boiling above and he says something in Arabic that despite his atheism might be Thank God, and he starts climbing, getting smaller and smaller until he calls from the topmost ridge that all he sees is more roofs in all directions, some lower, some higher. The Surveyor and I stand in the valley beside a small, glass frame that rots there like a mini greenhouse and peering into it, like a deep, dark mirror, we see ourselves side by side. Zoë Palmer pulls a wrinkled, reflected face, making us laugh.

The two of us try the walkway past the frosted windows, round a quad that plunges twenty storeys, before stepping onto a giddying steel plate at the top of a fire escape, from which, at last, part of Bristol spreads below us.

Zoë Palmer gulps the air, leaning on the railing, hair loose. She points at a housing estate arranged in curves that makes me want to run away. -Post-war, she shouts. -We've come a mile or more to the other side…

The steps twirl down two dozen levels into a wooded area, the trees flaky and brown, running the full length of the factory as far we can see it, on the other side of which, a cemetery prickles, and she's about to say something when her phone comes alive in her

hand, fizzing with incoming contacts.
A muscle in her face twitches.
-Let's get our stuff, I say.
She nods, retreating from the railing.

Inside, the others are at the dining table, where Mo 13 holds a framed photograph he found on a bedside cabinet, beside a suitcase, a wardrobe of men's clothes and a single, cotton dress. The room is tense.

He taps the photo: -Mother? Wife? Daughter... or... self?

The image is green with age. It shows a woman, Caribbean maybe, late twenties, in the same dress that's in the wardrobe, smiling with a cricket pavilion behind her. There are clues that place it in the 1970's but no identifying mark except on the back, in spidery writing: *My Love.*

Miss Morphine lingers over it. Zoë Palmer fidgets. Even Spooks is quiet.

Jonas grunts and goes to the kitchen stove. -I got pics like that. Mom, Aunties... get me? No big deal.

Blackwood stirs: -So do we get ready for a welcome..? Or...

Miss Morphine says she's done with running and if anyone shows up she'll speak to them herself. There's steel in her eyes that I've seen before, handling fighters who won't take her medicine.

The Terp says he's not sure about crashing a stranger's hospitality but we could share our food with them? No-one's in a rush to leave, except Zoë Palmer and me.

She touches Blackwood's sleeve and opens her tablet. A Lego cobra stretches from a tangled base to a matchbox head: -We're here.

She circles zones with an unsteady finger: — You can see now how wide it is but not how long or deep...

There's a catch in her voice and her eyes flash copper. -Satellite images of this factory are basically a smudge, and estate agents won't touch it...

-That's a silver lining... I say and she grins, making me feel like a million dollars and worthless at the same time.

-What about Ordnance Survey..?

She shakes her head and packs the tablet into her bag. She glances at the balcony: -I could come and go, she says, -So could you.

I bang my chair. She'll not return, unless Blackwood finds those mythical deeds, if the scam is to be believed. The floor vibrates and guns bristle from the corners but this woman is real. I get my pack on.

I go first, careful not to make a clang, and Zoë Palmer and I start our way down the fire escape while the wind bites to the bone and daylight strengthens over the city. It feels good to be doing this, with her, despite the fact I won't see her for dust when we're out. We pass windows like sockets that exhale moss and plastic, and I scan for hostiles. Seeing nothing real, we move on.

With three storeys to go, the stairs run out. The last stage swings on threads of rust, over a pit. I have rope but it hits the wall, gets snagged and won't reach. I swear I'm doing everything I can, but I also see the Defeated on the cycle track, moving like toys in a world that even if I reach it, has nothing for me. The factory seems relentless, full of power and promise, compared to that. Sod it. I'll do it. I'll escort her to her boy, say goodbye, find a hostel, get sorted, get out of my face...

Zoë Palmer pleads for the breeze to stop swinging the rope, but it won't settle, and needs to be twice as long. Even if we make it down without breaking our necks, we'd be in the pit that plunges into the foundations, back in the guts of the building.

I sink to the metal, exhausted, failure in front and Blackwood's madness behind. Zoë Palmer howls in frustration. Forced to retrace our steps, after two turns, the section we were standing on shudders and detaches, tumbling into the pit with a crash. I wipe blood from cuts in my hands, and we continue the long, hard climb past the empty watchers, back into the sky.

22: Day 2 Plus: 'Legitimacy'

Zoë Palmer retreats to a pile of blankets and I can't go near her. Blackwood's on the sofa, a blister pack of pills and the photograph on his chest. He sees our disappointment but is unsurprised.
-What now..? he asks.
Hell should I know? I want a drink. I want out of here.
He gestures at a kitchen cupboard that has been slid aside. Behind it, Jonas has found a third door with its latch working smoothly. It leads back into the factory. No-one seems pleased.

Mo 13 says what the hell is the matter with us? We're free! Miss Morphine needs air, he says, although she never said a thing, and he flings the windows open, changing the fug to ice. Blackwood sits up and breathes, says thank you.

Jonas makes brews using water from a rain butt. Ten minutes later they're bantering about who the Military Police want to arrest more: Spooks, Mo 13, Jonas, Work Experience or Miss Morphine, who protests loudest, so they settle on her.

Kerry "Miss Morphine" Sands was an okay medic. She came from one of those London boroughs where no-one can afford to be, where whole tower blocks dream of being sports stars or singers but she was too clever for that. She knew that every time you see a winner, there's ninety nine losers and she knew she was one of the ninety nine. But she was into her sports so she dreamt of having her own physio clinic one day; maybe she shouldn't have. She became a nurse and fell victim to the hospitals, and their sales targets. Joining the Army was her escape, too. Darling God though, knocked it out of her because of me, and where I lead her. Except this. If the world had given her a better chance when she left the Army, been a little kinder on her way back home, maybe she would've been okay... but the world doesn't do "dreams" for those of us who just can't face the day.

Mo 13 bickers with Spooks about freedom, and for some reason Marxism. He might be right but I don't feel free, and this world ain't getting equal any time soon. So I repack my Bergen, signal Zoë Palmer to wait here, and I go outside, take a hike up to the nearest ridge and like Mo 13, I see nothing but more peaks.

I gauge my position. Rain pats my skull and turns the tiles into speckled toast. Below me is the flat roof valley and the skylight. Balancing my Bergen, I find my phone and try it. No bar. I swing my legs onto the forward slope. If I carry on, the factory could twist, and I'd be lost out here till hunger and thirst get me. But maybe I'll reach the edge and find a way out. I study lumps of moss, bright and soft, zooming in, each one a forest on a hill, each tile a desert with lichen like splayed hands asking the sky for life, and the sky, bloody hell, the sky is freedom. Why stop now? Why go back to Blackwood, Zoë Palmer, and the rest of them down there who wouldn't give a shit if I lived or died, not really?

I hear the voice of all open country, the one that says: It's you and me now. But open country doesn't care. It'll kill you without mercy unless you make it surrender. So I scrape a return-marker into a ridge-tile with my knife and scramble down into a new valley. It's a gulley filled with crap and more roofs on every side. I take a swig of boiled water and move out, climbing the next slope, tiles cracking under my boots, moss bouncing back the way I've come.

I pause at a second ridge, scrape another waymark and advance. I do this a dozen times, catching my breath on new ridges and checking I can still see the last waymark. Tiles break off and skid to the bottom of each valley with a clatter. Crows peck at grit. Weeds grip on in the wind. Funnels poke up like trees on a battlefield and I know the guns that hide behind them.

The next slope has fallen in. It's left a skeleton of blackened timber sagging over a deep, dark wreck. I fight off vertigo, and climb carefully, fatigue kicking in, trying not to think what'll happen if a joist gives way.

At 1430 hours, I rest. The lower ridges of one of the glass-roofed jungle canyons blocks my route like a field of greenhouses, lethal to get across, too wide to skirt. I eat corned beef and think. My fingers are raw from gripping on, and the light will turn, soon. I could be caught out here at nightfall.

But I can't go back. I have to find something to hope for. I survey the furthest tiled roof I can see.

The glass in my path is a problem, but I can't leave here without knowing, so I go down and use the greenhouse framework to climb over sections that plummet into the factory, slipping, clinging on, I manage to get down the far side and collapse, heart racing. My chosen final slope has ragged gaps and decayed skylights. I plot a route, seeing faces at apertures and too tired to care if they are mob or not, I force myself up the hill.

At the top, a gale whacks me in the face and my stomach jumps at the view – the city! Bristol with its low lines of red-brown roofs, islands of pink and cream tower blocks, its spikes of churches and bone-pale, fort-like structures hiding behind stacked concrete hutches on a hill, and beyond it all, the misty idea of sea. I drag myself higher. Then hope evaporates. The down-slope of this roof is missing. I'm perched on the rim of a shell. I fight the urge to leap over, and I'm screaming for morphine, anything to lighten my load as thirty storeys down below, is the building site I saw on my way here; a wedge of land crammed with grey-topped houses, mud between them. But the site isn't silent now. The noise of engines and churning rubble pours up on the roaring wind. Through streaming eyes I see black and yellow machines advancing toward the factory.

I stretch over and not only is it hollow beneath me but vehicles with wrecking balls are destroying the building that supports me. Behind the attack, the nearest houses have scaffolding on them and workers in hi-viz cutting trenches, back-filling them with liquid grey. The ridge creaks and I freeze – the ripple of a wrecking ball somewhere out of sight. I spend a few minutes gathering intel and suddenly inside my jacket, my phone bleeps. It feels like a hundred eyes are on me.

Very carefully, I slide back down the slope to the greenhouse roofs. Shaking and needing a drink in my bones I crawl up the frames, as rain begins. Each pane is like staring through ice and algae into an ocean and I swear in one of them I see a darker shadow, a vast presence that slides across the depths, heading through the bowels of the factory quicker than I can move up here. Glass drops out from under my leg and I don't care which insurgent hears me now as I yell and grip on until I bleed, inching across, Bergen threatening to take me down until I slide off the last window frame and kiss the tiled slope in front of me. High up, my marker is barely visible in the storm.

This factory is being demolished right beneath us, and something malevolent maybe only I can see exists down there, to be cornered or released.

And that's my decision: "us".

23: Dark 2: 'Morale'

I suck up the pain and eat the distance, slope by slope, fingers numb and rain inside my skin, until at last I see the skylight in the valley below, reflecting a glow from the 'parlour' windows. It's the most beautiful flicker in the world. Nothing ever hit me so hard with longing. It's physical. It's human. It's home.

And it's her I tell first about the city and the demolition, before anyone else, like a betrayal of Blackwood, who's stoned on pills. Her eyes widen. I've seen the world she wants but what can I say? Touch it and die. I'm shivering like a casualty.

We sing the Teenager happy birthday - the filthy military version. Spooks whips out a pack of cards and Jonas produces balls he says are muffins. The stove crackles and gives us colour.

At midnight, no-one has arrived to claim the 'parlour' and Spooks says it's finders-keepers. Blackwood mutters doubtfully, but it's warm and dry. My outer clothes are draped on a chair and fresh ones from my Bergen are folded beside me. Flamelight smoothes the panic out of Zoë Palmer's face as she drifts asleep and I watch a protestor on fire, rising from the pavement with Coppers hanging onto him, flames leaping up their arms, desperate not to let him fly and show the world what could be done...

Remember him.

I resurface and relieve myself in a bucket, go to the door we'd arrived by, put my ear to it, and feel nothing.

I prod Lucky Jonas and the lads awake, deal with the cursing and sketch out a stag rota. Work Experience gets the first night off, as a birthday present.

We allocate the bedroom to Miss Morphine and the rest of us take bivvy spots, each near an entryway. I place my Bergen against the door we'd entered by, and the Terp takes first watch on the chair by the balcony, rubbing his eyes. Blackwood's comatose on his sofa, and Jonas pokes the stove yet again. Five British soldiers and an Iraqi agronomist? That fire doesn't stand a chance.

I take *Industry & Architecture* from my pack and slide it under Blackwood's elbow – I'll tell him my news in the morning. I trudge to my bag and crash, spinning for a drink, listening to rain on the windows making snaps of comfort... drifting into a hole with a fighter scarred by electrical welts... callsign Ugly... what unspecific desert... crawling... a man with an orange-stained beard... a child... a lawn... a vehicle pounding a wall... thud in my ribs, what!

-You're on stag, Psycho...

On all fours...

-Status...?

Jonas sighs: -Saw summink on the roofs but it was just a fox, innit.

-What..? Twenty storeys up..?

-Then it was a Lesser Spotted fuckin' Roof Fox, blud, because whatever it was, it wun't human.

I slide into my boots, and feel the old familiar sludge in my head. Jonas puffs his bag and bivvies down. I need to look sharp. Get busy. So I tour the position. A thinning moon and a stove burnt to embers. A bounce of springs in the other room and Miss Morphine stumbles out, slouches to the bucket, makes a waterfall and creeps back, silent. Blackwood twitches and his book falls on the floor. Zoë Palmer is motionless, face turned away.

I eat coffee granules to keep the ghosts away and listen to a rumble in the building. Demolition? At night? Mouth open, I hear it swell and die, open the door to the roofs and get nothing but the lisp of air on edges. Inside, the rolling bass is obvious now; brickwork like a drum. Blackwood fights off something above him, then slumps back, cold.

The rain. I think of Troy and the things I've seen, how the walls keep moving, the mob, the White Suit, the darker presence, the impossible roofs and Jonas' door to the factory. I mentally tear up the Field Manual and re-set the game. If this is going to work, we're going to need a few things sorted out. The rules of war are simple: Know your enemy. Choose your ground. Target his centre of gravity. System shock. Chaos. Friction. Simultaneity. Change.

As daylight arrives, I have a plan. Blackwood sees his book with something like surprise and fear, never asks where it came from, and I watch him hunker down and scribble. That's good. I need him to wake up. Like in Syria, I can't save these people – only he can.

24: Day 3: 'The Growth of Religious Extremism & The Primacy of Political Purpose'

Breakfast is noisy. Lucky Jonas heats up tins of tomatoes and burns bits of bread on sticks. The camping-gas cooker smell and sugary brew gets the chatter going.

Blackwood places *Industry & Architecture* on the table next to the photo of the woman, and he taps the book. He thanks us, using our real names, no ranks, nicknames or jobs, and there's a catch in his throat.

-I'm not going to run, he's says. -If it's okay with you.

He opens the book.

-Out there, they think we did something very wrong. Some of us even tried taking our own lives over it.

Lucky Jonas dips his head. Zoë Palmer looks at me, then away.

-So I've written this down, he says, tilting his head on its injured side. -I don't know what it means anymore but...

He takes a paper from his book – not the scrap I saw with a child's writing on it, but a fresh sheet – and he spreads it out.

"Deliver us from evil" it says in ballpoint pen across the middle.

Miss Morphine murmurs it, and the Lord's Prayer pours into my head like an old rhyme, drying up at the breads and trespasses, the will-bi-duns and temptations... Words for children and funerals.

-Is that the plan? Zoë Palmer is dismayed.

And I watch this band of misfits wiping tomato juice from their mouths, the lost Surveyor softly sinking and the pregnant woman stifling a burp, all of us hiding from judgement and business-as-usual. My designs in the night shrivel up in the face of it. I knew this feeling would come, and I'm freezing now, like out on the roofs, needing a proper drink. A gale bangs the windows. A piece of woodwork cracks but resists. I'm short-circuiting with emotions I don't even have names for. I need to run.

That's when I see a man standing in the room, pointing a spear at us, dressed in a cap and overalls, feet planted for war. I clatter upright. How long has he been there, teeth bare, creamy eyes and black old skin?

-What d'you Crazies want in ma house? he thunders in a West African accent. -Eh!

Zoë Palmer shrieks.

So I'm not alone. They can see him, too.

25: Day 3 Plus: 'The Importance of Local Leaders'

Mo 13 falls back as the man pokes the javelin at him, held from his groin like a six foot penis. It's only a broom, but the invader clocks us all in turn, rock steady.

-Eh! What you mess op ma tings for? Eh!

He swerves and jabs at Spooks, this time. I grab a fork. I want Blackwood to step up but he's fogged, like he's not even here, with his hand is on the framed photo. It's Miss Morphine who clears her throat:

-I'm Kerry Sands, she says, -a doctor in the British Army. We're sorry to intrude.

It's straight out of the manual.

The old man snaps: -Eh..? Harmy? There's no war, here! Eh!

Jonas leans back. -Matter of 'hopinion', old timer, innit.

I grip the fork. What damage this geezer can do with a broom – or me with cutlery for that matter – is not obvious, but there's no guarantee he's alone. He could be playing the fool while the mob are waiting to spring us. But the doors are closed and no other movements catch my eye. I can't see how he's got in.

He lowers his broom and tips his hat back at Spooks who brandishes a combat knife. Ignoring the blade, the man steps smoothly and checks the room, glances into corners, sizing us up. When his eyes peer into mine, I feel a rush of shame and my gaze drops. Only the best-of-the-best have that.

-You don't look rich.

-What? says Spooks, in defiance. -Is you rich?

The old boy shimmers and appears by the sink where he props

his stick. I wonder with horror if I've passed out for a moment because he moves like the building does, supple and lithe.

-Den how will you pay fah brekkages..? Eh? Tings you broke you shouldna broken?

Miss Morphine is quiet. The eyes of the others tick toward me but my head swims and the man moves on Blackwood. -An' who ah you, Mistah? It's a long time since I hear the ol' wahds...

Blackwood is stuck, and I wonder if he can even see this guy. Miss Morphine finally states his rank and name for him, and the old man halts, listening to a forgotten song. Jonas breaks the spell by getting up noisily and going to the stove, deliberately dragging a foot. The African watches him with amusement.

Miss Morphine asks what do we call our host, then?

-Eh! The lady in that pitchah she call me... a name you carn pronounce...

He draws the photo out of Blackwood's fingers, holds it to his chest, eyes closed, humming. Now's the time to jump him.

I cough, instead. -So is this your place..?

-Eh! he roars. -I am the Caretakah!

He laughs, his teeth like pearls, and I'm rooted to the spot. I can't do a thing about it.

The Caretaker makes a sideways click in his mouth at Jonas before turning to Work Experience, who has been sitting at the table the whole time.

- Eh! Your friend has got the limp but you have the bad legs..! Eh! Is your friend a malingerah?

I react: -If you're a caretaker, who're you working for? Have you been spying on us?

He slides like the factory walls and appears next to a terrified Mo 13. He cradles the photo: -Eh, mah Love, he whispers to the image. -Family...

I catch the Medic's eye – Blackwood must act – but he's seeing ghosts while the Caretaker talks to the photo, tracing the woman on it: -One biiig happy family, eh! mah Love.. that's what we wah...

He asks his photo what she thinks of these new Crazies – does she think they have the colour and smell of the crowds of people who worked here? Does she remember a generation having kids here, making chocolate, all the flavours of the world, and sending them out...? Does she remember how they worked hard, those crowds, doing the same thing, day in, day out..?

-An' they wah crazy. But they wah mah people, eh, mah Lov'... mostly... Ah these da same..?

Spooks makes a move but the Caretaker raises a finger and the Sniper drops like his strings have been cut, with horror on his face.

The old man turns and barks this time at Zoë Palmer. -Eh! Who you work for? The Harmy?

She sits, terrified.

-For the Family..! Eh!

I manage to murmur: -Let her be...

He turns on me, eyes like a furnace. -Soldiah bwoy... Who do any of us work for? Where can a man go if he has no job an no prospeck, jost his memories an' a littol coin for de collection tray, an' if they chase him or leave him, he's mad as a spidah! Eh! Why should he not drink himself to death an' destroction? Why should he not abandon all he lov? Why should he not tro himself out on the street? Eh!

I feel my jaw moving, but nothing comes out.

Blackwood whispers: -They forgot about you..? They left you up here? How..?

The old man leans on the table and it shudders. -Eh, Mista Blackwood. It's me who switched the last machine off. Ha!

Suddenly he's beside me, with the smell of his breath and armpits. He's been here so long, he whispers. But the Crazies never see him. Just like the bosses and workers who barely knew he existed, the invisible servant who fixed their fuses and stopped their leaks. -Not always in the way they want, he chuckles. -Eh! Mah Lov'...

A thought strikes me. -You know this place...

-Eh! When I move, nobody see it, soldiah bwoy!

-All over the factory..?

He taps the side of his nose, -Victory Cocoa have no secret from the Caretakah. Nor do you, soldiah bwoy, he says, eyeing the scar on my neck.

I lean away from his breath, which is way too sweet, and catch Zoë Palmer's expression. A question crosses my mind: -Was there a man who died on the machines here, maybe twenty years ago...?

There's a continent and all its kingdoms in the look he gives me. He sniffs the air around my face: -They are blind an' live in darkness, he says.

-What?

-People die for chocolate, soldiah bwoy. Not only here. You like to get dronk?

Saliva leaps into my mouth. I'm screaming to do that, but how can this old man tell? Lucky Jonas pipes up: -Give Dragonfly some Punch or Foreign and he's your bitch, Granddad.

I want to melt his face off, but the Caretaker silences him, tells him that if he think himself a chef, there is a cupboard set into the wall, so disguised that none of us had seen it, and as he points, it falls open, revealing stack upon stack of tinned foods. -Kill and eat, Lucky Mistah, he says, and moves to the wall by the stag chair. He kicks out a panel. Inside, a dozen demijohns glow.

I inhale sharply.

He pulls one out, yellow and misty like summer piss, and brings it to the table, unpops the cork with a thumb, singing to himself: -Oooold soldiahs nevah die... Dey onleh fade away... Eh?

He sweeps our mugs into a group and pours. Controlling my shaking, I take the nearest one. It smells of leather and apricots and

the heat rolls down my throat.
-I put a littol spice in, he says.
-Yes, I whisper. -I can tell...
He smiles and the warmth goes into my veins. He refills my mug and the second one goes down slower. The others are coughing, except the Medic and Mo 13 who refuse, and Zoë Palmer who's in disbelief.
-That's good stuff... I say, as it roars into my skull and I wonder how I did my thirsty stag right next to it... wow... I never knew...
-See, son? Dere's hope fah you, still.
"Son"? He sloshes his cup against mine, and I'm a mess.
Oh deliver me from sweet evil.

I wake up in front of the fire, boots on. There's evening light, rain on the windows and a silence in my head, like something is missing. This is no hangover, this is just a lack of horror. I sit up and Blackwood's gaze is on me.
-Where is he? I ask.
-Who? he coughs and I feel a terror that none of it was real, the warmth fading, and all my loathing, the stuff I lock away, gets shaken up again.
Jonas is clearing plates from a feast they must've had. He sucks his teeth:
-He went out, Psycho...
I leap up and jam a foot in the Sapper's chest for calling me that. Twice, three times, seeing him go under my boot and the others pulling me off, Mo 13 calling me Arabic names, and all I do is prove them right. The 'hit' came over me. I feel Blackwood's pity and Zoë Palmer's fear and I'm repeating: -Okay okay. My kind of apology goes like that, okay, okay, and I stagger off and vomit in the bucket.
I ache, one minute in heaven, the next in hell. And the ironic

part, the big fat joke is this:

My plan is for a war without violence. Clear. Hold. Build. But this time we are the insurgents. We have overwhelming numbers against us but like Che Guevara or the Finnish Winter War, the Stern Gang in Palestine, the Taliban or ISIS, like them, we will overturn the odds. Confuse and disrupt. Strike at the enemy's centre of gravity.

Yep, with this beast in me.

So I go to Jonas and tell him: Okay okay. I unravel the paper that Blackwood wrote on and hammer it to a wooden picture rail on the wall, pinning it there with a fork, between the balcony windows and factory door.

I mean it, I tell them, more than they can know. Let's make it happen instead of fighting each other or sitting around, hiding.

There are cries of "Psycho" and "Dragonfly's gone loco", but Blackwood gives me space, and they listen. While Lucky Jonas and I wipe blood from our faces, I explain my plan.

Zoë Palmer can think what she wants, but I will get us out of here because I will seize this place. Blackwood draws circles on the table with his finger, and when I've finished, he says: -Do it.

Jonas rubs his chest where I've bruised him, but he begins to write a list of the things I've said we'll need.

And the old man is the key. I'm sure of it.

But night arrives with no sign of him.

26: Day 4: 'The Importance of Local Support'

He saunters in through the factory door before Jonas has even tried to poison us with breakfast, broom on his shoulder, singing a hymn.
-Eh! he announces. -The old wahds ah sooo good. Eh!

He levels his tool at Blackwood's chest, dripping dirt, and his other hand goes for a pocket inside his overalls. I jump, but all he does is pull out a huge sheet of paper, lay it over the dining table and call for a pen. He says he'll stop the Padre throwing things into the darkness, 'coz the darkness is messy enough, and with a nod from Blackwood, I hand him the biro from my notebook. The African waves it away and tells me to do the drawing, starting at a point he jabs at with a sausage-finger.

I try to keep up while he dictates a scrawl of lines and loops, creating a tangle, and I'm not sure what he's getting at. He goes off on tangents and says nothing clearly. Zoë Palmer gets it, though, and offers to take over. The Caretaker however grabs my pen like a tradesman sketching the day's work and fills the sheet rapidly with angles, tubes, flows and islands saying, 'Don't go there', 'Crazies here', or 'This part need a fix-it-op'. He leans back with a click of satisfaction and says we can walk it twice as fast now.

Zoë Palmer tucks a strand of hair back and claps, once, saying he's drawn us a schematic – a map of the wiring and pipework, the power and water, earthing and sewage, air vents, lifts and shafts. They pass through walls or drop through floors, travel through concrete for a dozen storeys before shooting off at impossible angles. This isn't the boxes she gets on her tablet. It's a vast, kids' climbing frame of gas, leccy and waste, of vacuum tubes that once sucked money and messages around the structure, chutes that channelled products. This is what he remembers, it's what he's taken care of. What he's drawn is true, from the first water junction to the last.

He taps his teeth with my biro, then circles an X, close to where I started his scrambled up tube-map.

-Seek here, he tells Blackwood, puts the pen down, wet with spittle, folds the sheet and gives it to Blackwood, who tucks it deep into his greatcoat. -But you'll be with us when we look..? the Padre asks.

I say, carefully. -Remember our plan, Blackwood...

The African grunts, takes his broom to the piss bucket, shunts it aside with a boot and pushes open a door in the wall behind it that we'd never even seen before.

-Eh, he snorts, -don' use dat mop bocket for your moon-watah. Eh!

And he disappears into a bathroom, complete with ancient ceramics and a tin bath. Gobsmacked, we hear him gushing, presumably, his own water.

Miss Morphine collapses with laughter.

-Bagsie I'm next..! cries Zoë Palmer, bright with amusement and even my ghosts can't stop me smiling at her.

But we can't stay here forever. Sooner or later, the mob or cops will find us – if we haven't run out of food or torn each other to pieces, first. So the door leading into the factory is the only way we haven't tried. But even if we do make our way down there, this mad, vindictive building won't let us go until we've done what we came here to do, whatever that is, and we could spend eternity down there finding a window that doesn't move or a door that doesn't drop us into a pit.

I study my equipment list, and call Jonas over. I need everyone to go through their kit bags, and see what we have. He nods. Not because he likes me all of a sudden, but because he knows we have to act.

While they search, the African goes to the stove and the room soon fills with the smell of ginger and garlic. He sizzles, reciting tales from the factory's past, of workers' affairs, bosses, wars and rations, and chocolate mountains, until I gather the guys together.

The Teenager thumbs a DS and lays out his contribution: three hoodie tops, all black, and spray-paints in yellow, green and pink. What he was planning to do with them is anyone's guess but I'm glad of it; he cheers me up. Jonas combs through his own items, picking his teeth with a screw: a hand-powered drill, a million-candle torch, gaffer tape and a knife. Mine is the multi-tool, with its wire cutters. Zoë Palmer has her tablet and gun, Miss Morphine brings Savlon and bandages, Mo 13 an alarm clock and Blackwood has his pills and books – that's all I need from him, if it means he brings his true self. There is also the Caretaker's map, and several kilos of those silver sweets that Troy said the mob will do anything for. At least, those are the things the unit are willing to part with; and it's a sign – giving them up – because it means we are not Defeated. Spooks though, brings nothing but a gormless grin, high as a kite on something he's found. I'd rip him a new butt-hole for this, but given half a chance, it's only what I would do in his place. But it ain't helping.

As if it wasn't hard enough, Mo 13 watches Miss Morphine, every move she makes. I think of the way she gazed at me, and how the others have clocked me watching Zoë Palmer, who in turn keeps fixating on Blackwood. This unit could fracture under feelings like these, so when Spooks takes a roll of foil and exits to the rooftop, Mo 13 sidling after him, I let them go, before the appetite to numb myself takes over. Finally, I follow them out and find them kneeling and holding a lighter under a twist of foil, with tubes in their mouths. They seem bewildered, then offer it to me. I see Kats, her dealer, my neighbourhood, corrupt kandaks and the hostels. It makes my tongue tingle and I miss her. Suddenly I'm in the middle of the mess I made; her eyes and her dealer, all my fault, a loss of mission and the whole sugary self-destruction makes my head spin and it could happen again, right here.

-You pricks! I yell. -I'll throw you over the wall!

Spooks' eyes roll. -How's your Lightning, Sir..? and they crack up.

Hell.

I go inside. There's a curry fog and Blackwood's reading by the fire. I slap my hand on his book. He pops in alarm.

-Did you say those dicks could do drugs..? I roar, wanting them all the same.

He closes *Industry & Architecture*, rises and hobbles outside. The Caretaker kneels in front of a motor that he's stripped down on newspaper, tears tumbling down his leathery face. Miss Morphine emerges from the toilet as if she's done something wrong. The Teenager hides his legs and Zoë Palmer covers her head.

-See? says Jonas. -It's what you do, Psycho. You can't be "delivered".

Rain patters and Blackwood returns, dripping and vacant. What hope have we got?

The Caretaker is nowhere to be seen.

On the paper, though, is a completed diesel engine.

27: Dark 4: 'Night Vision'

Night comes, with noises in the floors and walls. A distant scream wakes Miss Morphine who creeps to my side and hugs my arm, tight, like Kats might've done, running to me for comfort. I'm a red blooded guy, but I'm in a wrecked building with no known exit, and a pregnant medic in my lap who saw my mind was on someone else. So what do I do with this trusting, female contact? 'Miss, I'll get you out of here.' Or: 'You touched me; I can eat you.' I take her to an empty sofa and place a blanket over her.

Even if I fight my way out of here, I've got nothing on the outside. There's no Kats waiting with a hero's welcome and no place to go except the streets; even the Army and Police want to lock me up. I'll help Zoë Palmer exit and once she's out, she's gone. There's no mission or meaning out there. People will still scramble over each other for stuff they don't even really want. Defeat is all I know.

The scar on my neck throbs and my tattoos writhe. My body knows what the job is, even if my brain hasn't caught up. Zoë Palmer is as tight as a walnut on her own sofa. Blackwood groans on his, and I don't believe in his chandeliers, but one thing is clear: Before it will let us out, we must possess this factory. I say it again: A war without violence. Clear. Hold. Build. We have to make it safe – even for kids. Then Zoë Palmer will bring Tyler and stay. It seems that's my war aim: possession.

Dawn soaks in. I wait. Waiting is natural. War is waiting. But do not sleep, as I have told young officers, or death will smack you out of the ground. Do not allow stray thoughts to go on loop in your head. Not of lost love, not at wartime.

I step outside, strip and pour buckets of rainwater over my skull, pits and bits, scrape my flesh clean of all longing. I stand naked in the valley, trying to remember the green hills and the day the kids came for me, the day I stopped running.

I pull my combats and boots on and return to the parlour, my top still off. Miss Morphine is up and Zoë Palmer hunches, tablet in hand. They look up at me and their eyes widen. I step aside and quickly cover my tattoos. I'm not ready to explain them, not yet.

I look for the African, but he's not here. Blackwood lowers himself onto a seat, breathing heavily.

-Prepare your plan, he says. -With or without the Caretaker.

28: Day 5: 'Contest Outlying Areas (In Other Words Don't Forget Them)'

Zoë Palmer takes some convincing, but I plead with her to wait in the parlour. I need to know what we're dealing with down there, even if I do find that restaurant door.

Lucky Jonas stirs a pan of smoke and I spoon flakes of his heated tuna into my mouth and feel the salt and oil burn home. He wipes his hands and picks up his gear, comes to my side as I shoulder my Bergen and lead him and Work Experience to the factory door. He unbolts it. I pull it open and a cold, dark breath pours into our faces. A flight of stairs disappears downwards, so I take point, the pair following on, sticks and blades at the ready.

We work our way into the building, leaving tiny markers carved into walls, just as I'd done on the roofs. We put gaffer tape on doorjambs and railings, and obvious graffiti on others, with a tic-tic, almondy shush of the Teenager's yellow can. We drill across doors, fixing them shut, tagging some with symbols that the mob follow in their manhunts. Ending in the grey-green light of one of the bridged, glass-roof canyons, I dump sweets in a cul-de-sac and we climb to an observation point.

It doesn't take long. My balls tighten as a torn-up girl limps onto the walkway. She follows our tags across it, stops by the sweets, then panics at a noise behind her. She finds the knotted rope that Lucky Jonas put there and swings herself precariously over the railing into fifty foot of air as her pursuers crash into view, jeering, piling onto the bridge after our tags. The girl climbs awkwardly onto a balcony beneath her hunters, who, oblivious, see only the silver wrappers.

They wear tight pants, heels and business suits. They crawl, tangle and grope, fighting over the sweets while below them, the girl lies still, staring up. Before I can analyse this, a new guy hobbles onto the bridge, clothes ripped, with a new group chasing him right into the first. He disappears under their bodies in a muffled scream. I hold my breath as the first girl rolls into cover and the group on the bridge finish with their victim, looking for more fun, whooping and waving their winnings – wraps and bottles from his pockets – leaving him motionless and naked. Three of them hang back; a black male in sports gear, an Asian guy in a hoodie and a thin, white lad in trainers who laughs at the cavern around him. They tip the naked guy over the edge like a sack of rubbish and he squirms like a peeled squid all the way down to the floor, where his head splatters into blood and muck beside the concealed girl, who shrieks. The males grab their crotches and head after the main group, laughing like hyenas.

Work Experience retches. Lucky Jonas lets out a stream of whispered curses. Me, I wish I had an SA80.

On our way back, we hear more groups echoing in corridors, step aside to avoid one of them and find ourselves overlooking the deep hall where the restaurant door opens and closes, throwing more people into Victory Cocoa. This time, it stinks of oil smoke, lit by flames in the centre, where a figure collapses inside a burning tyre and a small crowd dances to a rap artist, clattering and whooping as their prey stiffens in the fire.

We escape, running headlong into the back of a group of Defeated mob snorting and pill popping – a restless mix. With shock and horror, I see the White Suit who scared Zoë Palmer facing the group, holding a woman on a dog lead, telling them she's a politician and he announces new trails, in pink, because someone is fucking up the yellow. He yanks the scapegoat's chain, telling them that in the outside world she stopped them getting what they wanted. Work

Experience is offered a spliff by a bystander. I pull him back into the shadows before he – or I – can accept. White Suit senses it. Our lines are getting blurred.

We find her, later, lying on her back, injection tracks in her arms, barely breathing, naked except for scabs and dirt, so thin that her vagina sticks up like moss on a rock. Pills lie scattered and taped into a jacket, tossed aside. We place it over her. She moans loudly if we try to carry her, so we're forced to leave her with bottled water and corned beef. And I sense that heavy shadow again; a presence in the caves beneath our feet that puts a shiver down my spine. I move us on ever quicker, through false walls and doors Jonas has rigged, until we climb the last stairs and are let into the parlour by Mo 13, hoods up, filthy and shaking.

We look like the mob, says the Medic.

I stagger onto the roof, toward the shower.

Blackwood holds his head in his hands when I tell him how it was. I'm shaking, and everyone can see the state Jonas and the Teenager are in. Zoë Palmer bites her nails to the quick. How she thinks she'll get past the mob, let alone convince the factory to let her out, I don't know. But every hour we waste, someone suffers, and sooner or later, they'll reach us too.

The Caretaker is back. He shoves a plate under my nose, heaped with garlic and eggs. His skin glistens: -Eat, son, he says.

That word, again, cuts me to the heart. I never knew my real dad. I mustn't let on.

-Hit them, yells Blackwood, fingers ploughing the table: -Hit them hard, Marine P, no half measures. I want blood. I want you to break them!

Everyone is startled and I weave my hands together to stop their tremors, a sadness in my throat. The Caretaker twists, as if he wants

to leave:
    -Now James, don' be hasty...
    The Padre takes a knife and glares at him.
    I push my plate away. -He's right, Blackwood. You have to be different. You have to be yourself.
    -I am myself, Marine P, and 'myself' is angry. I don't have this other bullshit you want...
    -Eh! James! Remembah what you seek!
    -Seek? You mean ownership..? Of this purgatory?
    -James, seek the ol' wahds.
    -No! he shouts, stabbing the table so hard that his hand slips down the blade. Miss Morphine throws an accusatory look at me and Blackwood shrugs her off: -Get rid of those monsters..! he yells.
    -I want a safe house, dammit!
    Then he better be ready. I'll fight like an insurgent and hit their centre. I'll make it uneconomical for them. But if Blackwood acts in bitterness I won't do it. He has to give them a reason to leave, in peace. -You had something special, I say, -and you've pissed it all away. Remember The Hidden One..? Bashing heads is no big deal.
    He jabs at crumbs as if they have importance.
    Work Experience pipes up. There was something he saw today that he can't get out of his head. That rapper. The one those people were dancing to. The Teenager used to pump himself up on the guy's tunes back in Helmand. But that rapper was killed in a shooting six months ago...
    Blackwood's face twitches. He raises the knife at the Teenager, then at me:
    -I'm going to make this whole damn place vanish. I promise you that. Then it will be beautiful again. But go and empty it, first.
    Zoë Palmer's eyebrows rise. I groan and beg the Caretaker for sense, but his head is cocked to the side, listening.
    There's thunder in the floor and walls.

29: Dark 5: 'Nineveh Part Two'

Blackwood screws himself up in a corner. The Caretaker meantime sparks up the burner and firelight flickers. His leathery voice starts telling his tales; a soothing, endless chunter in the Parlour. For example there was Suez, he says, a war when Egypt kicked the British and French out of their canal. The quick witted Arabs blocked it with sunken ships, one of which was loaded with chocolate from this factory, going to the Eastern markets and old Mister Snow, head of the family, had a mighty temper. He was 'faithful' once, kept out of the wars, until his son ran away to fight Hitler. His faithfulness went bitter and he traded with any army in the world, and when his ship was sunk at Suez, he rampaged through the factory firing any workers he could find who were Arabs. There were three, and they weren't even Egyptians. But he didn't care. He made them pack a crate of bars for the British commandoes, in front of everybody else, then he made them vanish without wages. When the British won an airfield near the canal, he made sure they were photographed eating Snow's Victory Cocoa.

 -The Harmy made him their choco-man for all their wars aftah that... So if you want this place, James Blackwood, remembah the stories. Eh! One biiig, raggedy family, like the farmers back in Ghana, mah Lov. Ol' Snow treat them no bettah than Crazies. Eh!

The Caretaker says he has a more cheerful one, and he tells how long, long ago, before anyone had heard of ISIS, or chocolate, or Easter Bunnies, or Wi-Fi, the mighty Prophet Jonah was a rich and famous advisor to the king. He was told to drop it all and go to Nineveh. This was his enemy's capital and the most powerful city in the world, with many slaves and famous cruelties. He was ordered by God to tell his enemies that if they changed their ways, they would be saved from disaster. So what did the Mighty Prophet do? He ran away – to sea, when he could not even swim, the fool – more scared of Nineveh laughing at him than of his own Maker's instruction. But God did not give up. God chased him with a great fish, eh! which swallowed up the Mighty Prophet and spat him back on target. So Jonah trudged to Nineveh, frightened and smelling of fish guts. But he forgot that in those ancient times, people knew that Destruction hung above them like a power cut, or ebola, or militants, or a dirty bomb. They understood. The Caretaker chuckles. The scaredy-cat Prophet Jonah crawled into the city of greed, into their marketplace, stood on his box and… they dropped to their knees. No banking crisis, no Destruction.

-Eh! So! laughs the Caretaker, -Which is more ridiculous, eh, mah Lov? The fish or the forgiveness..? Pick one!

Blackwood and the Caretaker sink into urgent conversation. Zoë Palmer hugs her knees on a sofa, eyes wet with tears. I want to wipe them away with my fingertips but instead I lay my coat over her and power up my phone, not caring if I'm traceable. -Let's ring your kid, I say, but I can't get a bar, and luckily she doesn't hear me.

I challenge the African about his morbid tales. His hooch screams at me from the panel in the wall.

-Soldiah bwoy, he crinkles, -you know already! Ol' Snow must be tamed. Eh! Like a lion!

And I trace a new map in my mind, one I wish with every sinew that Zoë Palmer could paint, with her good sense and equipment, so I could watch her fingers turn my lack of hope into a Lego cobra…

The African clicks his fingers and calls across the room to her: -Derek Palmah! Eh? I remembah him.

And she sits up. She gasps and slides to her knees and I want to catch her.

The Caretaker's spoken out of turn and he knows it.

She pulls my coat round her: -Was he a good man?

The Caretaker's on his back foot. -Eh? That's important?

She nods, furiously, tears in her eyes, and he answers with a high-pitched:

-Well...

I glare at him. He needs to get a grip, and tell her what she needs to hear, be fictional if necessary but be compassionate, for pity's sake. It's the rules, mate.

He sinks to a crouch: -Your daddy... He... like to fight. He organise strikes. He get bettah wages for the workahs. So. Eh!

Her mouth moves, thinking of what to say.

He lowers his voice. -He was a littol violent but he got the money for his friends so... "good"? He mek enemies, though, him fightin'.

Zoë Palmer's head dips. -This place killed him.

The Caretaker rubs his chin into creases, and stands.

-Don't go! she blurts, but he rests his hand, not quite on her scalp, then continues toward the door, singing one of his songs in a rising lilt:

-For de Lord our God de Almi-i-ighty reign...

I go to her, thinking I must look after this woman and I must have no further interest in her, not wreck her, not do a Kats all over again.

She looks at me with her features filled with blood:

-He was good, right?

I tell her yes. A good fighter by the sound of it. A hero.

-I just want to go...

And so do I, to somewhere quiet with her, to give her all the comfort a man can give, into that bedroom but Miss Morphine watches me and Mo 13 drops a mug.

Zoë Palmer curls back into her sofa.

That night when all are asleep, I go on stag because no-one else will and anyway, I there's no chance I'll sleep. Suddenly her voice floats across the room.
-P, is he... one of them..?
I go and kneel beside her. I tell her I don't think so.
-He knows who James is.
-He's not the only one.
Her face is etched with worry, even in the gloom. Her blanket ruffles: -Are we dead..? Is that why we can't get back..?
Blackwood talks in his sleep, calling out to a lost God. I see soldiers dropping like fruit and a crowd at a barricade where a man ignites in orange feathers who even then, cannot make a difference.
-We can do this, I tell her. -I will get you out of here.
-I hit my head on a beam, she murmurs, -out on the building site...
The wall ripples. -This place will open up if we do the right thing, I say. -That's the mission, yours and mine.
She sniffs. Blackwood turns in his sleep and I tell her something I've never told anyone before.
-One time growing up on my council estate by the hills, we mugged this little kid. It pulled the gang together because he wasn't one of us. I stood over him with my hand held out, like all he had to do was slap money in my palm, when he had nothing, and everyone knew it. So someone kicked him. A girl it was. I felt weird about that because half an hour ago, she'd been – you know – getting friendly with me and to go from that sort of feeling to this, or if she was trying to impress me, I don't know... Then someone else put the boot in. Then another. In a matter of seconds it was over; there was no more hardness to kick at, except the scalp. One of the smallest boys

aimed at the kid's head but I told him leave it. They took the piss out of me, then, and I had to face them off. I pulled the kid to the side of the road and he was making this high pitched noise; his voice wasn't even broken yet, his face just a puff of claret so I took a tenner out of my pocket and shoved it in his trackie pockets, rang the bell of the house he was outside of, and puked. The others were watching me and I didn't care. Next day they came for me, more of them than before, so I ran to the hills but they kept coming after me. The hills were green, because it was May, and there were dragonflies…

Zoë Palmer is asleep.

30: The Hidden One, Phase 2: 'Compound 46'

The war in Afghan is business-as-usual.

The foreign poet – The Hidden One – has vanished, along with our chance of winning the locals over in a way that would've felt rooted, and honourable. The Rules of Engagement say we can only shoot back if we're attacked, so we patrol, nerves at breaking point, being ambushed again and again until even the Brass have had enough and they tell us it's time to take the fight to the enemy and bite them in their heartland, hard.

So three nights later, our convoy growls into the desert under cover of darkness, headlights off, apart from the sea of the Milky Way above us. We're crammed into these sweat-box vehicles with all our ammo and weapons, blindly trusting our drivers not to tip us into a ditch or river on the buckaroo trackway down to the harbour position. Once there, we tumble out and breathe again, piss and rehydrate, hoist our equipment and continue on foot to the forming-up line. An hour later, we penetrate the Green Zone under these incredible stars, spreading through a network of trenches, preparing to assault what our maps call 'Compound 46'.

Our target is a fortified hill raised on a rock in a bitter wilderness, built by Alexander the Great to guard the veins of the Helmand River. Now, it's the Taliban who lord it from there over farmers whose region was dug and watered by America in happier times, and from where they've struck at us relentlessly.

Our Terp translates their radio chatter, the sounds of them waking up and their nicknames for us. They know we are coming. They're excited, and they're comfortable.

They have no idea what we bring them.

We bring C-Company in overwatch with 40mm GMG's and .50 calibre HMG's, plus 30-mm Rarden cannons, coaxially mounted 7.62mm machine guns and 81mm medium mortars capable of firing smoke and illuminating rounds out to five thousand metres, with Estonian escort – whose fathers fought as Soviets, here – in Vikings, Scimitars and WMIK's. We bring the lads of A-Company and my own B-Company, with my platoon, moving through the ditches carrying SA80-A2 British Army assault rifles, thirty kilos of kit and ammunition on our backs plus UGL's – underslung grenades firing out to 350 metres – two per platoon Section. Corporal Luke 'Spooks' and Private Skinner shoulder .338 Finnish Lapua Magnum -firing sniper rifles that can hit a man between the eyes at two kilometres. Corporal Onuzo lugs our 7.62mm belt-fed machine gun, with an effective range of half a kilometre. Jones 270 packs our Javelins, fire-and-forget. Privates Mawson and Brown bring our 51mm mortars, Sapper 'Lucky' Jonas and his Engineers carry bar mines, claymores and grenades, on the attack for once. Sterling, Havelock and Nduom get away with standard kit, and Greenfield mans the radio to Bastion while Sands, our Medic, packs a hospital. This is what we bring. Waiting for our signal are JTAC-initiated half-ton bombs from American A10's, B1's and F15's, callsign Dude, with Apaches, British or American, listening in from Bastion, equipped with rockets and 30mm cannon, callsign Ugly, ready to deliver like a road drill from the sky.

Against us are their AK47's and RPG's, their IED's and on special days the '107' rockets of Terry 'Tally' Taliban.

Is it a fair fight? It's not supposed to be. 'A determined and resourceful enemy with a gift for coming up behind you,' the battalion commander put it, and there was a cheer when he said that this time, we are better armed and better prepared, and allowed to do our jobs. Our power is awesome.

I surveille a field of poppies, and satisfied, I nod to the lieutenant, who orders the attack. My country's wealth ploughs into Terry.

I do not remember every kill. Mostly we find them, blackened and mangled as we smash our way in. I drop two for certain. The first is a footsoldier. I put two rounds in his forehead before he takes a breath. Whoever paid him ten dollars a day valued him less than a Big Mac meal, supersized. I cost twenty times as much.

The second is a commander behind a hut. He begs for his life, when he wouldn't have spared mine – he would've videoed me for the world to watch. I put a round in his chest, two in the head. I do it to keep us safe. I know that. I do it and force back my vomit. An Apache circles above us, ploughing shells into the village until there's nothing left but crying and dust.

We fire 90,000 rounds that day, drop four tonnes of explosives, launch thirty rockets and fifty grenades, to kill two dozen Tally, confirmed, plus others we vaporised. We suffer three wounded, including Greenfield who dies of blood-loss on the operating table.

The Politicians declare the region pacified and we pull out before the stain has dried and the kids have stopped weeping for their missing dads. A month later, another Terry commander moves in, and lords it again, and strikes at whoever's in reach while our trucks pay 'taxes' to his border guards to allow our kit to retreat into Pakistan.

Waiting for the plane out of Bastion, the Padre and I drink whiskey, off-manual, to keep us glued together; fractured men.

That was war in Afghan.

And the Padre has no word of consolation; just a poem from The Hidden One on his phone.

Now follow me, child, to the plains of Nineveh,
Mound of heresy, offense to Allah,
Raised on idols and Crusaders' images
– no gardens grow, no waters flow –

where on the Day Of Vengeance, they say,
Yankees will fear and British know
that the rocks of Ramadi
Smoothed by the banner and its holy shadow
are hurled by The Hidden One
who weeps, my child, because
your only reward is 'paradise'.

It was the last part that got the poet into trouble, and made Blackwood want to save him.

But the Hidden One was long gone. Taken by his own.

31: Day 7: 'Morale'

I have to know our motivation, to be sure no-one will white-out. So after two more days of reccying the factory, I stoke the burner and ask them to sit. Nicely.
 -Tell me why you want this place, I say. -Each of you.
 Spooks, Mo 13, Work Experience and Jonas are in agreement. They have nowhere else to go. To the outside world, we are the Crazies, to be pitied while building charity houses on reality TV, or ignored in hostels and jail.
 Miss Morphine brightens with the old game. -We can make it nice up here, that's what I think, put up some art, and books, and... She throws her hands in the air.
 -Chandeliers...? I say. -Blackwood?
 I brace myself but what comes up is a slowly-releasing spring, not a leap down my throat:
 -I need a place that lets me know who I am. I never put down roots, so if I own this place and if it's full of 'history' then okay. I want to kick the history out and make it safe for us all. I'll fight for that no matter what it costs. Is that ok, P?
 The fire crackles. Jonas murmurs agreement but Spooks shuffles his feet; he's not been the same since I threatened his drugs. I turn to Zoë Palmer.
 She hugs her daypack, examines her nails: -I want to go home...
 That's not what I asked.
 She blinks, rapidly. I wait.
 -Okay if you must know, I still think we could make good money out of it... You, she corrects herself, -could make good money...

There's a moment of disbelief in those who've not heard her say this before, then Blackwood unravels, fast: -'Good money'? Goddammit! he bellows. -Surely somewhere should be free of all that madness? No-one can afford a damn thing anyway unless it cripples them...! What's your problem..?
-"Threat Equity", I mutter, and they frown at me.
The Surveyor shrinks, and there's more to her than this and I want to reach out and take her in my arms, feeling fire I have no control over in my belly and I want to tell her she can do it, she can be brave, and think again, be strong and beautiful and stupidly my words don't form up like Two Section given clear orders, they charge out of my mouth like rookie militias. If she wants pounds and pence and purchases then my story is of things taken, by force or neglect, of places scarred by loss, and pain not pleasure and because of all of that:
-My reason, I say, -is I don't want this place. I want you.
Jonas snorts and calls me Psycho. I ignore him. I'll take it as a test. Blackwood is dissolving into a world of his own when I need him most, the Caretaker hasn't shown up, our food stocks are low, I get angry at our food being rubbish, at Jonas' sarcasm and Spooks' negativity, the fact that I can't break into the hooch cabinet no matter how hard I hit it, and our quarters are an ice box of useless antiques. But I will go to work.
Zoë Palmer hides her hands between her knees, and looks up at me.
-The restaurant? she asks quietly. -We have to give it a try.
Yes. So that's it. She's shown us what we're worth, which is just enough to escape from, and I see in her what Kats was: a chaser after bigger hits. My heart will scab over when there's action, alcohol, and more action because there are no green hills here to run to, only barren roofs.
I rip Blackwood's note from the wall and slap it on the table

between us: *Deliver us from evil.*

Jonas spits. -With Psycho on the case...

I see the past in his eyes and the tremors in his hands. It's no small thing creeping around this maze. He's right. So I jam the paper back on the wall with the fork and head out to the shower.

This time, when I come back in, naked from the waist up, my shirt is in my fist and it's staying there. There's something I can't say in words but it's drawn all over me. So I hold my fists up and turn my back to them like a crucifix, slowly, while my tattoos, monsters and scrolls unwind across old blast scars and electrical whip-marks, surrounding the thing I am, spread across my shoulder blades and down my spine in red, yellow, and black – the dragonfly.

I cover myself and go to the sideboard, pour myself a mug of rainwater and bring it to my mouth, spilling it, shaking.

I may be dead by nightfall, but I will be a good man. A hunter. A protector. One who loves the ones he should.

Maybe I can do it, in this building, for them, for her.

And I can't let myself care what they think of me, not anymore.

32: Day 8: 'Best Practices in Counter Insurgency'

It's time. The false trails we've laid will mean we can strike back and take this place with a new sort of force. That is my deep and sincere hope, and I have briefed them all, including Blackwood, on what I expect. Today, when we see a gathered mass of mob and Defeated, instead of hiding, we will confront them.

And this time, Zoë Palmer brings her kit, map-making, and I lead her, Blackwood, Jonas and the Teenager into the belly of the factory. Mo 13, Spooks and Miss Morphine stay behind, on guard, to receive our wounded, or to decide how to survive if we don't make it.

It will be five of us, versus hundreds.

Blackwood doesn't make it easy. He brings the African's map and tries every door, and when I challenge him, he resists me. The Caretaker has given him a new obsession – finding the other half of the child's diary; a single page in this endless wreck. With it, he says, he will know what to do. Instead, we find lost souls we didn't need to: construction workers, office types, unemployed locals, dazed junkies, stag and hen do's, house-hunters, all of them Defeated, all of them hungry. Talk about impossible. But we need to pacify this place; bring it under our command. If the hope of a scrap of paper helps him do that, I will allow it.

We spray our last graffiti tags – in pink – ensuring our trails finish up in the hall with the restaurant door and tables, deserted now, no rap stars or burning tyres, but the tables are there, laid out for a mini-fiesta, al fresco style. If we can funnel enough of the mob through here… and if that door opens when we need it to… maybe we can send them home, gang by gang.

We take positions on the balcony; me, Zoë Palmer and Blackwood opposite the restaurant, the other two hiding on either side. We hold wires that Jonas rigs up, stretching into the roof. It's untested, but hey, that's war.

Night deepens and an indoor rain of leaks from faraway roofs comes and goes. I point out isolated clusters of partygoers gathering in the darkness.

I curse the Defeated under my breath.

-Why do you call them that?

She's dim in the shadows but her fear is crystal, and I didn't think I'd said it aloud.

-Tell me, she says.

So, with a bit of embarrassment, I describe how our all wars are defeats. Nothing changes. Banks still rob us and we do nothing. Big boys threaten to switch off our gas or internet and instead of thinking why the hell we let them rule us, we consume even more crap we don't even want made by people who hate us and then we consume each other. Call it 'a relationship'. Then we move on to someone else. And money stands over us all, laughing like Death laughed at me, and we see no other way out from it, so we call it 'normal'. That's being Defeated.

-But P, she frowns, -we pay our way and get something back, doing business, and it's not perfect but it's better than chaos... Am I defeated? she asks. -I don't feel like it.

-You dream of running from a cliff...

-I do my best...

-You what..?

-I do my bit ...you know... to be 'ethical'...... I recycle...

I can't even laugh. Her voice is clammy with fatigue and as we fall into silence, a heaviness grows, a feeling she's right, that there is only business-as-usual, and it defeats us all. Get used to it.

The restaurant door clatters open and in come the chefs in a blaze of light and noise, carrying steel pans like Army caterers, and down go the plates and the pots and kit, checking and stirring and following up with piles of breads and baskets of fruit. The smell wafts up against the damp of Victory Cocoa and the urge to sack it all and go down there and get that good scram is tough to resist. Then the door closes, and I hope the two lads in the balconies don't get ideas. But we don't have long to wait. The door flashes in rapid succession like a luminous gob, disgorging knots of ravers, ramblers, frightened couples, office parties, bodies falling through, spat into the factory, tickets in hand… They hover, bewildered in their own torchlights, looking to sit and eat, then the mob howls from the shadows and attacks, chasing them between the tables and into the echoing blackness where some are caught, others escape toward the backs of houses that have been swallowed by this place. In the dark balconies I hear the Teenager and Jonas stifle their voices, even Blackwood mutters from his catatonic state by the railing. They have recognised some of the newcomers; even a celeb or two.

-You still wanna go down there? I ask.

Her face is a mask.

I thought not.

Before any gangs can gather again, Jonas joins me and we slip down and move between the food tables, the smell almost overwhelming, in commando mind-set sticking to the plan, we jemmy all the exits, turning them into one-way traps, passing quickly from one to the next, and finally to a huge, sliding, goods-door that we pull across the route to the backs of the absorbed houses and we fix it shut with hidden chocks. The only exit now is the restaurant door. We creep back to the balcony and take our positions as mob start trickling in again, this time through doors we've tripped that won't let them back out.

Blackwood washes down handfuls of pills. I blag two, and

swallow them, feel the sunshine grow in my chest and head...

A victim enters from a rigged door, skidding, spinning as far as the tables, followed by two more torches. Thunder rolls, and a dozen lamps and mobile screens burst in and fall on the victims, followed by more people entering than we've seen before, a riot unfolding at the centre, bickering over the banquet that's not big enough for all of them and they're unsure why they've ended up here. So far so good.

Zoë Palmer groans as they pour in, jeering, high, confused, swirling down the length of the hall in waves of lights, cramming through the entrances we've plotted, eddying, confused, activists and bystanders both swept up in it, the weaker vanishing beneath the strong, hoovering up the food on the tables with Jonas' doors closing behind them like valves, and I have my first moment of doubt. They are only thirty feet below us, and their faces flash: fierce, afraid, old, young, hungry. Music buzzes from a box carried on the shoulders of a gang in black who cut through the rest to clear a space where White Suit steps out from between them and onto a stool, and he's lit up. Zoë Palmer yelps and my breath stops. We need White Suit. It shows it's working because he clearly wasn't expecting to be here. A victim squeals at his feet and he waves his arms impatiently – it's bedlam. The crush is so fierce that when the restaurant door opens with its gust of light, the people scrambling over the tables near it – suits, trackies, campers, townies – wedge themselves into the frame, pushing back the newcomers. It quickly blocks with bodies.

We need to shove them through; I give Blackwood the nod: -Engage!

Will it work? Can he do it?

I urge him. Now! The ruckus is turning to the White Suit. Disappointment grabs my chest as Blackwood struggles to move or make a sound, but he rises to his feet and a rebel, almost animal yell swells out of him, a cry that slides, hoarse and attacking something high above him, pouring out a howl of loneliness that I only guessed was in him.

The lights jostle – they've come to chase, not be herded and they are furious at anything that stands in the way of their enjoyment, and my heart sinks because we need to win this crowd but Blackwood howls again, like a wolf in the rafters and the White Suit, surrounded by his thugs, turns this way and the whole mob's attention is on our noise now, not on him. A torch picks out the source of the cry, followed by a hundred lights and screens. The restaurant is wedged open by silhouetted bodies, and tables have been overturned, food sliding off them.

Blackwood rises like helium.

I've no idea what'll come out of this medicated Padre, but he needs to command the mob. I'm worried...

He spins over the railing, which catches him like a tentacle and straightens him up. He glares at the mob:

-You scum of the earth..! he shrieks and I'm thinking: No, Blackwood, no no no....

More lights pick out the Padre. Maybe it's something they can Tweet, thinking it's been laid on by White Suit, who glowers, but then the lights divide. Those by the restaurant squeeze in harder, worsening the bottleneck. I hope against hope while angry clumps form up, flashing at White Suit whose thugs hold firm, their spots aimed at Blackwood while their leader bares his teeth and the Padre screams:

-You shits-on-my-shoooe! Haa oooh!

The activists force a laugh. Others stay on the fence – the good-time squad who didn't come here to be challenged, and they are separating over this cry of pain.

Blackwood crackles. People hammer at the exits but Jonas has sealed them in. The only way out is the restaurant, blocked with bodies. Blackwood lashes out, in whips of rage.

-Get out of my house!

I urge him to come back on track, to execute the plan, but: -Scum..! Scum..! Scum of the earth..! he chants. -I will lay my punishment upon you!

Come now, Blackwood, come on come on come on. What's the matter with you? Give them hope! Undermine their leaders..!

-Get your stink out of my HOUSE..! he raises his arms in the agreed signal, way too soon, and Jonas and Work Experience yank their wires and a hail of silver sweets drops onto the panicking crowd. The restaurant is gridlocked, no-one is getting out but they hurl more sweets until heaven help me Lucky Jonas lets off a firework. It's payback for the Teenager's birthday and it detonates onto the crowd, who bellow.

The factory heaves like a womb and I see bodies. White Suit holds firm, teeth blazing as the hardcore glue themselves around him.

Jonas is lighting another rocket. I'm furious.

I signal 'withdraw' and drag Blackwood back. I look for Zoë Palmer but she's not beside us. I call her name again and again, against all mission protocol, with no reply. I pull the Padre into our hideout while faces roar and jump. Work Experience arrives, swaying on his pins, saying she did not came his way. Two more rockets spin into the crowd.

I reach Lucky Jonas, his eyes wild, swearing that 'no woman' has got past him. I throw him into the darkness to join Blackwood and I scour the faces below, looking desperately for her, and there, I spot her, scrambling over the bodies in the restaurant door. The light behind it goes black, slammed against them in a billowing shriek while Thugs start smashing at one of Jonas' valves with an axe.

I see the stairs she must've used, but a scion of crazies have broken through and are heading up. I have to get us out of here. I have lost her. I have done it again.

The factory starts to rain, internally.

Bergen heavy, Tally and ISIS, Kats and Zoë Palmer in every shadow, I pull us along, the Teenager and Jonas struggling and tripping, Blackwood halting at doors. I grab him. His face is greasy and pictures slide over it: Poet, Commander, Girl...

We get twenty yards and the corridor flexes. Thugs appear. More come up behind us, with a Rottweiler.

I draw my steel and adrenalin fills my veins, sweet drug of choice, better than promises or so-called love. I drop the nearest Thug in one swipe and the Teenager kicks a second one down before a skeleton in a suit jumps out, waving its arms:

-We just wanna talk, innit!

Troy.

33: Dark 8: 'Causes, Aims and Elements'

We're led into an office where an angle poise lamp points at us from a desk that's loaded with steaks, cakes, pastries, fruit and bottles of wine. Behind it sits the White Suit with a skinny girl on his arm. She's distant and pock-marked, a gold patch sprayed on her forehead, wearing a T-shirt daubed with 'Scrounger'.
 -More tea, vicar..? he circles his hands.
 Ten Thugs – including the Crap Hats who abandoned us when the Sanctuary fell – one dog, and Troy stand against us, laughing.
 Blackwood trips. Jonas lets out a volley of curses at the Crap Hats.
 I'm not doing this without a fight. I twist violently into Troy and he hits the wall. Work Experience kicks a Thug in the nuts, flooring him.
 More close in but White Suit hollers for them to stop, and they pause. Their dog growls.
 I have my steel. Jonas has a lighter under a rocket and the Teenager keeps his hoodlum in check with – I cannot believe it – a samurai sword.
 I roar at them all: -Eleven on four. These are my kinds of odds, muthafuckas. Let's see who's standing in five, four, three, two...
 White Suit waves for calm.
 I don't take orders from him.
 I'm six foot four and there's not much left on my bones these days but sinews, teeth, fists, skull, scars and rage held together with tattoos and madness and I will be their nightmare because I have nothing to lose. I have ten seconds of this energy in me because

it's made of anger and anger eats its owner so I fly out of hell at them, tear heads from necks, spew venom, throw them into my underworld, two Thugs beneath me already. A firework skids into a corner. Bang! The dog leaps at the Teenager's chest and I get my blade on a Thug's throat.

I feel a hammer on my head with stars and pain while Blackwood goes down beneath another so I let the Bergen spin me to his side, plant a boot in the pig that's on top of him, get my knees beneath me and swipe at two Thugs who come at me from behind. My blade catches one who howls while Jonas gets trapped underneath four more.

White Suit claps. The knuckleheads stand down, all shapes and sizes, male and female, hungry and itching to eat us. Other ghosts only I can see melt away into the walls like rats.

White Suit's on his feet, cooing. I want his guts but my head is pounding and my hand is sticky. Instinct gets me upright. The gorillas rub their wounds, taking new positions – one has his boot on Blackwood's neck. Their Rottweiler, though, quivers in the Teenager's arms, growling at anyone who comes near him.

I lunge and knock Blackwood's assailant off him and three others swamp me, planting heavy punches in my face. Again, their boss orders them to release me.

I drop to my knees.

-That's more like it, he thrums.

I study the blood on my hands, fuzzy, needing Blackwood to act, hauling us up, coughing. I have my steel. Jonas holds his jaw but he nods at me: he'll stick with us if we can think of something.

White Suit reveals his teeth. He creaks like leather, slightly out of breath, posh vowels dropping onto Blackwood: -Is this a good time to talk, Rev'rend..?

I spray disbelief.

-A drink..! he turns and bellows at me. -Come, Soldier!

He selects a grape from the table, places it between his teeth and pops it. Hungry and parched, I wonder if Blackwood will accept, but the Padre murmurs:

-You shit, Whistler.

I give a low cheer.

White Suit swallows. -Come, come, Rev'rend. Who's the 'shit' here? I'm a very successful man. I've built a thriving business in this dump and we have hard-working people here paying good money to get a little excited and maybe get a little revenge on those who've let them down... their secret is safe with me - isn't that something you'd pay for? To hide your guilt amongst your friends..?

His followers chuckle. -So... he says, -How much are you making, Vicar?

Blackwood sways. I reach out and hold him, planting blood on his sleeve, my head floating. I think of Zoë Palmer and wonder what this slimeball did to scare her, and whether she got out, or if she's wandering in the maze. Blackwood has to talk us out of here – but something else is going on. It takes shape in my mind as I realise, rapidly, where we are. This is the centre of gravity. We are there. The very thing I said I'd hit, hard.

-You can't get out of this building, I smile at the mob boss. -Can you, pal...?

White Suit takes a sip from a wine glass: -We all escape in our own way, Soldier. We all have our 'sanctuary'...

The dog growls in the Teenager's arms. Work Experience rubs its belly.

I'm surer than before: -You're in hell, here. And you can't get out.

-Oh, really..? he wipes his hands on the girl: -I don't know about you, 'mate', but I'm in fucking paradise..!

His Thugs and Crap Hats guffaw. Light falls on his inky eyebrows, pale cheeks and skin so thick with product that his eyes are like coals in powder: -I fear we may have gotten off on the wrong footing,

Soldier, he says, stroking the girl: -For what matters most is love, sir, and it's practically wall-to-wall in here some nights. Isn't that right, Troy..?

Troy shuffles, targeted. Blackwood stares at the ground.

I recognise this Whistler, now. He was a politician, once, with banking interests – or was it the other way round? I never can tell. He'd even inspected our troops, with his open-neck shirt and body armour, a pizza bar just out of camera shot.

-The world is made of Runners and Chasers, he says. -Choose wisely, Rev'rend, and I'll give you twenty percent.

I kick a piece of debris across the floor. Blackwood looks up.

The businessman raises his hands: -Money is good! It penetrates places soldiers can't. Ask the Chinese! Or the Saudis!

Blackwood's shivering, his failure turning into shock.

Whistler sighs. -Look, I've had it with priests and flocks, Rev'rend – all that gay hate and kiddie fiddling. I could've made you my ultimate scapegoats, real-life Guy Fawkses. But no. I want more. You were pure gold tonight, Rev'rend, even if I say so myself, it was old fashioned, moral S&M. It whips people up and gives them something to bounce off.

-So here's my offer, he takes another drink and wipes his lips. -Tell them what little shits they are. They repent at leisure, wherever your crappy little office is, get a moral detox, and you send them back to me angrier and hungrier. Make sense? Soldiers, churchmen – you'll be sensational. Tell you what, I'll even raise the ticket price, and when they're done with you, they will always return to me – because my highs are greater than yours.

He grins. -I like it so much I'm getting a hard-on.

Blackwood growls: -Why the hell would I agree to that?

I grip my steel.

-Oh please, says Whistler, picking his teeth. -A certain Padre James Blackwood is killed, colluding with Daesh on an illegal, unparliamentary operation in Syria. Only a "Marine P" gets anyone out alive, and he goes potty in the aftermath, takes an overdose after killing innocent civilians. Everyone in power knows the story and I'm willing to bet you're the self-same chaps, which makes you a commodity.

-But here's the fun part, he indicates the walls, -while the Rev'rend claims this "house" is his, my builders – the delicious Ms Palmer included, Soldier – are tearing it apart. What was that word, Troy? "Intestate"? Lacking balls?

Troy grunts.

-So while you remain dead, my dear James, and unable to prove otherwise, you're irrelevant. I can enjoy your pain or we can have a relationship. Agree to my terms and I'll let you stay. Otherwise, I will chase you into the depths and you can sermonise the demon or whatever's down there for yourself.

Blackwood: -So you'd pay me to fix the people you've broken?

Whistler lifts an eyebrow: -You make it sound so bleak...

He clicks a finger and Troy shoves a sports bag across the floor.

-Let me care for your needs... says Whistler. -And avoid unpleasantness.

Work Experience looks to me. I give the nod and he unzips the bag, one arm over the Rottweiler. His eyes pop as he lifts out a foiled brick, a corner peeled to reveal Afghan resin. My saliva leaps. He takes out a bottle of whiskey, then a wedge of fifties in an elastic band. A box of medicines. A schoolbook in Arabic. A carton labelled: X-Box. He hovers. From the bottom of the bag, the Teenager lifts a canvas wrap, half a metre long. He hoists it to me with a knowing look and my skin leaps as I unfurl a British Army assault rifle.

-Whatever turns you on, says Whistler, sitting back with a sudden, weary crack in his voice.

Bullpup layout, full mag – no blanks – trigger-group oiled and smooth, fire-control, gas-operation, metal cocking – shclick schlack

– scuffed but maintained. Barrel five hundred and eighteen mil in length. Five kilos fully loaded, with scope, firing seven hundred rounds per minute, velocity one kilometre per second, effective out to five hundred metres, meaning death in half a moment. It feels so long since I held one of these. I swing it into my shoulder and pan across his monsters. They screech and tumble and I aim at Whistler's head. He closes his eyes, leans back and lets out a sigh. I squeeze off three rounds of live ammunition.

Blackwood yells. Thugs panic and the girl screams. Dust swirls from a grouping I've made on the wall just behind the businessman's head.

Whistler blinks, looks around and sees he's still here. He slowly digs a finger into an ear, regarding me with hatred.

He'd wanted me to.

I was right.

My blood surges and I get him back in my sights. I should kill him, yes him and all his gorillas, seize his girl and rob his stash, be king of this fucking pile, make Jonas grovel and Blackwood act like a man when I tell him to.

But why should Whistler be set free?

I swing the weapon down, click to safety, extract the mag, scatter the ammo and toss the gun back into the bag. Thud. It leaves my hands like chains but I want it back already.

Whistler forces a grin. -Health and safety never was my strong point...

His black eyes ball us, filled with uncomplicated venom. His fingers crawl to a peach and penetrate it.

-Be my bitch, Rev'rend...

Blackwood howls.

Whistler is furious: -My customers don't waste their time with 'god', or 'evil', sir, they just get on with it. But fuck me they love a good shiver... They just don't force it down anyone's throats..!

-Bullshit..! yells Blackwood and a piston rams his body. -Your god is: "What I want" and your evil is: "leave me alone to consume it"!

-See, Troy? says Whistler. -What did I tell you..? This priest is hired.

Blackwood dives and bashes the lamp, throwing shadows around. -Never!

Whistler leans away and rattles his Rolex, glancing at the walls as if he doesn't trust them. -It's my house while I control the door, he lowers his voice, -But I'm a reasonable chap, always ready to play fair, so here's my offer: I'll wait twenty-four hours to hear from you, then I'm coming to take what's mine.

His Thugs retrieve the bag. One of them shouts at the dog but it barks, preferring Work Experience. They shuffle, watching us with hunger, smirking, waiting to see us stripped bare, but nervous, too, knowing we're beasts in a paper cage.

-The girl, says Blackwood.

Whistler's teeth flash. -Filthy Rev'rend… why not!

He dismisses her onto the floor, brushes himself down and moves to the exit, dragging his people with him. He gives me a puzzled stare as he passes me, almost regretful, and they vanish like oil into the factory, taking their pale leader with them.

Work Experience stands at the table with an apple in his hand.

All the food is plastic.

And the heavier shadow crosses the door, following Whistler's gang.

34: Dark 8 Plus & Day 9: 'Dealing with Unknowns'

We reach the Parlour exhausted, ravenous and not with good news. Spooks shakes his head about the sports bag while Miss Morphine checks us over, slathering Universal Goo onto any tiny nick. Mo 13 throws sticks into the burner as if he can incinerate our problems and Lucky Jonas stamps in from re-setting traps and false walls, bars the door and collapses onto his bag. The Teenager crouches on his pins, his attention on the dog. I tell him to put his antique sword away before he pokes an eye out, and as for the mutt, just don't give it names. The Padre goes silent with pills and his book while the new girl is face-down on the table, asleep. She's dressed like a lap dancer, with lank, bleached hair. Spooks watches her when he thinks no one's looking.

There's no sign of the Caretaker, but a demijohn sits in the window. How I'd missed it is a mystery. I twist the cork like killing a chicken, pour myself a mug and feel warmth go down my throat, drain it and rapidly sink a second one, thinking:

What the hell have we done?

Horror and craving roll through me as I think of the gun, the recoil in my shoulder and the comfort it gave me. Would it be so wrong to have kept it..? Even to defend ourselves..? Just until the Padre has his awakening..?

And like a knife in the heart, I know that Zoë Palmer left my side, preferred her chances with the mob. Maybe she got out, but I don't see how. She'll be running in the maze, even though she has the only decent map of where we are, on her tablet. The ache in my chest is frightening. I'll have to go back and find her.

I ask Blackwood what's next and he bites:
-What choice have we got..?

Whistler was right about one thing: I was given a medal and the Padre was branded a traitor. The others would be court martialled or have their cases dismissed if they turned Evidence against the rest. Darling God was our WMD.

The Brass had a shitstorm on their hands in Syria, so they tried a low-budget, unsanctioned mission that went Pete Tong enough to have got them strung up like pissed paratroopers on a Friday night. Instead they had this perfect, dead scapegoat and a chance to pin a gong on me in exchange for my silence, disband Two Section and drive me to the loony bin. "Marine P breaks the rules of engagement" would be news enough. But it was much, much worse than that. I obeyed. They wanted a high value jihadi scalp so they used the Padre to find it, and me to execute. My orders were changed to maximum kill, just as he was talking me down from Kats' text. They told me to betray him. But I'd had it. It wasn't worth the cost in lads and locals, nor the strain you take when you kill someone you shouldn't. I was high on morphine that day because I'm a junkie at heart and I led Bolson to his death, hurt his lads, tortured an enemy, maybe two. Then I killed a girl and her lover. In that last part, I obeyed.

But bigger than it all, is what Whistler doesn't know. When no-one was looking, a tiny thing that meant anything was possible. One spark was bigger than a bomb: that girl lived again.

The Drone crew were ordered to finish it off with Hellfire from their laptops. Did Whistler see their medals, too? No. But I won't stop. I will pay my debt to Blackwood. I will be a good man if it kills me and if these field notes turn out to be my obituary.

Just two things remain: Blackwood did not give in to Whistler, not yet. Even if he didn't win the day with his hatred of the mob. He stood his ground, back there.

And now I miss her. I do not trust her and I know she can't stay. But I will be the hunter, the protector. I will do it again.

It's a restless night of no bass, no noise in the floors and walls, just the building flexing in the wind. I see Lego stacking into space, a tunnel in which a writer's head vaporises, rubble running through my fingers, pillars and missiles climbing at angles, crystals through which I scramble in panic, and–

-Blud, you gotta see this.

Jonas is kicking me.

First light. Day nine.

He didn't call me Psycho.

He points at a hole the size of a double door that has breached the walls from the door to the balcony, the wallpaper shredded like Christmas wrapping. I join the others, peering into a corridor that was simply not there last night. Blackwood leans on the brand new doorframe in disbelief at what lies beyond.

The dog sniffs. Mutts have always meant trouble, and this one jigs like a tick in a box. But we step through the hole, into a new corridor. There are windows as far as the eye can see, paced between solid doors. We push through one, and it opens onto a vintage two-up-two-down leading off the main passageway. As does the next, and the next, each door between the windows turning out to be an entrance to a new house. Where we slept last night is just a foyer to a colony of homes with receptions, bathrooms, kitchens, bedrooms and staircases climbing one, two, three storeys up into the pitched roofs all around.

And the village keeps on growing, with French doors at one

point bursting into fields spread across a roof valley, beneath a sky ripped by a patch of blue; cool air and grass on the tiles, rising and falling like the wild places of Wales.

Back inside, there's furniture under sheets: overstuffed sofas and wing-backs, sprung mattresses and iron bedsteads, wardrobes, mirrors, mahogany sideboards, tables and dressers, cupboards with linen, plates and cutlery on hooks, Bakelite electric connections, stoves and fireplaces, all abandoned, under wraps.

Back in the parlour to this residential warren, inside its new entrance hangs a chandelier, fresh as ice. It tinkles as we pass beneath it, notifying the factory that we are here.

And in the centre of the table is a crowbar with a bunch of grapes, and the note that I'd pinned to the wall, to which someone has added on the back in thick, carpenter's pencil: *Learn your lesson.*

I pick a grape. It's real.

This is the graffiti I saw when the factory wouldn't let us go. Does it think we're ready? Is that what this is?

We tool up and penetrate the warren. Blackwood limps, map in hand, breaking into doors, feverishly peering and moving on. We find tinned food in every kitchen – a generation out of date. I prise some beans open and they smell okay. There's no telling where this ends, but there's still only one way in and one way out: the hole in the wall where I'd once pinned the note.

-This is a problem, I say, thinking of that SA80, standing at a window with Blackwood, blurry from pills but fizzing with what we've accessed. Miss Morphine is sketching, sensing what this place could be.

He's spellbound: — We could take shelter up here forever, P.

I take a step back. -So it's over, then? Peace in our time?

He ignores me. -Zoë Palmer would love all this... Why did she run, P.?

-To reach her son, I sigh. -Wouldn't you?

He nods, slowly. -Do you think she made it?

-No, I say, and the admission hits me. -She'll be down there having to make contact with Whistler, that's for sure. He's her only connection to the world she belongs to. And you know she has a map of where we are, right?

-I wish she were here. It's a gift… he says. -I'm not sure why, but…

-We should've finished them off when we had the chance.

-It's shown us mercy, he whispers. -Victory Cocoa.

I recall the spark I saw in him, facing Whistler: -He left that room first, not us. They did not win. We had the momentum.

His eyes close. -This changes everything…

I punch the woodwork. -I should've killed him!

Spooks swears, nearby. There's hooch in my belly but I'm not drunk. This stuff doesn't to do that but it does make me want a purpose again. I should try Zoë Palmer on the phone and see if she made it.

-Marine P, he says again. -This changes everything…

We cautiously allocate apartments near the parlour. Miss Morphine chooses one opposite mine but Mo 13 ushers her on, saying the next one is bigger. The party girl, an East European calling herself Gracya, drifts into it instead, wrapped in one of the Caretaker's coats. She flops onto the mattress with a squeak of springs.

My billet is two rooms – enough to keep bodily functions separate. I enter it carefully. It's not a tent, a barrack or a hostel. I place my Bergen on the bed and my sleeping bag on the floor, nudge the window open and the night blows in. I deal with clothes that need airing and lie down on the floor, watching the war and Zoë Palmer, her boy and his father, Whistler's teeth and Kats, all my broken choices... The floorboards give hardness and calm.

The window lets an icy rain sneak in and a puddle creeps toward my hips. But this feels like safe haven; a place to think.

I stop myself. Someone will take it away soon enough.

The next morning in the Parlour, the guys are bantering. Jonas is at the stove.

-Look after the dog, Work Experience! says Mo 13. -Jonas is looking for meat!

-Waiter! hoots the Medic, -These eggs look like they're mine!

They laugh and Spooks glances away from Gracya. It's been a long time since I've seen warmth from Two Section. It reminds me of days when everyone came back alive.

Blackwood calls for attention. He has Snow's *Industry & Architecture* and the first half of the note he's looking for. He resembles a fire that's been started with petrol – fast burning, and who knows where it will go before it stops.

35: Day 10: 'Develop'

-What should we do with the things we've been given? he asks.

They tease each other over liberated cornflakes, not exactly listening.

-Share them? says Gracya, wearing the Caretaker's coat. It's the first time I've heard her speak.

Blackwood smiles.

I hold my head in my hands. Share? Share with whom? This sounds like Whistler talking.

-"Honour is the equity of kindness," Blackwood taps his book and Gracya sniffs. Maybe she understands because I sure as hell don't.

-So, he says. -We can make our own world, up here. Right? There's only a handful of us but listen, this is all we need: we could start all over again..!

They shuffle. Wind ruffles the curtains and the chandelier tinkles. Oh, no, I'm thinking, their 'sanctuary' game again...

-With cash and credit cards, club-cards, cafes, pubs and all those ways of organising stuff so that the aim is to give nothing of yourself away, just numbers and images of the State, like a wall against other people so they stay back, you can just carry on consuming whether it's ideas, foods, things, art, whatever... all according to your appetites, letting them rule over you and cutting out anyone who stands in your way. Even art is consumption unless we ask if it took us beyond our appetites? And if it did, where did it take us..? And what about people? How much do we consume other people?

-Honour, he says, jamming his finger into *Industry &*

Architecture, -is when you go out of your way to treat someone better, and they treat you better in return. That makes equity. See? Instead of squeezing what you can out of someone, you put extra effort in, and it's growth in the new economy because you gave that person a margin to grow into. And it's currency because if you give someone a kindly bit extra, the flow of honour returns to you later. If you carry out a necessity, you bank that, plus you generate a thankful extra. If you give someone leisure by your actions, the currency returns to you as leisure-plus. The risk of unpleasantness or danger on someone's behalf comes back to you as larger honour from them, whilst cooking and cleaning mustn't trap anyone, and neither must dreamers be crushed by pulling twenty-five hour days to prove themselves.

-So we get, like, extra baked beans...? the Sniper grins.

Jonas swings a spoon at his head. The chandelier tinkles.

-Or who does the latrines..? the Sniper continues.

Blackwood taps his book and agrees that dreams rise or fall on who shovels the shit. -This time, he announces. -Shit is honour.

It's bonkers, but my stomach leaps. He's coming alive.

-A long time ago when I was a trainee priest there was this jumble sale in the hall with piles of clothes on trestle tables and all these people elbowing each other out of the way to find what they wanted. I had this vision of them cutting each other out to find some sort of golden fleece at the bottom of the pile and I thought, that's how it is, everyone thinking there's this thing that everyone wants, maybe it's material, maybe it's rights, who knows, and we get shouty at each other and scramble for the golden fleece when it's not there. It doesn't exist. And what have we become?

-I want us to dream again, he says, -of what we wanted to be, and what we wanted to do. We could bring each other's dreams to life –– it will be our finest hour..! Honour will be our currency, not debt, like a promissory note flipped on its head...

He smiles as far as his wounds will let him. -I don't know where I'm going with this but it feels good. And we will not forget the things we think are free, such as daylight, and buddleia in bloom...

Mo 13 coughs like a Marxist and says what have we got to lose? Take a look around us, at the world we've come to know. We could be brave. Gracya hides in the Caretaker's coat. Spooks watches her and says that sort of crap is just an excuse for being poor, then at me: -'Specially now Miss Moneybags has gone.

Blackwood fires back: -Mo's right. We could live beautifully up here, but what would be the point? We could sit around like lords or we could go down and bring back the people we love. I know each one of you has seen someone.

Spooks clicks his tongue at a far-off target: -Why would civvies wanna hook up with us? Even the Crap Hats left, and Psycho's woman didn't stay...

I rise with a clatter. Blackwood puts out a hand.

-I'm offering rescue from Whistler's kind of despair.

-And what if we hate them..? Spooks curls a lip.

Blackwood sighs. The warren of houses gapes behind him, chandelier and all.

-Don't expect to think it's normal, he says. -Normal is dead and gone.

-How does that make sense? says Spooks.

But Blackwood's right. Even Zoë Palmer could see that, if she were here.

'Normal' went up in Hellfire about a year ago.

I wear the black for the poor and the beaten down, livin' in the hopeless, hungry side of town, I wear it for the prisoner who has long paid for his crime...
- Johnny Cash, *Man In Black*

Part 5: Asymmetric

36: The Hidden One, Phase 3: 'Darling God'

Syria. The lines are shifting. We're not in Afghan now, with regular units throwing their weight behind us. This is stealth, not wealth. We are the 'advisors', deniable, caught in a tangle of local alliances. If the folks at home knew about this, there would be Protests.

Lieutenant Bolson is under my wing. He's dispersed Two Section well, in trenches a hundred metres from the target, establishing three firing points. I climb to the edge and survey the village that ISIS have taken, shivering with stolen morphine to stop the text she sent me last night from looping in my head and colliding with the Padre's consolations.

The sky is approaching dawn. I'm scared about what it will bring. In the mountain beyond the village sits the monastery of Mar Petrous, like a vast, medieval visor. Behind its walls, the last Syriac monks watch the progress of modern jihad and shelter a handful of kids who fled there when ISIS arrived in the village that sits between us. I shoulder my weapon and peer through the scope, calculating my sprint. 'We'll be back for breakfast, Boss' I tell Lieutenant Bolson.

The first missile flies in, and GPG's thud in from the foothills, above which a handful of Kurds rim the last defences of Mar Petrous with rifles. If ISIS hold the village, that monastery will be their next target. For now, their slaughter is delayed by our unexpected counterattack. Both types of Peshmerga, plus Shiite Militias and Sunni Tribes, a mishmash of deals that could unravel any moment agree the assault, drawing fire away from our sector. In the ditch with Bolson are my hand-picked team: Sapper Jonas, gunners Havelock and Nduom, Sands the Medic, Jones 250, Padre Blackwood, a Teenager who impressed me back in Helmand and our Iraqi 'terp Mohammed 13, who says with the radio pressed to his ear that Jimmy Jihadi doesn't know we are here. I see the shadow of a vast beast pass over the monastery. Sod this morphine.

If they capture me, I will not play their part on TV. I will not read their script. True horror is having your killer's tongue in your throat in your final moment. I'm sure some have resisted and seen children with pistols at their heads. But I have no-one. Any pain they can give is physical only and when they have finished I will go where they cannot reach me. I will advance to England's hills and they will be beaten because they will remain here in the desert with my hollow corpse.

My heart is buried and my word is worthless. Switch me off. You'll be doing me a favour.

I'm ready to fight, now.

Bolson is wary of me and I don't blame him. I'm under orders to extract an asset from this village so I've dragged the Padre onto the team, off-manual, to ensure a smooth ID and 'rendition'. Two Section are here to assist. They hide in the ditch below me.

Two weeks ago, a jihadi came forward with intel about their leaders, including The Hidden One. My ears pricked up. Was this the poet who vanished? Was this where the trail led us? His name was traded across the bazaars, his verses relayed on MP3's and sung on videos winning fans for the cause with his bloodthirsty verses but recently he'd changed to hymns of peace, and was causing rifts, making local Sunnis and foreigners think twice. Our informer said The Hidden One was ready to preach a denunciation of the ISIS butchers, but we'd need to get his 'bride', the girl he's betrothed to, to safety first. I told the Brass what I knew, and about the man in my battalion back in Afghan who'd known the poet, even counted him as a friend, and how he'd made a similar offer once before. Our spooks checked the intel, confirmed by an ISIS boy from Brighton fed up with wiping Chechen arses. The Brass flew Blackwood in, and using voice recognition he confirmed the ID and described his crazy plan: fly the poet to Qatar and get him on the biggest Arabic channels, let his voice plough the culture open, sowing doubt and a love of life into the death-cult's supporters. Many others would join such a leader. He'd be the first in a prestigious new court of cultural heavyweights, denouncing victimhood and discussing the truth and beauty in living. The Brass were impressed by the potential defection, and Qatar – who some say regretted funding ISIS – might well agree.

Then came the news. Instead of vanishing like he did in Afghan, to be near his fiancé here in Syria, the asset and his wife-to-be – the muse for his most famous poems – had been taken hostage by ISIS at Habiballah, a village they'd ethnically cleansed of Christians, below the monastery they now laid siege to. This village we codenamed Darling God Farm. The Brass said they needed a team "to advise the locals", covert but budgeted, to extract The Hidden One before the crazies could behead him on YouTube and sell his girl as a sex slave. The Tribes, Militias and Kurds will neutralise the fortified village – with our air power – and One Section will cover our exit. So I speak to the Padre at length, and throw him into our night march, because he alone can confirm the asset's willingness to switch. He talked me down from Kats and he will help me decide which plan to obey.

Guns crackle on the far side of Darling God and shells fly in from the hills below Mar Petrous. The diversionary action has begun late.

There's a snap of fire and Bolson says One Section have taken a casualty, three hundred metres to our rear. This is bad; they will lose more men stretchering the guy out, aborting the assault. We, however, have not come into contact. I'm reluctant to pull rank on Bolson, who wants Mawson and Brown to lay down suppressing fire for One Section. I jump on him not to give the order. The enemy mustn't know our position. We're not in Helmand now. One Section will have to suck it up.

Jonas cowers. A cook who loves jerk chicken, they say no bird is safe. Find your anger, I tell him. No more roadsides or ambush, it's go go go, it's the reason you suffered and waited; to hear me say: Engage! Get the bastard who's trying to kill you; mow him in half for blowing up your mates.

Whatever else, he mustn't think of home.

The village is hit from three sides; the local alliance giving it everything they've got whilst we've not fired a shot. Bolson wants to abort but he pauses on the radio. He's been asked by the Brass, watching us from drones: Are we on, or off?

We're a hundred metres from the bricks; grey with murder holes through which the enemy can fire. I see no movement, and I see a way in.

If we delay, the balance between drawing fire away from us and chasing the enemy into us will tip. ISIS will murder the asset and upload his last words to the internet, and they will be less than poetic.

-Attack at state red, I say, and begin my sprint across the stones.

37: Days 15-15+: 'The Importance of Operational Design'

I can't rest. She's not here and I can't even try her by phone. So I stand at the factory door, tooled up and ready, when Blackwood asks:
 -Where will you go?
 I tell him I don't know.
 -All this, he says, -is nothing without her, is it?
 I speak into his blue eyes, pinched with burns. -Deliver us.., I say. -That's the mission I'll sign up for.
 His gaze widens, and snaps shut again.
 -Marine P, the mission is love. You want to be delivered from something and I think it's a lack of love.
 -You sound like a pop song, mate. If I bring her back then it's for more than something I can't have. I've got photos of 'love' and me with our toes in ashtrays. Maybe all of this is nothing without her but what if she's here, and it still is nothing…? I'll take that risk but you need to remember the God who fired you up, Blackwood. You need to be big. You need to disobey. That will help us all.
 -I need proof, first, Marine P.
 -No, mate. Proof is a luxury. It's time to act.
 He nods, and I don't like seeing this. He also wants what he cannot have.
 -Bring your book, I say. -It's a start.
 -Shit is honour?
 -Exactly. Normal is dead and gone.
 He brightens, grimly.
 -Okay then, I say. -Get your stuff and let's go.

So the two of us descend, him using the Caretaker's map, crowbarring doors and shaking his head, me with my steel ready. But all's quiet. We meet no mob, only their detritus. Even the export hall where we failed is deserted so I hustle us to the restaurant door, which shows fresh signs of attack from this side. I place my ear on its coldness. Nothing.

A shadow dashes across my torchlight, a hundred metres away. I pan and see pillars, wreckage and houses. Nothing but a serpent sliding round a column: *Learn...*

There's a click by my ear and the door explodes, blazing us over as two figures fall through, grabbing each other and shrieking when the entrance slams shut behind them. They cry out as Blackwood illuminates them – a man and a woman, shielding their eyes.

-Don't be afraid, he says, getting his feet beneath him.

They ask if we're 'the organisers' and Blackwood chuckles. -No.

-Then who are you..?

He lowers his torch and says carefully:

-We are the insurrection.

I'm gutted. This search patrol is over, because the couple agree with Blackwood to come to the Parlour, on the promise of shelter rather than staying in the darkness with Whistler's tricks. Spooks swears when he sees them enter, and I'm thinking he could be right – this is bad. They stand together as if they're ashamed of each other's presence – a boyish guy in his late forties in skinny jeans and expensive jacket who's somehow familiar and a younger woman with her hair pegged up by pens, hands held like she's missing a clipboard. They've brought the outside world with them and that world does not want us to win. The Sniper can see it a mile off.

After a brief turnaround, Jonas and Work Experience join our next patrol, but again we return, this time with five newcomers. I'm frustrated but at least I'm doing something. The Teenager says he knows three of them: two lads and a lass, pock marked and pale, hungry for a hit, frightened by Whistler and a batch of bad gear they took before finding the factory. The Teenager's dog is subdued, and I agree. I shiver with my own, sweat-streaked hunger for gear. We cannot have junkies around, or they'll vampire us like Afghan Po-Po.

The pattern repeats the following day and the newbies we bring back are a married couple in fleeces who stick to each other and wolf down Jonas' custard and carrots. They'd lost hope whilst wanting a baby, they say quietly, and locked themselves in a garage with the engine running, before finding themselves here.

Other stories start coming out. The couple that arrived with Blackwood and me quietly say they were, or are, having an affair, when someone attacked their hotel room. I recognise him now, different in the flesh with no makeup: he's a TV scientist, and it turns out she's his producer. Normally he can smile and tell us we're toast – or was it stardust? – but there's not much chirp or wonder in him now. They keep a nervous distance from us and each other. Blackwood brushes crumbs off a sofa, making space, and instructs them in his three-part mission: honour for currency; sanctuary from threat; building a new life. I gesture at the note on the wall and its crumpled: *Deliver us from evil.* They blink and shuffle.

Blackwood gives each newcomer a blanket and a towel, and shows them to an apartment stocked with food, and what I see is this: As surely as once he waved souls on their way, he is bringing back his dead.

The following morning, Work Experience's junkies leave. They'll be back, they say, but they need to get something sorted, first. He steers them past the improvised devices at the foot of the stairs and returns, diving into his DS with a fierce focus.

The Caretaker is there although I never saw him arrive, regaling the TV couple with tales of cocoa and Ghana. The TV Scientist's leg jiggles. He asks Blackwood about 'the ticket price' and if the 'experience' will, you know, 'go up a gear'.

The couple in fleeces emerge from their nest beyond the chandelier to huddle over bowls of whatever Jonas throws at them. They describe the outside world – the protests crushed in every city, the bankers swaggering free, the refugees piling up on islands and their murderers spreading poison and bombs into bars and shopping malls. And then there's the house they cannot afford and the child they cannot have. They vanish back to their billet, and I think of Kats and what it would have been like to face that world without giving in or getting off our faces, and having our own kid to raise and teach how not to be Defeated, and it aches, but I'll bring Zoë Palmer home. I'll pay for my mistakes.

Each day, I descend into the wreckage, going it alone now, facing drifting bands of Whistler's souls who grow in number, lying in comas or watching me pass by. Their supplies of gear and sex has not gone down, it just seems not to work anymore. It's like the week before the stronger stuff arrives in town. None of them are what I'm looking for, so I climb back at the end of each day, while the factory swirls and beasts grab at my face, with limbs blown clean off their owners and loose wires twisting around me. Hooch helps, but not as much as the Caretaker's tales.

He tells of a girl of seven or eight – none can be sure – in the gnarly forests of Africa where barefoot, she cut the cocoa pods from the trees, working with her father, her mother and brothers, all of them hungry. The spider Anansi was disturbed in the canopy and came down beside her. He told her he was rich and powerful and that she'd offended him by hacking down his home so what would she pay to replant it? Python, leopard, fairy and hornet were the things he'd paid for the stories he'd traded from the sky god, and they don't grow on trees. Can she match that? A child in rags who should be in school instead of harvesting beans, she told the spider to be gone with his possession of sky-high things. I'll match your price with a Queen, a King, a Knight and his Slave, she said, and between them they'll buy your forest. If not, I'll plant you a new one and put you in the canopy with all the stories of men. How will you do this, little girl? he sneered, and she answered: My spit will reach them. Anansi saw profits he couldn't refuse, and agreed. She spat on a cocoa bean and with a smile, she put it in her sack for the weighing station.

Brer Rabbit and Bourne Ultimatums – the Caretaker knows what he's doing, humming the old songs, coughing, coughing...

38: Day 21-ish: 'Positioning'

Three hipsters arrive. They have awesome beards – apart from the girl, whose tattoos make my eyes water. They clutch estate agent leaflets for things they can't afford. They offer to pay rent, dragging suitcases and laptops with them and they bring more news of how it is on the outside, or was, before carbon monoxide got them in their shared flat. The world is making some people very rich again, they say, while others have dropped off the edge. And many of us who cling on, they say, throw even more energy at what we hang on to, by, like, trying to find the best coffee, or local nano-brewery, or by scraping haikus into the dirt on vans – anything to make this time we call life seem full, and worthwhile.

-So dream with us, is Blackwood's welcome.

Instead of rent, they get to work on their laptops, designing things for the Parlour that probably won't get made, and films of us and the Caretaker's stories. They bring a projector into the Parlour, which the Teenager sets up. The first thing they show is a silent film called Metropolis – a weird kind of operatic sci-fi with scenes missing, which leaves the Teenager hungry, and his dog baffled.

The second film they show is:

Wessex Film Institute. Black & white. 1933. Director unknown.

Interior. A factory.

A hall is filled with women in white, singing beside conveyor belts.

Shrill choir, not in tune: Pack. Up. Your troubles in.

Their hands work fast, straightening boxes.

Your old kit bag and.

Close-up on caskets lined with silk, onto which the women paste pictures of a knight in armour resting in peace.
Smile. Smile.
A male voiceover, plummy, tinny:
What feyne voice the women are in. Of course, what they do is eunly a side-shew in a chocolate factoreh!
A man cranks a wheel and grey tar is folded into a tub. Pulling a lever tips the contents into an alloy bin. Men in white coats hold up test tubes. A rack on a conveyor belt fills the screen and a machine squirts pale grey stuff into it from a row of udders before it slides into a tunnel that drapes it with more liquid.
In-genious, isn't it?
Women in white, close-up, stoop over the rack as it comes out. They twirl black paste onto each square, one per second, without spilling a drop.
De-lightful wiggly things. And the chocolates too. Hullo! Let's see the foiling machine.
A carousel with a brushy hole poops out a silver sweet.
I'll bet your mouth is watering, now. Mine is. And I expect we'll find the girls in a propah hullabaloo.
Shrill: La-la-la boompsie-eh... My lover flew away...
Machines turn, caskets slide, pasted with dead knights, moving off to the horizon.

39: Days 27-37, maybe: 'Civilians'

The more I hunt for Zoë Palmer, the less I find her, and the more souls the factory gives to Blackwood. So I go with him, to see if she's among the ones he reaches. When he sees the Defeated, he tells them we are the insurrection. Most aren't interested. But some are, like Punk Dayz. He takes up Blackwood's offer because he's bored, he says. His gang laugh at him for getting off the floor. Or there's Surf Dude Freddie, in beads and combats, who shakes Blackwood's hand with swollen fingers. His mates go: -Yeah, we'll touch, innit, after we got sorted.

But no Zoë Palmer.

There are people cooking up, comatose, or growling of how their pride got offended. I despair, if this is all that's left.

Then in a jungled canyon, a community of men, women and children who've been holed up there, making the best of it, they up sticks and follow Blackwood and when they arrive at what we've started calling 'the Mansions', the houses beyond the Parlour absorb them without a hiccup. They pass beneath the chandelier and their kids run down the corridor, excited by the light and valleys.

But still no sign of Zoë Palmer, and no way to call her.

Mo 13 goes red in the face and asks: Would we like a school up here? Some kids' clubs? His dream was to be a head teacher, he says, but in Iraq it was impossible because his family was from the wrong tribe. Would we back him up?

He explains his credentials and the parents love him. But these are nice kids. What if he gets hard nuts like I remember? Idiots with blades? He looks at me like I'm twelve, and says at least they're not packing Kalashnikovs.

Each day I come back from looking for her, I find a growing security nightmare. There's junkies on the dry-out promise, trendies with views on the food, gormless squares who've never lit a fire, and others who act like tourists. The whole thing is becoming murder to manage. In the first week, a laptop and some cash go missing and so does Surf Dude Freddie.

A quarrel breaks out. A Spanish anarchist and a mate of his from Finland mutter about cyber warfare and tracking apps. They're accused of theft by the TV Scientist. They quote one of their heroes and ask what's property anyway? The childless couple, who've put up a decent bookshelf, go nuts about the note on the wall that says *Deliver us*. I tell them it's our tradition, from the days before they got here, and if someone comes up with a better explanation, that's when it'll come down. The argument sparks higher when a political newcomer and his earnest girlfriend say who are we "crusaders" to tell anyone what is evil and who needs rescue? Why be ruled by soldiers? We're killers like the Tally and ISIS, and what about the Israelis? What about the refugees we made? Blackwood tries to raise his voice. They jeer and say the road to hell is paved by people like him. He says: -By levelling us, you make yourselves imperious.

They see a kind of madness laid out before them, and so I do, but I can warm my cockles over it.

Some stay, many go back downstairs, and Jonas' walls close behind them.

The TV Scientist and Producer also have a problem, with the note and with Blackwood for not being what they'd expected, and above all with the Caretaker for digging at whatever bugs them then vanishing. They threaten to leave, but she, the Producer, sees a telescope lying in polished pieces on a newspaper and she quietly sets it up in the valley outside while the Scientist rants on. For a few nights, at least, people traipse outside and are displaced by wonder, and kids join them at the lens, finding Saturn, its rings, and moon dust.

Then a foursome looking for loft-living, with money they can't spend on organics, with designer clothes and deejay bags, they leave too, saying they'll look elsewhere, and Blackwood does nothing to stop them. It's a final straw, for me.

I tell him, if we want people up here, then these are the people we need, the ones with brains and taste and cash, not the trash with mentalness and guilt.

He pins me with a questioning look and says the ones who stay are the ones we need.

What for? To prove something? Even to Whistler? Is anyone even fixing themselves of the problems Blackwood loves so much?

He looks at the Lightning in my hand, and munches a fistful of pills. A gang of kids tear past, chasing a football.

With sadness I wish the Caretaker was here to tell them tales, but he's been gone three days already.

It gets worse. Searching for her, I enter an office, open plan, wrecked, but broad and bright, with one wall made of windows in metal frames. I open one of the windows and taste the air that rolls down from a square of sky above a quad with more windows opposite. A sense grabs me and I spin around. Two figures are standing in the sunlight. I know their clothes. I know their looks. I know. Fury and hatred flow at their black bandanas and combats; ready to cut anyone's throat who won't pray the way they do. Two youths - one Asian, one Black.

ISIS.

Fascists.

I plant myself, steel drawn and ready.

They have sticks and urban accents, London and Birmingham, telling each other this place is crawling with undead kaffirs, fam.

I'll be their angel of death, then. Or whatever Islam For Dummies told them, page one.

-Welcome to paradise, dick heads.

They're old enough to have put a bullet in a civvie. Big enough to have shot fathers in the head. Adult enough to have taken girls as slaves and starve a village because it has a different god and bulldoze its ancient places. Or just You Tube the shit.

-You shoulda stayed at home and played X-Box, you pricks.

They wave their sticks in a street-fighting way, but without the advantage of semi-automatics. I close in, fast, and throat-punch one, hit the other in the septum, dropping them. They roll away, spurting claret through fingers pressed over their wounds, moaning like it's unfair. I give them another taste, then tie them together with flex pulled from the wall, blindfold them with their own bandanas and make them stand while they try not to choke.

-I have a friend, I tell them. -And you're gonna be his project.

One of them coughs in a way that tells me he's done this to others. His mate curses me with his god. I poke them forward. -Move!

At the Parlour, there is fear and recognition, including at me for tying these kids up and getting them covered in blood. They get a lot of sympathy and even Blackwood gives me a piece of his mind.

But Mo 13 stares.

-There you go, I say. -Keep them under lock and key until they get a GCSE in Get A Proper Girlfriend.

I go to the bathroom and vomit.

If we're going to be delivered, we need to do it for ourselves.

So I wait by the restaurant door and when it opens, I dive for it, forcing my way in, Bergen and all, into the dizzying kitchen where I drop to all fours. The aroma is insane. An Indian chef with an apron soaked in blood aims a cleaver at my skull... but slams it onto a heap of meat. I scramble toward a furnace where a Mexican pulverises chillies and a North European stirs a fryer of boiling gold. They pivot, shouting and sweating and bumping me because I'm unexpected, but somehow okay with it, yelling orders at servers who face a crush of customers with desperate faces. Two of Whistler's Thugs, their backs to me, lift a section of the counter and let three customers stumble through to the door at the back, which catapults them into darkness. I'm jostled toward the counter by a babushka with earrings down to her shoulders who shovels pastries into an oven. I take cover by a bin and scour the faces pleading for food, wriggling my phone into my hand. My Bergen is struck by a cook but I've got two bars – at last! – and is that her? Hungry like the rest? Eyes with circles under them? The faces shuffle and she's gone. The pain that hits my stomach when she turns away is furious. I have the text written already; obsessed with it for days:

We won. You won't believe it. There's even a school here. P.

I drop as a Thug sees me and goes ape – and my phone stops sending at ninety percent. I smash my way back past the chefs and into the factory, hoping my message got out.

I collapse into the Parlour, to be confronted by a six-foot Christmas tree and a handful of residents watching ancient Cockneys chatter on the wall – a black and white film called Passport to Pimlico. They're startled by me and I don't know who these people are. But the stove is roaring and the warmth is real. Two construction workers, though, sit uneasily in hi-viz. I scare them and they quickly know who I'm talking about: She's like, one of the consultants: 'a suit'. I ask them when and where, and the answer they give is one I should've guessed, but they haven't got a clue how to get there. Nor have I.

The Caretaker's generator purrs outside. Patrol kit sits on the table, mixed with festive paper and scissors, and there's mistletoe in the chandelier. Half-empty mugs of hooch lie around, so I collect and drain them, fatigued and frustrated that someone else can fiddle with what I consider to be mine and before I do any damage I head out to the roof, to the wooden booth with its watering can, strip and douse myself with freezing rainwater, trying to wash away what can't be touched.

40: Dark 40: 'Into the Transcendent Frame'

I ran scared for my life from those kids on the estate, up into the green hills where I knew the trees and streams better than any of them. I could hide there and split them up – not all of them would bother with the climb, not on a hot day in May.

I waited by a stream while the sun clattered off the water. There was a stick in a niche, pointed at one end, so I took it, crouched by a bush and held it like a pikeman in a civil war story I'd read. Two of the biggest kids came puffing up. They saw me and laughed. One of them pulled out a knife.

A dragonfly landed on the tip of my stick. The span of its wings were as big as my hand. It took my breath away. I'd often tried catching them up here but never seen one like this. It lifted off and landed on my arm, the colours of oil in its wings, its head like a helicopter cabin, its wing-blades twitching down, up, and I understood. Sun dappled the nettles around the trees. This insect was a hunter, a protector, not the hunted, not protected. I thought of the kid I gave my last tenner to, and I got to my feet, on my green hill, and faced our enemy with my stick, my dragonfly whirring above my head.

There's a shout in the Parlour, followed by cries for help. I run in from the shower, still damp, to find those who were watching the film are clustered in the Caretaker's bedroom doorway, hands over their noses while actors bicker on the wall. Punk Dayz is on his knees by the bed, the Caretaker is sleeping on the covers, fully dressed, and the smell is nasty.

I elbow my way through, fists ready, but the punk is in pieces.

The Caretaker's on his back, in his Sunday best and boots, the picture of his beloved on his chest, hand by his side. He's motionless and bloated. God only knows when he stopped telling his tales.

The voices quickly become opinions. The newest residents don't know who the Caretaker is, and others think Punk Dayz has done this. I call for hush as Miss Morphine enters, covers her nose and goes forward, examines the African, looks for a pulse, pulls an eyelid open, and waits. My heart hammers in my chest.

The old man's skin is greenish black and the stink is strong.

Miss Morphine sets up a team of first aiders and nurses from the newbies. They clear the room and give shocked Punk Dayz a blanket over his shoulders and… I dunno. Bollocks. Really. Anger rises in my chest.

Death doesn't give a shit for dignity, but this is the first time I've seen a man dead in bed, kit in order, no nine-liner or helo requested, no panics. I want to stay here with him; when Blackwood arrives I tell him we should fetch our crew, the guilty from Darling God Farm. Just us.

He agrees, and they come, Work Experience leaving the dog outside, Jonas wiping motor oil off his hands, Mo 13 folding his palms in echo of his childhood Islam, Miss Morphine closing the door, each of them trying not to hold their noses. I ask about Spooks, but the Medic shakes her head. He vanished after a row with Gracya, didn't I know..?

-Blackwood, I whisper. -Say something.

He doesn't want to be this person, not again, but reluctantly and fearfully, he lifts his hand until it hovers over the Caretaker's head. After a pause, he mutters: 'Thank you…'

We need more. The odour in the room is repellent.

-The old words, I tell him. -Do them.

Blackwood wipes his face and sighs, dragging verses, in pieces, up from his gut and into his throat: -He gives and takes away...

Yes, Blackwood. That. Keep going.

-Bless... Blessèd be the name of the Lo--...

His breath hangs in the air, chopped. I reckon this would be important for the old man so I push Blackwood again, and he closes his eyes, inhales, immersing himself in the stink of death and he recites the lines, tears falling down his stubble and off his chin like a snot-nosed kid.

Miss Morphine says 'Amen', draws a sheet over the African's body and we regard each other, all of us in this room. Outside, Gracya is crying her eyes out, hugging the Caretaker's coat round her.

-Peace, whispers Mo 13, -be upon us all.

The Marxist holds out a hand to Blackwood, who shakes it, and we all do the same, as a group, even me and Jonas, our pact; the final act of the Caretaker.

I go to my billet, lie on the wooden floor with the window open and drink hooch until the last enemy blurs.

There is no marked grave. He lived here long before us; chose not to leave. He unlocked the factory's secrets to us, gave Jonas his generator, Blackwood his map, me his hooch and that word: *Son*... He gave us something, each of us, even his tales, and he crowbarred the Mansions apart for us all. Why would we throw him out to the city, even if we could, where the Defeated would shove him into an oven?

Mo 13 enfolds the body in linen. We place hardboard beneath it and invite everyone to join us, forming up behind Blackwood, torches lit. Me and the remaining men of Two Section, plus two residents – Punk Dayz and the Finnish anarchist – we carry the

Caretaker down, Blackwood humming a tune in a cracked voice, slowly, and as we descend, he adds other songs, gathering strength, a hymn, all the way to a room in despatch, with ledges of the right size. We encrypt the Caretaker there, with his beloved on his breast.

That night, after hooch, the Caretaker joins the spectres in my room, the accused and mistreated, crying for justice, reaching for dreams they'll never see, loving people they'll never hold.

It feels like today we've grown up, and remembering the old words, it's time to write tales of our own.

Rigor, Livor, Algor mortis. Eyes. Stomach. Vitreous potassium. Insects. Plants. Putrefaction. This is my hymn. Sing it with me. Do justice.

Decay is eight times faster in air than underground. Too cold or too hot and it won't happen, like saints. In deserts and mountains, the body will mummify, if not eaten first. In the Arctic, it'll freeze like chops. Fat people decay faster. People who die of bacterial disease decay faster. Poisons, however, preserve us.

Sing with me.

2-3 days: green staining on the abdomen; body begins to swell.

Sing.

3-4 days: staining spreads; veins go marbled, browny black.

Louder.

5-6 days: abdomen swells with gas; skin blisters.

14 days: abdomen tight and swollen.

21 days: tissue softens; organs and cavities burst; nails fall off.

40 days: tissues begin to liquefy; face becomes unrecognisable.

Sing.

100 days: adipocere, if in a damp place, the fat goes hard and waxy.

Deliver us, I hear myself.

Deliver me.

Deliver the beautiful Zoë Palmer.

41: Day 50-ish: 'Transition to Self-Reliance'

I can't stay. It's that simple. At 0500 while everyone sleeps, I fill the Bergen with food and hooch, pass the unlit Christmas tree, pinch one of a pair of construction hats on the table, slip it into my pack and open the factory door. The wreckage claws at my face with a cold wind, and my torch barely penetrates it, bouncing off walls that drip with ice and webs.

I step down the stairs, leaving the Parlour and Mansions, without turning back. I can't do this 'peace' thing – this 'home' thing – I need to move – I've lost too much; way too much. If I can't reach her and she's down here forever, then so am I, in which case I'll find Whistler and kill him, so people can sleep at night.

I put distance between me and upstairs. I don't trust myself with Blackwood who'll plead with me to remain. He's coming alive, bit by bit, but he's slow and keeps giving in to what's possible. I need him to face up to things that are impossible, to light a spark in me; but no, he's... Anyway a hundred metres in, I sit, aching from boots to shoulders. I eat codeine and spam from the bottom of my Bergen.

I'm an insect in an alien hive.

The Defeated, the people Whistler cons, they are back. Their noise rumbles in the depths and a group rampages past, ravenous and sucking each other. Perhaps the good stuff has hit town at last. I keep moving, a ghost to them, being graffiti, fuzzing this way and that, their beat as low as the pulse of a whale, my steps moving in time with it now, my chest filling with noise and hunger, till I feel the pain, like splints, a reverse altitude sickness, pressure increasing, when all I thought I wanted is to get through here and find her. I pull out a bottle of hooch. A dozen Defeated in suits and football scarves block my way, awake to the thumping blast now, passing smoke between them, stinging the air with bud like lemon that drips up my nostrils, and I press into them, swing a fist and contact one who reminds me of a dealer I knew, so I feel the hurt in my knuckles like joy as his head bobs back and they stare together, squinting at my torch while he blinks and licks the blood off his lips at me. I douse my light and reach for his spliff, brush it past my face, draw it back to crush it, the shot of it in my senses like petrol and kandaks are there, the local police and the villagers, their boy, their prisoner, muzzle on his head, while the damp-ended joint is swapped for a pipe, a wet thing the size of a bolt, and I work hard to bring myself back, because in this belly of the beast, there's a dog looking up at me in sympathy, a mutt bred for this place, and it twitches into a hole, to chase rats. The Defeated move on, leaving me against a pillar, and I rise with the pressure of my Bergen comforting my skin with abrasions, the weight of action, the thunking metallics of it all make me want that hit, so I move forward, one foot after the other, to speed, to stagger into a hall where dancers sway in fire like trees and I take a bottle that rolls my way and put it to my lips, knocking over its previous owner. The hot sugar of the liquor, and bitter smoke on foil that follows, and more liquor, and someone offers to go down on me for what's in my pack and none of this is the hit, the thing to bring me back, and I move on, where is the thing that will drive this agony out and I know it, have always known it, and through a passageway lit like a mine-shaft I see them coming and going, it has to be this, the greatest hit in the world, and I draw my weapon and adrenaline floods my soul, I yell and charge them with my steel and swipe, slash, see two go down, I whoop and twenty gather tightly against me, with dogs, and a homeowner strides out of the back of a house fused into the factory, blood for eyes, black turban and his beard bursting in orange over his vest top and he's the one, we know each other. I attack him at state red, and pain rains on me tasting of wet iron in a crunch of metal into sweet skin this is the risen me this is my empty grave my ashes and my hurricane. Nothing now exists no doubts no loyalties love nothing but the furious thump on thump as I take them down before they finish me and the flash of a hit in my face this is my hallelujaaaah..!

-The fuck? the homeowner burps, fat and smooth, his words glued with sleep and booze and I peel myself off the ground, tell this fat sack of death in his tracksuit and vest top something he should do to his mother because he is me, his face is different but I know this bag of shit I know this reflection just thicker under his turban unravelling like ink, and I see it before it happens; he plants a hand in my chest like a battering ram and I topple backwards, dazed by blood. I've seen it all before because it's what I would have done.

-We don't want no fuckin Big Issue here, he says. -Fuck off.

Then he's: -Wait. You a Runner...? Fuckin junkie-monkey. Get me some coke and keep it comin' or I'll Game you and getcha. Feel me?

I hold the wall seeing dust and body parts; this is one I should engage, put him down, but a kid's at the window above us, bare bulb above him and my strength has vanished – nothing I can do works against what I see, sour breath, bloodshot, this lazy Defeated homeowner gut in the do-nothing tracksuit and orange beard, his crewcut bare because it's the easiest, angriest thing.

-Who is it..? a voice like hers inside the house.

-A Gamer from the fact'ry. One a Whistler's, ain'tcha..?

He swings a fist at my face, gets a massive contact and I drop, starry, to the floor, and never once has he raised his voice, but he reaches inside my clothes, rummaging for what he wants. I roll away and there's shouting.

-Save me..? says a voice.

I get my knees beneath me and face the Homeowner, the black cold of the building inside me. I will kill him but drugs and drink have burnt my heart. Mob are gathering.

-Runner..! caws the Homeowner in his tracksuit and vest, spraycan at my head, sovereign ring on his pinkie, spraying gold on my forehead before I can get away, shouting: -Game on..!

The Defeated turn on me. There's no steel in my hands, just crack in my nose like a murderer's pillow. I don't even try. I curl up and see men rise from IED's and others facing my gun, pleading for their mothers, see my own, see dolls flung in the air, see rats walk away unharmed, smoke poppy resin with the kandaks.

Someone leans in and asks: -Save me..?

I run, stumble, pursued by mob, deep into the centre where a darker presence waits, hungrier than the rest, all devouring, a great beast with an RPG and I don't remember much until...

I vomit over a ledge into fresh, night air. The city glows. Searchlights under a thudding chopper strafe the housing development below. How long I've knelt here, watching this, after days of running without aim through dereliction, to find myself high on the outer skin of it, here on the floor of an office that's open to the elements, I don't know. Cold. Grimy. Beaten. Anchored by my Bergen, remembering sanctuary and Blackwood's pain, the Caretaker's skin, I retch again.

The bird makes slow rotations over the houses until it judders away for easier pickings in the city centre.

I lean into the world. The home with the flag is at the front of the houses, the leader of the siege.

An excavator with a wrecking claw sits on a nest of broken wood, while three bulldozers rest their grabbing arms into rubble that stretches from beneath me to the houses.

The roof I once perched on, has long gone. Gaping slices have been taken out of the flanks that remain; honeycomb onto the open air, rods and pipes like frayed ends, sliced rooms, stairways and insides including mine exposed to the city, while liquid pours in a stream from one of the cuts.

The building has taken a mortal wound.

Through my fog, I assess the heaps of brick, smashed and scooped; the hardcore they use beneath their houses, on space that was once inside Victory Cocoa.

I drink my last swig of hooch, shaking and surprised by it, thinking about those adverts, those smiling people with commercial eyes. Could I be one of them? Marine P, who came from holding off the enemy to find a Fuckwit who worked for the Shareholders by day and dealt coke by night drinking my beer and watching my flatscreen and being smothered by my Kats? Fuckwit wasn't filled with piss and rage. He saw no Terry at the foot of his bed. He was the goodtimes; low risk, rent paid, cock and chardonnay. 'My Kats' – how those words I've buried shoot up inside my chest with the memory of what we were fighting for.

I wonder if she fought him. Or if she faded like a face on a banner.

I pull back from the edge. The machines lean their jaws on the ground, asleep inside their fences and I'm thinking I want that SA80, now. Or make it an AK. Because that's the side I'm on, now; the side of the Kalashnikovs.

I eat from a tin and piss kneeling in a corner as dawn arrives with hard hats and hi-viz. The machines wake up and growl at the factory, making it shake and when they hit it, thunder rolls through its empty rooms like a drum, the messy beasts flinging bits from their teeth with a fart of exhaust, walking on their food, spilling what they don't consume. Workers scurry over their backs, pecking worms, while the creatures push forward; and I see her, in a hard hat stumbling over the rubble with a tripod and her daypack, pointing her kit at a wall that the demolition targets next. She goes down on her arse in mud. The men laugh and she sits there, and one of the laughing men is Whistler, bellowing, and I am in no doubt as to what I've seen and what I guessed. I stay in cover in the smashed office and watch her work, clearly weeping, until day dips into evening and she lets herself into the show home where a boy appears at an upper window. She is tearing this place apart as instructed. And she is being trampled underfoot as she does it. She cannot get out.

The Defeated lock up for the night and I see her moving about in the house. I find my phone and get a bar of strength.

I text again:

You won't believe it.

Moments later, she replies:

I can try.

My thumbs mash the keys to give her the RV, then I turn and head back in.

42: Day 51, maybe: 'Native support'

Virtually every seat in the restaurant is taken and customers cram into the spaces in between, waiting for an opening. Others pass straight through to the back, where the sound of the factory door is regular. I eat for fuel, and to force away my nerves, jigging and shaking like I'm under fire. But the taste is rich and fast and better than anything we have upstairs.

She takes the seat opposite mine, where I've occupied a tiny table by the window. Her face is jittery and shadowed. She's out of her skin with fright.

I have a beanie pulled low to hide the paint on my forehead. Nobody in the crush must see it; not that they'd notice a customer keeping his head down. It's loud in here and full of steam, and it's taken an effort to keep a seat free for her after I insurged my way in wearing the stolen hard hat that I've chucked under the table.

She nods at me and beckons someone from the crowd. I'm alarmed until a young boy starts moving warily through the throng. He reaches his mother and looks at me with saucers for eyes and I guess that's the way I'm looking at him, too. They both carry bulging daypacks and he grips a plastic toy – a Transformer – all spikes and armour.

-Is it better up there..? she asks. -Than what I've got out here?

I tell her how Blackwood is fetching people in. -And you should be fetched in, both of you.

She reaches out and touches the side of my face, puts a fingertip on the edge of my temple. Electricity travels to my feet.

-You look tired, she says.

Her finger leaves me and I feel lost. I wait, surrounded, while she decides.

I smile at the boy, and his mother nudges him to do the same. He says his name is Tyler. I pass him a chapatti and he crunches it to fragments.

I tell her there's kids up there, and Mansions, a million miles from the Defeat down here, and no-one can find us. Blackwood is building something good at last, and he needs people like her. I need... She'll be a celebrity. There's even a Christmas tree. The boy grins. Will she come? Will they?

I fold a naan into my jacket, hoist the Bergen and hold out my hand. There isn't much time, I say, and madly, she takes my hand, and Tyler's in her other, and we leave the table. Four people pile into our two seats, Trustafarians every one of them; the downturn dodgers. Meanwhile, her grip is firm, and I squeeze it thinking this is my grime over your soap but I am not losing you again. Pulling my hood on, we weave our way through, and join the queue shunting through the flap in the counter where Thugs ask for cards, swiping them, but I have resisted Defeat, so I hold out the twenties in promissory cash I was given once upon a time, by Zoë Palmer to help her escape and here I am, taking her back in, so I indicate the three of us. They focus on the customers who are complaining in the line behind us and we are waved past the cooks shovelling whatever the Defeated command them with their debts, and through the door into the factory, under a neon sign saying: *Enter The Game.*

There are fruit machines and crap tables on the other side now. People in climbing gear wait for a guide to finish strapping equipment onto them, and a guy in a pinstriped suit gets his pockets filled and head sprayed gold. I pull us down a side alley. Someone says something, but I've killed our torches. I lead the boy and his mother through a gap that the Caretaker showed me once and when we're in, I pull some sheeting back across it, drive away my ghosts and press on.

It's a shortcut, but it's not an easy one. I grab the boy to lift him past an obstacle, his wrists like iced twigs, and I steady Zoë Palmer around a drop. She grips my sleeve, looking into the void like it's the cliff in her nightmares chasing her.

We take a break after twenty minutes. There's railings and blackness either side and I'm knackered by the slow climb, thinking there was a day, back in the day...

Tyler's breath suddenly tightens and whistles. Zoë Palmer drops to his side and empties her bag onto the steel plate we're standing on. A compact bounces out of her fingers and over the edge, but I spot the inhaler, snatch it and hold it to the boy's mouth. Zoë Palmer grabs it and takes over.

Squish, squish. One-two, three-four, deep breath.

The boy's wheezing continues, and Zoë Palmer shakes the inhaler to see if it has what it should have, and is about to start again but I tell her to listen, he has eased off, and in a few more seconds, he gulps back throatfuls of air.

Zoë Palmer sighs and flops. I hold the lad with an arm around his back while he blinks into the present, water flowing into his eyes. His haircut is clammy and wholemeal, but his eyes are crystal, not a dull cell in them, not like ours.

She gathers him into her arms, her own dark hair plastered down her face, saying that's better, that's better, sweetheart...

I move to a railing and keep myself there. So long since I've held a child, so long, so far from here, so wrong. I see them lost to dust, ammonia and oil, hands held out for chocolate... She's asking me if I'm okay.

I wink: -Good lad well done.

Like a bouncy ball he's back again, putting us adults to shame. Who'd've known, from the glow in his cheeks? A piece of life has gone out from us, into him.

43: Day 54, apparently: 'Love Part 2 (Money on the Battlefield)'

Midnight. I lean on the Parlour doorpost while Zoë Palmer and her boy get a crazy welcome from Miss Morphine and Work Experience. Mo 13 and Jonas hang back. Blackwood staggers, hands outstretched. The residents who don't know, hesitate. Tyler sticks to his mum and watches the other kids.

Her eyes grow huge. A lot has changed, here.

They're taken around the Christmas tree to the sofa where Blackwood ushers residents out of the way who've been listening to him. They watch us like we're his words made flesh and he grins. Zoë Palmer drops into a heap, crying with her son held close while Miss Morphine brings cocoa and triage.

I look for a drink, every part of me in agony, seeing mother and son huddle there as she tells him who's who in a low voice.

Lucky Jonas carries some kit past me: -All hail the returning Psycho, innit.

Pride and shame well up. I head to the roof, and feel my tattoos writhing under fresh injuries I don't remember getting. I know what I became, to get them home, and Whistler is still down there; still free. I will find him and kill him.

"Home?" Did I just say that? There's clatter and laughing. People I don't know are clearing away china, others washing up, settling down for a night by the fire or filtering off to their rooms. But "home"..?

Jonas asks do I know how long I've been gone?

I'm in no mood for an argument. It was a day or two...

-We been huntin' seven days for you. Do you even know what day it is..?

Tuesday..?

Miss Morphine intervenes: -It's Christmas Eve, P. Let me look at you.

Christmas Eve... I've lost a week down there, doing God knows what... I dig a greasy half-bottle of vodka from the bottom of my Bergen as she checks me over, seeing Blackwood's face as I empty most of it down my throat. Miss Morphine swabs a cut on my eye and pronounces me lucky.

He says: -Sanctuary can fill those hollow parts, P.

I wipe my lips. -They're demolishing it.

-It's no use just telling people to be good.

-Did you hear me?

-I need to find the missing part.

-Well, I tell him, -I've failed to be different. I want blood. To kill or to be killed.

He asks: -Is it okay to have hope only, P..?

-I failed, I tell him. -I ran, and they're smashing their way in.

-She's here. You're here. That's good.

He throws pills into his mouth while I drink, hard. His eyes are alive.

-I have something to show you, he munches. -After Christmas.

Zoë Palmer cuddles Tyler. He grips a Transformer and stares like he's way past his bedtime. A trickle of kids come through in night-gear, put mince pies for Santa by the burner, leave with their parents again. Beside the tree, a group has formed over bottles of wine, and are getting louder. Where they got them from, is anyone's guess. Another group cluster around Work Experience, who thumbs a game on a tablet. They cheer as men get murdered by his action hero.

-I know what you did, Blackwood tells me suddenly. -In Syria. But I still trust you. Go to her, P.

I hear Miss Morphine drop her kit but Blackwood urges me on, to look after Zoë Palmer and Tyler. But I can't move. This is worse than being in a ditch in the Green Zone.

I look around. It's like a hotel in a power cut, all tinsel and tealights. Lanterns swinging where people come and go. Mirrors in ornate frames ping the light around. Blackwood tells me the Anarchists wrestled a mobile phone dish onto a roof. The Spaniard welded it and the Finn created an app he says will hide us on the dark net. But it means people are sending Christmas messages. If I'd only waited a few more days, he says, I could've contacted her from here.

-Too late, I say. -Pretty sure that would've been too late.

So I take a breath and break cover. I go to Zoë Palmer before Blackwood can speak any more to me, and I usher her into the mad, mad world the Caretaker left us; her eyes widening as we move through drawing rooms and lobbies, kitchens and libraries, pointing things out to Tyler, gasping at the sights.

I start finding faults, cracks, and mould, and how we have no mains or water.

-It could be nice though, she says. -You'd make a packet if the rest was safe.

-It is safe, I counter. -Blackwood struck a deal.

A red mark on her cheek meets a flush from her neck. She glances at the floor, and it's clear, to me, across all of Blackwood's wild dreams: we are tramps; squatters in a warren at the top of a wreck; the rejects, the poor, the insane, the guilty and injured; hiding amongst antiquities with camping gear and rigged-up kit, eating out of tins, lighting fires, washing in rain, shitting without mains sewers, water or power, or any safe way in or out, the mob and criminals and vaguely recognised faces infesting the voids beneath our feet. My hands are scabbed and twisted like my face, boots and torn fatigues. Blackwood is a sick man too soon out of hospital, possibly dying; even Miss Morphine's cap has a rim of grime while Lucky Jonas, Mo 13 and Work Experience are chancers in cheap sports gear, and Spooks the Sniper has given up and gone.

In front of her, I see us for what we are.

-It's fine, she says, -it's better than what's out there, for now.

"For now". I go to the door opposite mine and swing it open. Gracya's moved further on and I've kept it clear, since then, and ready. A reception room with teak table and high back chairs. Upstairs, beds on Edwardian legs with curling frames, puffed pillows and quilts. A washstand with a white jug and bowl. A brown metal trunk with linen and room for clothes. In each room I light a candle in a holder on the wall with a silver scallop behind each one that flickers back with seven flames. I take an unopened pack of Peek Freen biscuits from a drawer and hold them out to Tyler, who grips his mum and his Transformer until he gets the nod from above.

I leave them to it; close their door and go. Images of Kats. Times I'd slammed the door and left her there, pack on my back and off to war or full of liquor and blood, to sleep out. Kats herself shut the door in the end, staying inside with her Dealer.

That night throws everything at me: the Caretaker's prophet and blondies exploding next to newly built houses, boys in rubble – I reach for a bottle, not his hooch, feel its fire suck my warmth away, so hungry is that stuff. Voracious.

44: Day 55: 'Christmas'

I lie on the floor of my billet before first light, hearing kids shrieking with happiness, feeling the ache. I'm interrupted by a knock at my door and when I pull it open, it's Tyler, with blue eyes and a Spiderman dressing gown and his mum's too-big trainers. He holds out a colourful crumple the size of a book. Behind him in their open door, Zoë Palmer hugs herself in a towelling gown, smiling through her caution when she clocks my derelict state.

-He wanted to, she says, deflecting me.

Maybe so, but Tyler is itching to get back – Christmas paper has exploded all over their room – so I bend down and unglue my words: -Thanks, big man.

He scoots back and we grown-ups hold each other's eye for a second. She turns to go and I call out: -Thank you.

She pauses, and lets her door swing to. I wrestle for balance as my head detaches from its ghosts, throw on some good, clean clothes from folded piles near the window, scrub teeth and face in ice water.

I hold the paper ball Tyler gave me and memories crash in, of Army Christmases, of false boobs and cheap whiskey from guys in the regiment whose arses I'd dug out of trouble in the year, of boxes that charities sent us with labels like 'From the Fowlers' – people I'd never heard of, asleep in their beds as I sweated on high alert in a cargo container. Or when Kats gave me Simpsons underpants and a multi-tool saying they weren't unconnected, and further back, my Mum, who today has nothing from me because I've had my head fragged, and the whack of shame that pours up my chest is huge.

Scalextric, I remember that one, those palm-sized cars that clattered round an electric track in the days before video games turned a kid's life 2D, and I whir up the phone, scroll to Mum's number and thumb in a text, send it over the Anarchists' dark-net, so she can feel I'm out there somewhere, in a desert I can neither confirm nor deny, be proud on Christmas Day. Maybe.

I take a swig of alcohol and unpick the paper – it feels wrong to tear it – and out drops a grey Transformer. It stares at me with the face of a warhead and fists of wheels, has orange flames on its torso and a diagram of how it turns into a truck.

Sadness burns me at what Kats did, and the drink in my hand turns sour.

I grab a pack of Jammie Dodgers and a book off my shelf filled with architectural photos that I found called *The Junk-happy House*, wrap some of Tyler's excess paper over the book and cross the hall. I take a breath, and nudge open the door she's left ajar.

She looks up from where she sits in her gown at the dining table, feet sunk in a pool of paper where Tyler plays with his presents. I give him the Dodgers, say thanks for my cool Transformer, ruffle his hair and she pours out coffee, the aroma feeling healthy as I take a seat opposite.

-Merry Christmas... I slide the book toward her, -took ages to find some paper.

She smiles, brushing a finger through her ponytail. I tell her she doesn't have to open it now, but she pulls aside the wrapping and her smile deepens. -I know this guy, she says, tapping the author's name. -A classic of the Seventies...

I apologise, saying I'm not exactly used to this sort of thing and thanks for making coffee, not a brew, and–

-He made houses out of recycled junk and gave them a 'happiness score'... she falls quiet: -Thank you, she says, -for coming and finding me. Us.

I swallow. Heat rushes over my skin and I hide behind the coffee. It's good and strong and I resist the thought of adding something to it. An elder sits at the table, blowing twigs off his tea. I look away, back at Zoë Palmer, whose eyes are filling up. She huddles, so alone it seems, while Tyler crashes toys on the floor, and she jumps up, rushes out to the kitchen. I get up, and find her by the butler sink and she turns to me. I put my arms around her and she puts hers around my shoulders, and I hold her as she sobs into my shirt, the clean smell of her hair in my nostrils, the softness of it against my jaw and her body shuddering inside her gown, pressed against the basin, I grip her and desire stirs when Tyler calls from the other room: -Mum? and she pushes me aside, wiping her face, -Yes sweetie..? He's hungry can he have these biscuits, he asks, and she calls back yes, and she buries herself into my chest, then looks up into my face, regretful, and I know that this, too, is not true.

-There's something I have to do, she says.

I step away. -Does he hurt you?

She turns to the sink, and pointlessly arranges cups. I reach out a hand but draw it back as I spot her tablet open on a shelf, blinking with an incoming message.

I leave, go back through the room with Tyler eating Dodgers, give him a fist-bump on my way to the door, Zoë Palmer rushing up behind me. I swerve.

She holds the book over her breasts, her dark eyes asking me to understand, but we're on opposite sides of a fence, it can't be any other way.

-Thanks, P, she whispers, hoarsely, -It's the only present I'll get, that I didn't give Tyler, to give me. Stay. Tell me a story. Tell me how you got that scar.

And I feel guns pointing at the back of my head; a hand slipping out of mine.

-Not today.

I hide in my billet, drinking, reading Andy McNab for technical errors and finding verses on my phone: 2 SAM 22, and poems by the Hidden One, by which time I'm trolleyed on my final bottle, and next thing I know I've got a cleaver out on the Christmas sprouts, worrying Jonas in his kingdom but what can you do? Blackwood rambles on at the stove about JF Snow – the black sheep of the family that owned this place – disinherited in the second world war or something. "These three are my enemies: Ignorance, Repetitiousness and Gravity" he quotes, to which I add: And Irish cream liqueur. You prat, he says, and lectures us on pacifists, economic decline from Suez onwards until I tell him knock it off since Herodotus mate it has always been about money and Tyler sweeps in with a new warplane that fights my monster truck which was in my fatigues pocket where else would it be? Then he runs off with his new friends, more kids.

Turkey twizzlers. And the Queen's speech. I think.

Zoë Palmer stays in the background, as I recall. I can't approach her, and she cries and talks to the Medic, I think.

So I laugh my veins off with Mo 13 being a Marxist Muslim dressed as Santa staring at me over a cream liqueur. Like I said.

True meaning of Christmas: Monster truck.

And Blackwood is on his feet saying prayerful words while a thudding begins in the bowels of the factory.

-This is a Rescue Mission, he says. -From now on.

I wake up with my head against the door Two Section first entered by.

There's a Boxing Day walk across the rooftops, with pigeons and lichen, kids playing tag and football in the valleys outside, while others slip into the factory, unable to face Blackwood's note on the wall.

Zoë Palmer returns from wandering into the warren of workers' houses with her laser, fascinated by the endlessness of the Mansions. Tyler meantime exterminates the universe with a new Transformer and his mum talks with other mums, introduces him to other kids, about forty of them now.

I have a word with Work Experience at lunch, thinking he'd know about these things, give him my twenties and he returns later with a yellow thing that is armed to the teeth with teeth.

I wrap it and give it to Tyler at the table, who's ignoring Jonas' bubble and squeak, and moments later the toy has been twisted into three shapes. -Cool, he says, -thanks Mister P.

In my room, straightening my head by trying to write, Tyler bursts in and he pulls me across to their apartment. Zoë Palmer sits in a corner bathed in tablet light. On the sideboard are a dozen Transformers, in wrangles and frozen wars.

-Choose one, he says.

I refuse but he insists, saying it takes two to make a proper game. I pick out the smallest one.

-That's my favourite, he says so I put it back, -he's got rockets, he turns into a car and guess what? he can go invisible.

-Wow.

-Have him.

He presses the toy into my hand and we play, escalating from AK47's and RPG's on my part to nuclear bombs and force fields on his. I'm wiped out. No strategy prevails. My base on a nearby cushion is overrun by the boy's tactical and armed superiority.

-Keep it, he says when bedtime is called.

I close my hands over the toy and give the kid a high five.

In my billet, I place it next to my notebook and sluice my system with hooch, but when I come to, the toy is beside the Christmas Transformer, glaring past my shoulder, on guard against my unseen enemies.

45: Days 56+: 'Provincial Reconstruction'

I've not known "home" in a long time but I still can't rest. I stagger about like a street drunk as the place takes off around me. It's been doing this for weeks, if only I'd stopped to see it. But Zoë Palmer's here now, surveying and recording, thinking carefully and calculating what she sees while Tyler plays with the other kids. I should be satisfied. Mission accomplished.

Even Blackwood has come alive, fizzing with energy I haven't seen since we first went in to capture The Hidden One. He tries to collar me but I put distance between us; I feel the opposite, like I'm losing faith, sitting still, not much of the home-making type, not prepared to populate this place with losers and Whistler's victims. And if she never knocks on my door, nor do I on hers. I hover outside it, many times, then decide against it; she has something to finish that is nothing to do with me. I can only feel pain, and suspicion, if I think about it too much.

Blackwood and the Teenager meanwhile bring people in every day for the next three days, each one thunderstruck and filthy, fearful of what they've escaped, sad that the outside world has nothing for them and desperate to avoid joining or falling victim to Whistler and his mob. I feel like a lodger amongst DIY-fans, cooks and artists taking over: people with goggles making murals and structures from scrap that Blackwood praises, Punk Dayz and the Anarchists restoring furniture, others covering the walls in fairy lights and coloured drapes.

A chef laid off from a swanky restaurant is among those who've arrived, and Jonas is helpless as the new cook shoves him aside with knives, and uses stuff he calls 'in-gre-di-ents'. Things happen, like baking bread, and food piling up on stoves, china and seventies tablecloths, whatever the Caretaker saved, whatever is found in the Mansions.

Other newbies bring books that fill the libraries: *The Divine Comedy, Even The Dogs, Dead Men Risen, Savage Lands, The Book Of Strange New Things, Home, Capital*... books on urban planning, chocolate, Garden Cities, Arts and Crafts, Anarchy – things I never had time to think about and they give me a feeling of vertigo even now.

People blog, do instagramming, tweeting, whatever the thing is. The patrols keep going, several each day in that week between Christmas and New Year, and I lose count of those given Blackwood's welcome before deciding whether to stay. Some do, in this holiday season, others head straight back, or wait, deciding if they can afford to believe in this.

I drink hooch, write in my notebook, try Kierkegaard and Dostoevsky, anything huge that my crap schooling never told me about, fighting off images, avoiding Blackwood, Tyler, and Zoë Palmer who never knocks on my door, and my evil vibes increase, while Transformers keep watch on my window sill.

It's engage or run, and if you run, expect a bullet in the back. So the choice is clear.

I creep out one evening and find the new cook. We drink hooch on the fire escape, guessing the recipe, letting it replace whatever else was our poison. He'd fled into the factory after an overdose, he says, showing me the track-marks in his arms; a kitchen hazard, he says. We talk about cocaine and blades, and places where they kill what they eat, and of using, and not starting again.

He's not going back to all that 'scuse-his-French, he says, to people tearing each other apart when the point of food was to find enjoyment. He's stubble and bones, fidgeting. -Call me Chef, he grins, and we shake on it, and I wonder if maybe, just maybe, someone can recover from being the Defeated...

It sticks in my head and the following day, I grab Mo 13 and ask him about the jihadis.

-They're watching YouTube, he says.

I swear in disbelief, but he holds up a finger like he's hearing chatter, says the Hipsters have made a sequence of movies showing the victims: the families and children of the executed, backstories of various kaffirs, Christians and impure Muslims. And Atheists, he grins. He's made his inmates calculate how many hours of jihadist venom they'd watched, and he's making them match it with this; the minute by minute consequences of what they'd been part of, until they learn their lesson. When they're ready, he'll introduce footage of medics, aid workers, police and engineers. -They need action, he says, -and meaning, just like us.

Yeah, whatever. I'm not sure they'll get anything by watching more blood.

-Ideology, he hisses, -must hear its victims, P. And one day, he says, -these fools will beg us to help them fix what they did. And do you know why, P? Because they wanted meaning, and they will see that they were just a fart in history.

Earlier in the week, Lucky Jonas' team had hauled up a second generator from the basements, thick with slime like Victory Cocoa coughed up a pellet. They'd wrenched it apart until it roared on cooking oil and Jonas danced in the smoke.

Since then, he's been assembling machinery somewhere near the bottom of the Parlour stairs, with busy noises coming up through the floor, and packages arriving in the kitchen until late in that week between Christmas and New Year. Chef sets a pan on the boil and bitter sweetness fills the air, unknown in the building for a generation.

The walls swell with it. A tray is set on the table and Blackwood breaks the contents into pieces, holds one up, says something reverend under his breath, then calls the kids in. Tyler is among the first. The glee on their faces pokes me in the heart, then the adults have their turn, one square per tongue. Zoë Palmer's eyes light up, and Tyler feeds a crumb to his Transformer.

The ingredients are simple: Sugar, cocoa powder, cocoa butter, condensed milk...

Chef adds an armful of foil-wrapped slabs that he dumps across the table, announcing our first, mechanised production. I see Zoë Palmer applauding in the crowd.

Miss Morphine, in the lull, says that the Caretaker would have loved this, and she chokes up. I feel the loss, too, and wonder if he set this up, for us to find it and revive it. She puts her hand on her bump and nods vigorously, while Zoë Palmer glances away. A bloke in a pork pie hat picks up a guitar, no woman no cry, and thirty or forty voices sing it, including Blackwood, until an Asian, cross legged on the floor uncovers a stumpy drum and the guitar cheers up. Four men push a piano down the corridor, like thunder in a box of bells, and an elderly woman locates its honky-tonk. The musicians are joined by a floaty girl who christens their band The High Rises. Her voice is like astonished birds, and seventy people soon join in with the one about a day like this a year will set us right...

The singing is interrupted by an exhausted group from the community we'd found in the jungled canyon. They lurch into the Parlour, asking for Blackwood. They say they went looking for the back wall of the Mansions, to see how much we have, and they've found themselves back here, tired and confused.

The news forces him to sit.

I pull on a jacket, glad of some action, and tell the explorers to get some scram, chocolate and a breather while I fetch my Bergen. I gather them together and we move through the Mansions for the rest of the day, keeping as straight a line as we can, until we enter a dance hall via one of its side doors. The long wall opposite has no more exits, and rises through wallpaper churning with vines to a moulded ceiling packed with baby angels.

-This is it, says one of the community, calling himself Marek. -Anywhere you go after this takes you back the way you came.

I ask him how solid it is, and Marek shrugs at some sledgehammers leaning against it. They've tried.

Back in the Parlour, Blackwood's scouring *Industry & Architecture* as if it holds the answers, twisting in pain. An argument flares involving the jihadis. Mo 13 has brought them in from whatever 'lecture room' he's held them in. They look drained after two weeks of his lessons, but their dispute is not my project — these idiot kids are part of what killed men and girls and put heads on spikes in Darling God. To me it's simple: make them suffer till they see their ghosts. Whatever it takes. That's when they'll be safe around me.

The Asian drummer sits on the floor, watching me, so I face him. His name is Arun, with a low-pressure handshake. I ask him what he's running from. People in the Sanctuary mainly do tell, if they're asked, but I feel like an idiot as he swings into a wheelchair that someone else jumps out of.

-'Arun in his chariot', he says in a Welsh accent. -I don't need any more irony.

Irony? An Asian in a squat without his family probably is running.

Because that's what this is. A squat, however glorified. I watch Blackwood scouring his book while a kids' film is showing. He rises on a walking stick and has a word with the adults drinking heavily and sucking on joints, snogging at the back.

-Not in front of Charlie and the Chocolate Factory, he says. -C'mon guys.

And he touches his stick to my chest.

I take a step back.

-I have a mission for you, he says. -Tomorrow at 0800. Full kit.

I'm about to tell him it's only the idea of all this that he loves, not the actual trouble that his squatters bring with them, but I feel my attack crumble. In my own ears, I sound like Whistler, whining, accusing him. He taps Zoë Palmer on the shoulder, too.

-Talk, he grins, -both of you..? said in a low tone like we're the only people who matter in the Universe, before moving off to be host, and I'm left like a scarecrow in too much wind, reeking of hooch beside her in an awkward silence, everything in me wanting to hold her and to step away at the same time.

So I ask her about Tyler and she bats it away, says how endless this place is, and how she hasn't seen this 'back wall' yet. She carries on watching the movie.

I'd forgotten how bitter that film is, with its sugar and morality.

But look, I've also seen newcomers arriving with hope in their eyes, seen residents helping each other find a bed, offer hot food and tea, open their bags and even the doors of their apartments to each other. Some pause by Blackwood's note, some return to it. Some wander in the valleys like refugees, but the space indoors seems to expand the more it's shared, and I see people cleaning latrines, cheerfully.

Shit is honour.

Something, somehow, is being delivered.

46: Day 61: 'At the Centre of Gravity'

At 0800 on New Year's Eve as commanded, I'm ready. I'm jumpy, chewing coffee granules and thinking it's only a matter of time before Whistler finds us, and when he does, he'll come in force if his demolition doesn't get us first. So I've packed the Transformers into my Bergen and call me dim but it strikes me I've got a choice – to become a fighter taking this battle to its proper conclusion or a dump truck carrying my crap around in circles.

So I'm here, Blackwood, I'm waiting.

Zoë Palmer has her kit on too, edgy at leaving Tyler with some parents while Blackwood says good morning and promises us a swift trip. Her eyes meet mine and fear passes between us; down there are things that shamed us both. A hundred volts of indecision shock me and I want to touch her, and say it'll be alright.

But I don't know if it will, and I don't think I should.

So Blackwood, Work Experience, his dog, Zoë Palmer and me, we head down, passing the new production room, with its machines getting ready for work. She steadies herself with a hand on my chest and although I've known armour and kit, thorns and blades and bullets, her contact drives through it all. Then it's over.

We press into Victory Cocoa, pointing our torches into gaps and cracks where faces turn away in puffs of breath and smoke. Blackwood asks if they want to be "rescued" and they tell him to eff off. Zoë Palmer seems relieved. Me too, because in an atrium where objects moulder in the dark and Work Experience jogs on the spot,

his sword protruding from his pack, even the dog is nervous.
There's a clang of metal and I wish I had that rifle.
Blackwood grips my arm. -Marine P. Come.
The Teenager holds his sword at the ready, while Zoë Palmer does a 360 with her laser and I lean away from it.
Blackwood has the look of a hunter, squinting, with no map or slingshots this time. The air is rotten and our torchlight is sucked away by hollows. This factory is having second thoughts, throwing all its ancient fear at us as we close in on its heart. He has been here before, I realise, without backup, and I tick him off for it.
-If you hadn't gone missing, P, he retorts, -I wouldn't have found what I was looking for, okay? I went searching for you, and instead I fou--.
There's a shriek and an answering call in chambers off to our left. Blackwood chuckles.
A pinprick of blood-red laser hits my chest; it's my saviour or my full stop so I dive to the side with a curse and clatter into Zoë Palmer, who cries out and I steady myself – it was only her kit – and I say It's fine, it's fine... but it's not.
Blackwood pleads for hush, glowing with excitement. The walls breathe in.
-Stop, he whispers, -we're here.
He leans on a door set into a porch with pillars and shadowy gargoyles. It scrapes inward, swollen with years of damp.
I stride in after the Padre, pass in front and listen – mouth open to reduce my own noise – strobing a torch at corners and high ceilings – the empty hallway of a Victorian house like those in the Mansions, but grander. I'm happy to proceed. Blackwood hums a tune and walks ahead, touching vases and cabinets. The red dot dances across my face, making me swear again, getting apologies from Zoë Palmer.
I regret I've been so sharp with her, and maybe to relish a

moment's warmth, I brush past to shut the door, joking that there are few things I hate more than an open doorway that's not filled with British Commandos.

I send Work Experience with his dog to accompany Blackwood, who's clumping up the stairs. Zoë Palmer follows them. I have a head torch, a spotlight and a steel strip in my fist. I check every entrance in the hallway. Locked. The door at the end, though, prickles my skin. I extinguish my head torch and give the wood a nudge. It swings inward. I drop to one knee and hold the spotlight high, heart racing. I see faces snarling from the darkness. I roll aside, kill the light, and colours swim. With any luck the beam has blinded them, too.

I rise and attack, headlong, smack into an enamelled poster screwed to the wall saying *Snow's Cocoa, Bristol & London*. I gawp like a fool at the hundred year old picture.

Five boys in sailors' suits with straw-coloured hair stare at me from an image as wide as a window. They are all the same child, his expression changing left to right, from anger to stupefaction, with words from an Army Field Manual under them:

Desperation
Pacification
Expectation
Acclamation
Realisation

then in brackets: *It's Snow's!*

The last boy is doped out, fed by an invisible hand. A shit-stump shows between his teeth. I tap the image in relief and disgust. The artist must've had something else on his mind, like Cockneys on their way to the Western Front, half dead already with a fifty yard stare.

The boy is pester power, industrial in every way, but also he is utterly real. His faces watch me from the darkness till I kick the door shut on them.

I mount the stairs, damp and broad, the landing decayed. At the top, the lad pats his dog and aims his torch at Nineteen Eighties pastel wallpaper. I grunt and go to Zoë Palmer. From now on I want her in my sights as she studies her tablet, lost in maths, standing in the dark with three ex-army lunatics. She turns the screen toward me, sensing my suspicion and points at the heart of the Lego. She whispers: -We're at the centre...

Blackwood carries on past pictures of the Laughing Cavalier and blue-faced beauties until he pushes a door apart and steps through.

Our torches zip across a room with a quilted bed in the corner, a mahogany wardrobe, a white sink, and everywhere a layer of silt, with posters of wrinkling footballers with big hair, and a stack of mouldy Beanos on a dark, bedside cabinet.

The weight of the ruin presses in from all sides and I sense a presence, heavy and determined, cold and repelling us if it can, but only the bed screeches as Blackwood sits on it, leans on the cabinet beside it and lights a candle. From a drawer he pulls out an exercise book with a footballer on the cover. Photos drop out, which Work Experience scoops. They're curled and greenish and they show the boy from the poster downstairs, but on the beach this time.

I signal the lad to be alert, while Blackwood takes the photos back and opens the book, filled with scrawls and doodles.

He produces *Industry & Architecture* from his coat and from it, the page of child's writing that I'd seen before, telling of a summer's day in a factory teeming with workers in white, and he fits it neatly into the schoolbook, matching the rip precisely, like two halves of a contract.

The damage proves they belong to each other.

Zoë Palmer bites a fingertip, waiting for Blackwood to confirm what she knows.

He reads, like a declaration.

A child tells of staying with relatives he has never met before, during a summer holiday, of Auntie Bea's puddings, of Grange Hill on TV. Of being breathless and covered with eczema. Of his mother telling his Aunt off for giving him chocolate because it makes it worse. "But I'm in a factory of it!" He's been told not to scratch, he says in his diary, but now he's bleeding. "I hate it," says the child. "Really really really really hate it." Auntie Bea changes his sheets which have blood on them. He hates the cream she puts on his body, face and neck, saying it smells like Plasticene and doesn't work, and he can't get his breath. He's made to wear gloves, even though it's sunny outside. "It hurts" he says: "IT REALLY HURTS."

Blackwood turns the page.

The boy mentions "granddad Joe", who's died far away, and his Mother and Aunt crying and arguing. He says he wants to play football.

Blackwood turns the page as if it'll crumble, and him with it.

Zoë Palmer sits beside him with a rusty scrape of the springs that makes the dog spin round.

Blackwood shows us text and doodles by a nine year old spending his days ill in bed, and he reads on.

The Mother and Aunt come into his room and both have been crying and promise him treats.

Zoë Palmer stares at the floor. -It's this room...

Blackwood announces: -"The Elders came and laid hands on me. Auntie B told them what was wrong but they already knew. They prayed in tongues and sang happy songs and it was weird but nice and they told me to trust in Jesus."

Zoë Palmer peers into her tablet. It's making me uneasy, too.

The child prays. He wants to scratch, but he mustn't because then he won't believe, "But now it stings…"

The dog growls and Work Experience hugs it. Zoë Palmer flips her tablet open, shut, open, shut. Noises from the factory are growing.

Blackwood turns the page. He reads, thickening: -"I can breathe and I didn't scratch today."

He shows us a smiling sun across the middle pages: -"Auntie B cried again."

A tear rolls down his broken skin – "Why do grown-ups do that?"

-I got better, he lowers the book. -I was healed.

The boy in the poster is sitting here, grown up, damaged, with that same, middle-distance stare. It's him.

I blurt it out. Zoë Palmer glances at me like I've missed the bus. She asks if we can go now.

-No, says Blackwood impatiently. The boy in the poster is his grandfather Joseph Snow, painted when the boy's father made him the face of Snow's Cocoa. He's the one who grew up and went away, and died. He wrote *Industry & Architecture*. -I thought these memories weren't real... There used to be gardens...

Zoë Palmer puts out a hand, to help him leave.

-I was nine years old and I got better...

-But your name's not Snow... I murmur.

He frowns. Beatrice Snow was his great-aunt. She was visiting from Ghana where she lived at a mission station with doctors that she paid for with her chocolate fortune. She was old, even then. After that summer, though, she always sent him a birthday card, no matter what address he had, even though his family moved a lot for work, a card always found him, even as a student, a salesman, a curate, a soldier, and then in military hospital six months ago a package arrived from her. It contained *Industry & Architecture*, written by her brother – Blackwood's grandpa Joe – the torn page, and a letter.

It said she was dying. She begged him for forgiveness for the pain she and her father had caused his family when his grandfather, her brother, was disowned for going to war in 1940, first in Finland, against Stalin, then in France, against Hitler.

Blackwood looks up. He never knew the reason for the 'going away', he says. Only the Caretaker had remembered, he adds, his voice cracking.

The family were supposed to be objectors, the letter said, but the good intentions spun out of reach, and old Snow became angry, with his son gone, as if everything was suddenly futile, and the factory turned a blind eye to cruelty here and abroad, behind the smiling face of a boy, an icon he doted on and kept, and the old man said they must be like the firms around them, and let the money off its leash.

The letter said how Aunt Bea had spent the last years of her life trying to make up for all the agony, judgementalism and trouble this place had caused Blackwood's mother and all the anguish the factory had inflicted on Africa and its workers here in the city, for its hypocrisy and greed, colluding with corporations and governments in poverty and child labour while the older Snow became ever more cynical, even during the war itself, selling chocolate to soldiers about to die and getting rich from it. Cocoa was a health drink to their great-grandfathers because it replaced alcohol with nutrition, but look at what it had become. Old Snow hired managers who no longer built pavilions for workers but threw up a block schoolroom for African kids at the edge of the jungle that fell apart after the photographers left. They'd kept the farmers poor, sold the customers cheaper sugar, making money for its own sake in every conceivable way, until bloated and drained of life, in debt piled upon debt and trading in pain, old Snow passed away and she inherited this monster with a child's smiling face.

But she'd run away, and had no idea how to stop the beast, which staggered on for two more decades until it simply breathed its last, became a carcass of memories and ghosts, leaving its guilty heart exposed beneath the pleasure. Maybe James, the great nephew she'd met when he was a boy of nine, could put things right where she and her people had got it so wrong.

The letter confessed that while the Aunt had hidden herself in Africa, her brother, the estranged Joe, struggled with what he'd seen at war and brought up his little girl – Blackwood's eventual mother – in the shadow of a naval dockyard, writing a book no-one would read, the one in Blackwood's hands. When he died, the great-Aunt came back and tried to give the factory to his Mother, that summer. It triggered a massive row, in which his Mother called it dirty money, and out of control. But something else happened. Auntie Bea had asked forgiveness and she'd got it, at the height of the argument. That's why they'd come to him crying and asking the Elders of the old faith to see him.

-The old woman saw something in me, he says, voice breaking, -and if I could be the boy I was that summer, I'd know what to do. Otherwise, the faith was dead, and the banks could have it - there'd be no point resisting.

He opens the drawer and takes out a manila package like the one I saw before, but this time addressed to James in spidery writing. The Caretaker, he says, was told to put this here in case the boy should ever return. He slides out a folio of creamy paper, which he holds in one hand, the diary in the other.

Zoë Palmer seizes the folio and flicks through it, lips trembling.

-So nothing can be forgiven, Blackwood says. -Only paid for.

She catches her breath. -My God. The title deeds. We need to talk.

He rounds on her: -You're not understanding this, are you?

He raises his burn marks, rigid and angry: -I was dry and raw and bled all over. I couldn't even breathe. I was just a boy, he cries. -A sickly little boy.

Zoë Palmer pales.

-I was tormented by it.

She says sorry, slips the papers back into their envelope.

-No, he slams the diary into the cabinet. -I'm sorry for you.

I tell him to bring it. I tell him the noises are loud outside and I've got a bad feeling...

He bellows: -I got better in here! You haven't understood a thing!

I back off. He stays on his bed, torch fading, insisting: -I even ate those silver chocolates, to test God and make it real. She knew that! And I got better! And do you know why I knew I could get better..? Because I heard my family forgive each other..!

And I remember the Padre I when first saw him, in Afghan, fit as a fiddle from his Commando physical. Now, I see why he boasted about it online.

-What about the ones who don't get better? Zoë Palmer murmurs.

His scars fill with fire: -What? Of course you fight for them too, it's a war for our existence, against despair, it's... Why don't you get it? I really wanted you to get it..! I brought you into my most personal place... I could've just brought up some title deeds and been done with it... But I'm talking about the impossible, the things that happen when we act for love, even to those who stand in our way..!

The walls fold in, ready to vomit us out of here.

-Anyway...he says, -the job's not over just because one kid got better and it's not a blank cheque to behave like an idiot but we can get better. Anyone can.

-Maybe 'praying' gave you a warm feeling, Zoë Palmer persists. -You relaxed, those conditions can be brought on by stress. Believe me I know. You got the attention you needed and you got better. Kids are like that.

Blackwood stuffs *Industry & Architecture* into his jacket. -Sure. You're right. That's it. That's all it was.

He hobbles to his feet and she takes his elbow, the manila in her other hand. When I look at her face, she's flushed with conflict.

Work Experience whispers on our way out: -D'you think he'll let us stay if he sells it, P..?

I want to drink Lightning, lots of it. Before I pull the door shut, I retrieve the schoolbook, slipping it into my combats. Mad or not, he's going to need this because we are not coming back.

47: Dark 61: 'Breach'

We put a few corridors between us and the house. Blackwood angrily questions two people we find – a writer and a call centre worker, both of them tired and thin. He asks them if there should be more to life than this? Would they pray for him, for us, for everyone, for anything, and the writer says perhaps not, but the call centre worker says yes, whatever it takes.

Blackwood pokes me: -See? You'd be better at this than me. You'd know how to convince them...

But I know I belong here. That's the difference. I don't want to sink but it pulls me down. Hard. The hipsters, flipsters, finger-poppin' anarchists and chocolate-makers have built a scrapheap fantasyland which Blackwood has blessed while down here on our way back from the belly of the beast with his schoolbook in my pocket, the sound of hammering around us, mob structures emerging in the depths, passing junkies carrying tools, do we know what we're up against? A swell of radio somewhere. Thugs dragging chains. We take a break in an alcove but I'm restless so I track two Defeateds carrying a beam. They stop to smoke some crack where they can do it without being begged by anyone. I think of mugging them, the hunger pulling me. I've seen enough. A whole Bible of pages won't stop them.

When I re-join the others, they've moved on, Zoë Palmer with Blackwood, inputting into her tablet, held away from his view. Work Experience watches his feet, lost in thought. Even the dog has no idea I'm approaching them. I'm a wraith. I could hit each one in the head and drop them before they even knew. The thought makes me go cold. They're under my skin and unreachable, and I want them out. I scuff my boot and they jump as one.

I wave them forward.

-This is war, not a picnic.

At the stairs to the Parlour, we halt. Work Experience holds the dog, suddenly skittish. The trips and alarms aren't there. The manufacturing room is empty and unwashed, and voices tumble down the stairs. A chart song is playing and the door at the top is open. It raises the hair on the back of my neck. Blackwood fiddles with a blister pack.

Zoë Palmer breaks away, rushing up the steps. -Tyler...

I follow, two at a time, climbing against the pain in my knees but as the door gets closer, the smell of skunk sucks me into a cloud of downtime and RnR, a Humvee, the Yanks and Kandaks, and BLAM we tumble into the light, Work Experience following with his sword.

The Parlour is packed with strangers, the Christmas tree in their midst, bottles and cans everywhere including the Caretaker's cupboard ransacked and leaflets I've never seen before trampled under the crowd's feet and that tinny sex-music, the one that goes: Uh Uh Uh and Oh Oh Oh.

Faces, faces, faces. Who to yell at? Who to grab? I don't recognise any, jostled into the crush where a woman presses up against me, then changes her mind as she sees my stare. I hear Work Experience calling for his dog and I spot Zoë Palmer elbowing her way to the Mansions. I follow her until Thugs block my way like meaty statues. I pick up a leaflet, no time for a fistfight but my blood is up, there's a woman being mauled, hippies fighting townies, leaflets swapping hands – and there is Spooks the Sniper, I could knock him down and ask what's going on, but Zoë Palmer has vanished. I have no eyes on Blackwood or the Teenager either, so I drive my way past the gorillas and into the corridor to find her.

Here, residents rush about in ones and twos, lost and bewildered.

A blonde woman shorter than most with urgent eyes who helped me once and who works in the manufactory blocks my way. She's frantic:
-What's going on, P.? They say they're here for their "free apartments". Where did they all come from?
-Where are the kids?
She points and jogs beside me down the corridor.
There are faces we pass, I have no idea who, drinking-smoking-crawling, and others who've been here for weeks. She reads me the leaflet as we move. It's an advert for "Self-Finish Apartments", and "Start The New Year With A Bang", on Twitter and Facebook, for pity's sake. I have my head torch on. I switch it off, then on again, take a spare from my pocket, give it to her: -No really. If the power goes... – and then I see Zoë Palmer, streaked with panic. We reach her and she regards the new woman – who gives her name as Sheena – with a conflicted expression for a moment before her anxiety pulls us deeper into the Mansions.

We hear the shrieking long before we burst into a large, hexagonal lobby with a sweeping staircase, filled with kids having a riot of their own, running rings around scattered adults including parents who can't seem to pull them together. There are Thugs in reindeer antlers, Gracya huddled in a corner and a Santa in the centre handing out sweets in green foil – ones that were not made here. I'm panting after running but my chest tightens at the sight of kids chasing each other in gangs and arguing over sugar, hitting a piñata with sticks or sitting, sullenly, and there's Tyler, his face and lips rimmed with brown, a Transformer in his hand. His mum sweeps him into her arms and to my horror Santa steps aside and there's Whistler, orchestrating everything, checking the Mansions out. He sniffs a line of powder on his fist; and I want some.

-Happy fucken New Year's, blud! says a voice in my ear.
A Reindeer outfit. Troy.

-Whatcha menna do, man? We can't all be fucken preachers..!

There's a gap in the reindeer's neck where Troy's face is circled, grey and greasy. His teeth are slick with brown. Too late I feel his fist hit me in the solar plexus with pain I didn't expect because I was too arrogant to think he would do it. He drags me down like a drunken brawler and Sheena cries out as he kicks me square in the face-head, again and again, not missing a beat or a wasted shot, the pain is shocking, my steel gone, and I curl up, must fight, grab an ankle or someth--

... momentarily blacked out, but I kick his knee and he screams as it pops. I yell at Sheena to stop telling me to stop it, kids in a fog and Thugs in antlers approach, see Whistler hooting with laughter and Work Experience with his dog as they chop his pins and bring him down and something hits me from behind, my eyesight bursting like a firework–

48: Dark 61 Plus: 'Plan Zed'

It's calmer, with a rhythmic thumping nearby. Whatever I'm lying on is hard and a light shines in my face. My head hurts and my ear pings. I'm slapped, and I feel like this has been happening forever and the breath chuffing down on me smells bad but I know the odour.

Liquid fizzes onto my lips, with a sting of yeast.

-Yeah man, says Jonas. -Psycho got his ass kicked by Rudolph, innit.

I spit. -Food poisoning from you... prob'ly...

He slaps me in the face again. -Maybe if I do this a few more times...

I'm pulled into a sitting position, groaning, pain shooting through my ribs, head splitting as I open my eyes, in a corridor. I can't make out who's here.

Zoë Palmer...? Tyler..? Blackwood..?

Stars flash. I mustn't sleep.

Lucky Jonas moves away from blocking my world and my eyesight adjusts. I see figures huddled round a lantern. I take my time. They might be my people or they might be the enemy. It doesn't matter. I need time. Awareness builds a little stronger. The thumping sound is the noise of a party coming through the closed and barricaded Parlour door, fists hammering on wood, while we're in the Mansions corridor, the Caretaker's things being trashed on the other side. Work Experience's face is tickled by the lamp light, stick in hand, feeding the dog. And there's Blackwood, against the opposite wall. But no Zoë Palmer. I wonder which side of that door she is.

I pull myself together. The Teenager I can trust, so I shuffle on my haunches toward the lantern and they make space for me with a rumble of approval. I accept a brew, warm and incredibly sweet. Blackwood passes me a crinkle of codeine and I crunch it in with the liquid sugar, squinting at him, his dream in tatters, again. Damage everywhere. Artworks smashed and walls graffitied. Books on the floor. The group around the lamp include the Spanish and Finnish Anarchists, and Punk Dayz. They tell me about the fight that happened after a Thug put me down, how they cleared the Mansions and slammed the door on the Parlour but now we're trapped. It's just a matter of time before they break in. So this is the nightmare I'd predicted but I was too self-pitying to prevent. Defeat turns my guts inside out.

-And Whistler?

Blackwood murmurs: -I never did a deal with him.

It's not what I meant.

I struggle to sit and pain shoots through my skull. I'm cross as hell and I tell them I want to know who let the mob in, who unsprang the traps, and what the arse we're going to do about it.

-Relax, says the Terp. -Don't break your piss-bag, old man …

-Mo…! growls Jonas.

I look at my surprise defender, who says: -And you, Nutjob. We're gonna pull back, innit, and let the fools have this section. Padre any big ideas?

Blackwood blinks. His dream has burned, big time, but I can't stand his silence.

So I call out to him, telling him what he needs to hear, like the time I told the Caretaker to do the same, my words arriving in bursts, repeating it, until it hurts:

-That summer. Blackwood. I believe you.

I throw the diary at his feet and he stares at it like it's a snake, his scars livid.

-Pray. Or something. Blackwood. Please. Don't die off.

He scoops the book to his forehead and dips forward, groaning, and Jonas can't watch, has to change tack:

-Someone grassed us up, he says. -Like Spooks or some man else or maybe not a man.

And as he speaks, a figure enters the light: Zoë Palmer, tablet in hand. -He's asleep, she sighs and slumps onto a crate to warm her hands over the lamp.

She glances around. -Did I interrupt...?

Miss Morphine denies it quickly, holding her tummy, says we're talking of withdrawing, just as the pounding on the door becomes a chant: "Let. Us. In!"

Zoë Palmer speaks without looking up, says I told her it was safe. She turns to Blackwood, drifting on a summer's day, gets nothing, is about to say more but is cut off by Jonas:

-Listen up, party people, it ain't lost yet, he says. -Come an' put your eyes on a ting I been cookin'...

-Not now, mate, I groan. -My innards have taken enough punishment...

-Psycho stop your mouth, he says. -Bwoy, he nods at Work Experience, -Watch that door. Innit, do not fall asleep or play X-box. Come the rest of you slackass mutherf-- sorry, Padre...

Some stand, others remain. Zoë Palmer checks her tablet, shuts it and says she's going back to Tyler. I offer to escort her, the headache and codeine fighting and she says she'll be okay, and I watch her leave me, again, while Blackwood stays impassive. I neck another handful of his magic beans.

-Come on, though..! says Jonas. -If I was the 'Caretakah' you'd do it!

He's right. And I'll do anything not to sit here listening to the mob at the door. So I stand.

Jonas' apartment is nearby. He unlocks it while Mo 13 quips about the probable piles of porn. The Sapper clicks back that if the Terp is feeling lucky there might even be a goat catalogue. The banter is exactly what we need, cutting fear down to size. Blackwood's morphine is doing its work in me, too, and I walk on air, straight into an Aladdin's cave.

If Aladdin were a scrap dealer, that is.

There's a couch with a hold-all on it while all around the perimeter is a workbench piled with offcuts of metal, brick, wire and tools like a biopsy of the factory, all its tissue concentrated in this room, reeking of sweat and diesel, dominated by an object under a dustsheet in the centre, as tall as me.

Mo 13 whistles: -That is why you can't get a girlfriend, bro...

Jonas gives him the look: -Ladies. Come see our regimental band and armoured British whip, all in one...

And he yanks the dustsheet away and there's a stack of boxes in a metal frame painted black and a chassis with car wheels, wires criss-crossing it like veins.

-Ow, winces Mo 13. -She ugly for a first date...

Jonas snorts: -At least she ain't woolly or my first cousin... And he points out speakers, amps, a platform and a generator; the one the Caretaker fixed.

-Innit the trick, he says, -is man get the bass, mids n' tops balanced so they shake your bone but don't blow your sides off. Unless you want it to.

-But what's it for? says Mo 13.

The Sapper is dumbstruck: -You never been to carnival?

And Mo 13 falls quiet, being the first to understand. Jonas was planning to celebrate, and built a carnival float out of rubbish, put skill and effort into it. It's his baby, unveiled just when all is about to be lost.

I clear my throat. -So where are the decks or whatever you call it?

Jonas taps his phone. -This lickle bubba is the brain, fam.

-Small enough to be Mo's, I say, seeing a thing in Jonas that is stronger than me, but the Terp doesn't take the bait. Instead he caresses a speaker: -You have tried it, bro..?

-Do I look like a ball, Jihadi-lover? I wanna live to a ripe old age like Psycho, but I ain't got no use for it now so the plan is we break it up, like Hesco blocks, and build a wall across the Parlour door. They won't get past unless they got explosives, and we go up into the Mansions and start again. Plan?

But Blackwood has come alive: -This is the storm before the still, small voice...!

We stare at him.

-The thunder, he says, -before the empty cave...

Lucky Jonas takes a guess: -So I play some nasty white-boy rock and they back off, like Tora Bora..?

Blackwood sighs. -No, you ignoramus. Just move it out but don't destroy it...

But there's a flaw. It's bigger than Jonas' door. Blackwood studies me when I say so – like I'm the one who's nuts – takes a sledgehammer off the workbench and says: -We don't have time for negativity, Marine Sergeant...

And he laughs, huge and hearty, puckering, pointing at the wall.

-We can smash our way through a few old bricks, o you of little faith..!

-At last, says Mo 13. -A religion I can understand.

49: The Hidden One, Phase 4: 'Extraction'

In Syria, the lines are murky, with morphine to smother my pain and my injuries from home and the revised orders I took in the night, for my eyes only. This is no heaven-sent rescue. Darling God is the wrong translation. This is a hell of skipping metal, shot by those who want to feed on us, and we do it back to them, showing our common zeal in killing.

The attacking half of Two Section have joined me at the wall, with news from Bolson's half still in the ditch, that a force of jihadis have fled the village, heading for the monastery in the mountain. The Peshmerga should nail them there. It means a few less guns are pointed at us, so Lucky Jonas keeps his nerve and lays a bar-mine to widen the murder hole that Onuzo silenced earlier with his GPMG. We pile in through the Sapper's explosion, the remains of a Jimmy and his RPG, blood sliding in the rubble like an abattoir, and we are in. Me, Sapper Jonas, the Padre, Terp, Jones 270, Havelock and Nduom enter the village and its horror-show of corpses with their throats cut, executed from behind, beheaded for having a different creed and all of it on You Tube by now, poor bastards. Then we come under fire.

I kick in the door to a house, declare it clear and we dive in, slamming the tin sheet shut behind us as the metal is punched like a cheese grater, the morning sun adding rods of gold every time it's punctured. If we stay here, we'll die, so I plan an exit using more bar mines. The Sapper meantime is trembling on his knees and the Terp is fumbling his re-load. I order them to get a grip when there's a warcry from the back of the room. I hear the Syrian bee; the bullet that comes so close that I'm a nod from death and it ricochets into the Padre's armour, winding him.

I open fire and my target drops. I move in and he rolls away, screeching. His shoulder is a mess. But instead of finishing it, I press my muzzle into his wound and drag the Terp over: -Where's the Hidden One?

The enemy's just a teenager with bum-fluff on his chin, his turban burst like a ribbon of black ink, screaming uncontrollably so I take my autosyringe and jab it into him, yip it out before the full measure has gone in. It's not always pain that gets results. The Terp is by my side: -Bloody ask him now!

When we get the answer, three times in a row, I can't believe I didn't see it coming.

-He says, the Terp insists. -They've taken the hostages to the monastery... and they will take more hostages when they get there.

I have precious moments to make a decision. I will not let this slip through my fingers like it did in Helmand. The monastery I'd observed at dawn is less than a mile off, halfway up the mountains on a network of tracks. It's guarded by a handful of grizzled Pesh but they're not the ones we've trained on our long range guns and they're only lightly armed. I order the Sapper to radio Bolson for further intel, and the Terp to monitor enemy chatter including social media if he can get it.

Both of them confirm it. The dozen Pesh guarding the site came under attack an hour ago; no-one has heard from them since, and ISIS say they're cleansing the mountain.

There are kids in there who escaped the village. I get Bolson on the radio and tell him to try and sleep at night if we stand by. We have taken no casualties, have not been identified and the target is on the move but visible. He calls me Psycho down the airwaves but I don't care; it means he's agreed to tell the Brass we're on for a secondary assault, target Mar Petrous, one kilometre out. That's a decent sniper shot away. A drone makes a flypast and confirms via Wiltshire that there's inactivity on the ramparts of the monastery, but smoke, casualties and infantry damage. Beware of traps. I fix Padre Blackwood with my question: Is he willing? The look in his eye affirms it and so I move us out, covering each other, leaving the village the way we'd entered.

We move fifty metres at a time, the topography rougher and rising for an hour. Behind and below us, the village is smothered in smoke and the gunfire is fierce; the enemy has not been dislodged and the militias and tribes will soon unravel, so time is against us. Sweat pours out of my helmet into my eyes and my rifle has never felt heavier. At a water-rest, shielded by boulders, I give myself a quarter-shot of morphine to kill my aching heart and stop her words repeating and as it slides in I look above us, at the slotted battlements of the sandstone monastery, breached low down, with scorch marks and behind them, the ranks of pillars that give it the grill-like appearance. For a thousand years, locals have fled here from invaders, to pray for salvation and today, instead, they're getting us.

I am gonna finish this. I am gonna fix who I am. *Don't come home* loops in my head and I stumble in the grit for a moment, holding it together. I give the lads one final talk at the breach and fist-bump each one, call them by their names, face to face, my eyes stinging and ready for this, so high on the jab that I can barely feel my soggy, blistered feet or my torso baking inside my armour and I lead our attack, state red, into the brief darkness of the hole in the wall and its shelter from the Syrian sun, then we're through to a piazza and in the glare again.

The broad courtyard is littered with chunks of masonry and

dead Pesh still dripping. We take cover and listen to the gunfire and screams coming from deep, dark gaps between the grill of pillars in front of us. Jonas is shaking and the Terp has vomited. The Padre seems propped up by Nduom beside him. I tell them to take on water while Jones 270 scans the pillars, rifle at his eye. There's a trail left by the bloody intruders, who have placed no rear-guard. To the left is a patio table and chairs, with a flowery, plastic tablecloth and tea set undisturbed. Off to the right, the walls have bullet-ridden icons and every pillar has bullet marks in it; two of them have scars at human-height. The entrance into the mountain is dead ahead.

-So, I say. -How d'you lads fancy a nice, cold cave on a hot day in Syria..?

And I give the order to split up and approach the entrance from either side, Jonas leading the half that settles opposite me as we use the outer pillars as our final cover. Like me, he has an underslung grenade fixed below his rifle, and sweat like rivers that streak down his face. Distant shots and shouts echo in the darkness within. I tell him: -You're cooking tonight mate. Promise.

And we step in, sticking to the walls on either side. A domed roof becomes visible above us, and as my eyes adjust, I see the walls are smothered in frescoes of saints holding books and crosses; guys in robes that could be old as togas, each of them with their face shot out, the dust still trickling like stony blood. And at my feet lies a monk, in black, a short guy twisted like he's been wrung out and dropped, his life splashed in dark pools around him, with footprints of it that run into the cave.

We follow the prints into an arched passageway lined with images, heading toward the noises.

Bullets crack and zip from nowhere so I burst into a grotto trimmed with beams and chairs, dragging a roaring Jones 270 in with me, the Padre and the Terp lifting his ankles, hit already, claret trailing. On the other side of the passageway I see Havelock and Nduom kneeling in cover, ready to return fire; I need to think and my head can only hear her words.

We'll need more than the field dressings in Jones 270's pocket. I tell the Padre to pull him into the shadows and use his autosyringe to stab the guy's thigh, hoping morphine will kill his pain but not his respiration.

I give the nod to Nduom and after three rapid breaths go to my doorway, so I crouch and fire my grenade down the passageway in the direction of fire.

After the explosion, Jones 270 starts laughing about ice cream. I tell Havelock to come and cover him while the rest of us advance, treading on a child's shoe as I lead them, rifle in my shoulder, blinking in an effort to see and feel and think...

We enter a chapel covered in paintings and smashed pews, with chandeliers like broken fountains and a hole in the highest wall sending a spotlight of sun through swirling smoke and dust onto a dead priest in the middle of the floor. I gaze at the scene and maybe it's just the morphine talking but I think how shit, this is unfixable. I've come here too late to get any peace from the God they built this ancient place for. I never gave this sort of thing a proper, second thought and now... two black-bandana figures in a doorway kneel and fire at us. We return a dozen rounds and they drop; but four more in black combat gear burst out and it takes a good enfilade to stop them getting anywhere near us. I advance and secure the room they came from – a destroyed library with a bonfire of icons and scrolls smouldering in a grate; cries and shouts from elsewhere. I pull the guys in with me and post Nduom on watch, drag a last-gasping ISIS butcher in with me; he won't have had time to booby trap himself, and I call the Terp to my side again:- Where is the Hidden One? By now, I'm cursing the effort we're putting into finding a poet in this holy cave, thinking we should forget it and locate the kids, when the darkness takes an almighty clatter as an RPG hits the doorframe we entered by, skips past Nduom's head and demolishes the opposite wall onto my prisoner, flooring us as plaster pours in from a deeper room. Deafened, I get up and see an ISIS guy standing there brushing down his pirate beard, stunned, armed with a pistol. I swing my rifle up and drop him with a double tap to the forehead, advance to the gap with my ears ringing, click my gun to automatic and pepper the darkness, sweeping right to left in the recess until my eyes and chest ignite at the sight of a couple, huddled and bleeding on the other side of a table. I've shot them.

Padre Blackwood is back on his feet. He leaps in ahead of me, recklessly, and yells in confirmation and distress.

We need to move but Lucky Jonas is frozen – that RPG missed him by a whisker, the second won't. I clout him round the helmet and tell him to radio in our position and report the asset. Mo 13 can't get off his knees beside Nduom, who's going into shock near the dead jihadi instead of returning fire at the source of the attack. So I grab the Terp by his straps and with every sinew straining on adrenaline, throw him into the room, then pull Nduom with us toward the Padre, who's fumbling his first aid over the couple.

Blackwood yells: -This is The Hidden One!

The couple are a teenage girl, screaming and bloody from my shots, and a guy in his thirties in a beard and black bandana, bleeding from his head and shoulder, also by my shots, bawling in Arabic. The girl's pain is piercing. Blackwood cradles her. I feel through the gore in her neck for a pulse and the male attacks me, roaring into my face with snot and fury. This is the jihadi commander whose men killed Finchie and others in Afghan, raging while the Padre holds his fiancé. She is fading.

-I will get you out of here, Miss, I tell her, -I promise.

Lucky Jonas jumps as his radio crackles. Getting a signal into the monastery is a miracle but the news is not good: Russian planes are initiating a bomb drop, cluster and 200 pound. Bolson got word they were coming, before getting shot in the face – which puts me in charge.

One Section has aborted. Bolson, though, will not leave his Psycho on the mountain, he says by radio, and has ordered the rest of Two Section to reach us; they'll be here in fifteen. I ask Jonas again, does JTAC know our position and the asset's confirmation? He says yes, but JTAC are hampered by the Ruskie warplanes that are on their way from the coast, and they're less fussy about what they hit.

We are deniable. We need to get out.

I tell Lucky Jonas to blow us a new arsehole. He does it, and powdery light crashes in, revealing a new room full of shrieking children – and a narrow, shorter passageway with, literally, daylight at the end.

Shots crack into the room behind us so while Nduom returns fire, I order Mo 13 to join me with his pistol. The choice is clear – be pinned down here by Jimmy with our dying casualties or break out and risk the Russians dropping ordnance on whomsoever they please.

My radio comes alive and I give the Brass our status: nine liner, wounded civvie, a dozen minors and one enemy asset. We need immediate extraction as official military advisors caught behind an overrun Pesh position. Plus the Terp is in pieces; he's only a schoolteacher, after all, he's swearing so much it's screwing up the comms. I order him to belt up till we're past this shitstorm, and send him with Jonas to escort the children out – the Terp can reassure them and Jonas can lead the way on point, ensure no hiccups. -Just aim for daylight, I tell him.

We have to get off this mountain. Fast.

Back in the library, Nduom is returning fire and the Poet is yelling while his fiancé slumps in the Padre's arms, her blood all over him. I approach, knowing she was beautiful before I did this to her and her hand grabs my neck and her nails dig in, hard, pulling herself up from the depths, cutting me deep. I yell and pull away from the slot of fire it makes; she drops and I try again to get her pulse, get nothing except my horror. The Padre flips his head and cries out over the noise of war and the Poet's curses: -The Lord is my strength and shield...!

It's time to go.

Nduom fires his grenade to keep Jimmy's head down and takes point while I drag the Poet, bellowing at us, down the passageway vacated by the children. I'm hoping Lucky Jonas had the sense to find some cover out there, as the Poet punches, kicks, bites at me. I ask Nduom to restrain the asset as we reach the daylight, and Blackwood staggers behind us with the dead girl in his arms.

Solo, I edge outside into the courtyard with my weapon in my shoulder, my neck burning, scoping the rooftops, taking short, rapid steps, unsure of myself. I spot the kids sheltering with Jonas and Mo 13 under a portico, my soldiers jumpy and vigilant, and I clock the drone that swirls above us, piloted from Wiltshire.

Darling God burns in the plains below and the Russians will arrive any second. Havelock appears, leapfrogging the pillars toward us, carrying Jones 270 over his shoulder, who's laughing about a stag do in Cardiff. Behind him to my relief is Bolson's half of Two Section who've made it up here, with my boys Mawson and Okonkwo panning the courtyard for hostiles. I order them all into cover, but I need the Medic who sprints the hundred metres into the tunnel we came out of. Gunfire crackles and Havelock tumbles, fuck, claret bursting from his face, dropping Jones 270. The drone banks and slots a rocket into the source of fire, destroying stone and modern murder together, and my boys, my lads and lasses, they're caught out here in a brutal storm because I wouldn't let this mission die.

I order Mawson and Okonkwo to get Havelock and Jones 270 into cover, fast.

The Padre stands beside the Hidden One and Nduom in the tunnel, his expression a horrorshow. He turns and goes back in. The Medic is there already. More fire cracks out from the monastery rooftops, must be half the jihadi cohort from the village, mad as hell. Jonas and I crouch and pummel the ancient parapets while I scream into my Bowman as if it might help. The drone sweeps round. Nduom arrives with the Poet who falls against my shoulder, reeking of diesel, sweat, blood and lamb fat, and the Medic surfaces in the tunnel entrance, soaked like a surgeon.

-The girl? I yell.

She shakes her head.

I have no air, no muscle, no position. I push the Hidden One down and call for the Padre to hurry. ISIS are encircling us, despite the drone, and the Ruskie drop is a minute away. The Poet hits me and yells his beloved's name, Aisha, and the cut she gave me rages in my neck. I crouch and call the Padre again but the noise out here is intense as the firefight gathers pace. Jimmy has understood who we are now; we are YouTube bait, while the Pesh we did train, posted on a neighbouring mountain, decide to pump shells into the monastery to avenge their fallen. My radio fuzzes and the Poet howls, punching, clawing at my neck all sticky with blood.

I call to Blackwood, several times, get nothing, scream: -Come out! until he appears at the entrance, bare headed, black with gore from chest to knees and holding the girl like a mess in his arms. There's a wildness in his eyes. I tell him to leave the body and he lowers her, feet first. But instead of dropping to the ground, she steadies herself on the Padre, like someone waking up. The Poet cries out and she steps toward him, soaked in life. I run to her and stretch out my hand to pull her into cover. My glove and her bird-like fingers touch. Then the Poet thumps me aside and drags her into the open, thanking Blackwood deliriously.

I train my weapon on the jihadi Poet and glance at the Padre, who's gawping at the blood-soaked commander and his girl.

-She was dead, he laughs, -And now she lives..!

I do look. I take careful aim, all voices from home eliminated from my head now and I squeeze the trigger.

The commander jerks and begins to fall.

The drone whines. Blackwood runs to the collapsing lovers and the un-manned aircraft releases another rocket. The explosion takes all three of them out in a ball of fire that throws me into a coma.

It was barely 0900 hours.

That girl lived again.

And I did not disobey.

50: Dark 61 Plus: 'Overwhelming Force'

The pounding on the door is fierce. Whistler has promised them cheap houses. He's told them they can sell them later and escape the factory but it's an illusion. They'll come and do exactly what they were doing before, thinking we're denying them what they want, like they have victim-status, but we don't have what they want.

I stand with Work Experience. I will not let them pass. My head hurts from where the Thugs whacked it but I will go down fighting. They will have to come through me.

Desperate to get his machine into the corridor, Jonas' gang hammer away, bursting bricks like orange bones while the chandelier above us shivers. -Don't tickle it, Ladies! Hit it..! the Sapper yells, and the hole bites at the ceiling. -It ain't a supporting wall, he adds. -Prob'ly.

And graffiti above the Parlour door that I never saw before, reminds us: *Learn...*

A crowd have jostled forward, including Zoë Palmer with her hands over Tyler's ears. She gauges Jonas' work with a surveyor's eye as Blackwood tosses bricks aside. Hunger flashes between her and the turbulent priest. She blows away a strand of hair, grabs a brick, curses it and tosses rubble faster than the men. I've told him about the demolition but not how I saw her there. Now she's tearing this place apart herself with her bare hands.

Jonas barks out cocktails of insults to sexual prowess, family trees, hygiene, haircuts... the works. He fits ear-defenders over Tyler's head and gives the boy a fist-bump, tells Zoë Palmer to take the child aside and Blackwood agrees – as if this is no time to be reckless. Sighing, she collects the child, as if she always has to do this, just when she gets her teeth into something.

Jonas assesses the breach, judges it big enough and the Punk, the Anarchists and Mo 13 put their shoulders to the apparatus and roll it bumping into the passageway on under-puffed tyres, front axle on a tow bar.

Jonas climbs amongst his speakers with his spanner to take them apart but Blackwood tells him to wait. There must be two hundred men, women and children here, stretching down the corridor with torches. Punk Dayz, Chef, the Anarchists, Sheena, Gracya, teachers and nurses, hipsters, designers, scientists, jobseekers, refugees, brickies and painters milling about. They're either brave, or stupid. Even Mo 13's jihadis stand nervously with him, in tracksuits.

Blackwood crackles: -I see the darkness.

Walls shimmer. There's a murmur in the crowd, audible over the pounding on the door.

-You can go, he announces, -and shelter further back if you want. But if our currency is worthwhile I will not hide and neither will I join the world out there. With you I can scale a wall; I will not despair. We still have hope in each other, and a way of being free, here. We can take all our histories, our guilt and our waste and turn them into joy, not by consuming but by giving. So come! Tonight! Let's turn this world on its head. Let's tell the darkness and all that stalks within it that we are not afraid. For we are the insurrection and we are the life. A single match can dazzle in the night, and you are more than a match. You are a hundred lights, so shine like the stars in the firmament! Let's raise a rebel yell: We are not! Afraid! Of you..!

A whoop goes up from Gracya, thin and alone. A hand clap begins beside her, tentative first, then growing, spreading into applause, moving down the passageway with more whoops and I can't help myself, I call:

-Three cheers, hip hip!

And the boom hooray that answers me makes Tyler jump. It roars in the passageway and makes the chandelier clang like bells and the banging on the door cease. Blackwood climbs onto Jonas' machine, and calls again:

-Now anyone who ever had their heart broken, anyone who's done what can't be undone, shine your light this way, on this door. Burn your way ahead. This night belongs to you!

He gives a word to Jonas that surprises the Sapper who pulls a cord on the generator. It coughs into life, much to his astonishment. He trims it, connects his phone and fiddles with the amps. The corridor mists up with cooking smoke from the motor and the mob resume their pummelling. Suddenly there's a loud pop and the speakers thunder with a ragamuffin bass-line that makes my head hurt.

Blackwood punches the air.

On his signal, the team attack the brickwork around the door, hammering in shifts. I take a turn, replacing my pain with adrenaline and beside me, Mo 13 works with furious laughter, his jihadis holding his torch for him. A woman who hated them takes up the Terp's hammer when he tires.

Jonas tells Zoë Palmer, Tyler and the rest to stand back. He pokes his phone. The volume rises, and when the lyrics come it's pure power, a track about the blind who lead the blind.

The wall cracks. Blackwood pushes the door and when it resists, Work Experience throws his skinny self at the wood and it collapses outward, revealing sky-high homebuyers in the Parlour, their noise drowned out by Lucky Jonas' speakers. We step through, tools held high while Punk Dayz and the Anarchists push the trolley over the threshold. The mob falls back, crashing over artworks and furniture and I can only imagine what it must be like, chanting at a door to be let in, having a knees up in the candle-light with a snort or two when the wall collapses and blokes with lights on their heads and hammers in their hands stride in with a tank set to overwhelming volume, a hundred torches blazing behind them, cheering.

Blackwood limps through with a walking stick, in ear defenders and greatcoat, his spotlight sweeping the room. People collapse as Jonas' machine attacks with sound and our residents flood in, hollering. Even the Thugs are stunned. The shock and awe is beautiful, and no one is getting hurt.

Whistler and Troy – his Reindeer costume tied around his waist – are already by the exit but Blackwood pins them with his light while fleeing homebuyers pack the stairwell. I give Mo 13 a shout. Blackwood and Whistler are eye to eye. I join them. The Politician wipes his nose, face twitching as the tide behind us reveals a dozen people tied to chairs with golden spray on their heads.

Whistler's lips separate, liquid stretching between them, sneering past Blackwood and me, calling for all to hear:

-Careful with the kiddies, Rev'rend...!

It's more than a cheap jibe. The Parlour is filling with smoke like an over-cooked chip shop and the mob who remain are spluttering while Jonas plays a tune about war and what it's good for. Zoë Palmer and her boy step through the fumes. She sees Whistler and colour drains from her face but she has no time to think as her boy starts wheezing and drops to his knees. The throng gets away from Jonas' machine, coughing.

I elbow my way to the boy, and the volume is shocking. Zoë Palmer flaps her pockets, shouting at Sheena and Gracya who're trying to help.

Whistler howls with laughter behind me and I spin and aim my hammer at him but Blackwood gets in the way, diving to join the child on the floor. He lies down beside the youngster who's having a full-blown asthma attack, pale and panicking while Whistler hollers if only we'd done the deal with him. I block his advance on Zoë Palmer and Gracya whom he swipes for, and yell for the Medic, who's stayed away. Whistler jeers: -No expensive aircraft here to mop up your shit, eh, Marine P.? Guilty as fuck you fucking squaddies..!

I ram the hammer across him and his hands slip over mine, wet like his black eyes, his hair greasy and his skin sweating fly-eggs, his breath reeking of sugar. I push him while he licks his lips and tells me what I need. I'm losing energy, head thumping.

-Kill me, I say. -But you won't lead me.

-Kill what's already dead..? he tongues. -How..?

I twist, every muscle screaming and he's forced back. The floor tips like a ferry. I turn away.

The boy is on the floor in his mum's arms, fighting for breath. Jonas lowers the volume and his crew rush the generator, still connected, out of the balcony door. Remedies for the boy are shouted and with two hundred people, someone should have what we need but nobody does. Whistler is held at bay by Mo 13 and the Teenager and I hope they have what it takes to keep that devil back while a burnt man lies down next to a suffering boy and turns his icy eyes on me and I understand.

I reach for Zoë Palmer's shoulder.

-Is your room locked? I ask.

She hesitates, even now, but reaches into a pocket and I seize the keys. Blackwood, on his back, lays a hand on the boy's chest and cries out in a language no-one knows, and I reckon he's calling down a summer's day.

51: Dark 61, Near Midnight: 'Helo'

I run. I trip on bricks and shards, throw myself around corners, clatter her keys into the padlock she's added, fumble until a voice in the dark offers help.
Sheena.
I let her prise the lock off, burst in and tumble over bags on the floor.
Packed, ready to go.
A second body rushes in.
Gracya.
-Look in the small bag..!
She gives me a lighter and I bring the flame close, tip everything out of the bag: hairbrush, tampons, papers in a folder. Inhaler.
Gracya snatches it and skips to the doorstep. -Gonna have a party after this, right?
-Just run!
I scoop the contents up to re-pack them as Sheena takes the lighter and plants a candle so I can see. These are the things in a woman's life that touched her, have her smell, her hair, her prints, and papers, things she's thought of... Printouts, scribbles, spreadsheets with walls of numbers. I ask Sheena to bring the candle closer.
One sheet is thick with maths, labelled "Snow's, Option D: Elemental", with a list: Demolition, Removal, Substructure, Frame, and suchlike. The last entry shows a budget in the multi-millions, and a familiar logo at the bottom.
Beside the money, she's written a formula, full of crossings-out that gives a score. Above it is a question that she's circled, over and

over until the paper's broken:
Is this the Happiness??
I stuff the papers back into the bag, zip it up. My headache is returning.

Sheena says she'll do the padlocks, catches me with her arm, and smiles.

-Go.

I thank her and move, and when I pass the chandelier, I hear the clapping, enter and see residents cheering at a huddle by Miss Morphine's feet where Zoë Palmer faces Tyler who's coughing, sitting, drawing breath, Blackwood beside him. Lucky Jonas kneels as well, tears in his eyes as Zoë Palmer hugs her boy and Chef leads the residents in celebration. Only Gracya is distressed, saying it wasn't her fault that thing was empty, the inhaler now in Zoë Palmer's fist as she rocks little Tyler back and forth.

I scan for hooch, for anything in this blast zone that will numb my emotion.

Jonas crouches beside Gracya, says loudly over his music: -He was good before you got here, a'ight?

The people nearby agree and Blackwood smiles.

That in itself is a miracle.

-I'm tellin' you, Dragonfly, says Lucky Jonas, rising to his feet, face bright. -That boy got better.

And he climbs back to his machine to crank up a tune with an Asian flavour while Gracya wipes her tears and Mo 13 puts his arm around Miss Morphine, who's shaking her head. -It's like before, she keeps on saying. -I saw it...

I find a lager with a fag end in it, slug back the fizz and there's Whistler, propped against the wall, ashen under his makeup but whatever he's witnessed, he's judged it away. Four of his Thugs think otherwise, though, and they manhandle their boss and Troy out, slamming the door, looking like they've woken from a long dream.

Only then does someone notice the time – midnight. There's a cry of 'Happy New Year' and people look around, startled at nearly missing what so many of them would've spent all day waiting for. I keep myself out of the way of the congratulating, the surviving of another one.

With Tyler recovered and Whistler gone, the residents celebrate, laughing and straightening the place out. I go across to Blackwood who sits, though, exhausted, at the table.

-It's not over, I say, wiping my lips while my headache creeps back with force.

-Thank you, he breathes. -You are right and I was wrong. Now be with her, he says. -Please?

And I'm standing in a ditch again, shaking. What? That's not... She's not mine to be with. She's leading Tyler away, the boy drinking pop through a straw, spoilt by residents on every side, including Sheena. With a heavy heart I know the best I can do is guess what game she's playing, and see if she'll agree to the one that's forming in my head. I grab a half-empty bottle, step onto the flattened Parlour door, chandelier above me, and as they walk away, surrounded by supporters, I call out, bottle at my hip, and she halts.

I take a swallow and call it again:

-*Is this the Happiness..?*

She turns, and comes straight at me, jacket around her breasts, boots high, features deciding, hair drawn back and she doesn't stop until she's taken my breath away, with eyes that flash into mine.

-Thank you, she says, -for helping him.

-He's a good kid.

She touches my hand and my fingers respond. Contact.

-You're a good man, P.

And if she'd punched me in the belly it would have had the same effect.

-But I can't rely on impossible things, she whispers and her gaze drops. She turns away and re-joins Tyler, and I don't call her back, or go after her to tell her she's wrong. And I've missed a chance to share something fresh and new because I am, in the end, just like Whistler and his closed world of consuming 'hits' and what's possible. I deserve to be locked in ice, not here where people get scandalously better, where Jonas' machine hums a gospel number, one that goes: Oh Happy Day.

52: Day 62: 'Gain and Maintain Popular Support'

I sit by the burner while hooch and codeine smother my pain. Tyler is okay. I don't know how it happened but I write in my notes:
Go to a supermarket, get milk, get certainty. Go to Blackwood's way of doing things, get words, get a mystery. Which one sounds more alive..?
There are no dreams.

I wake up in the same seat, with a couple of residents still sorting out the damage. My headache has died down a lot, so I get my notebook, and as the others drift off to their rooms, I plan the takeback of Victory Cocoa, in full, and how to stop the demolition from devouring our home, because that's what this is, for good or ill, and I hope to Blackwood's God it is for good. So I nominate teams, tactics, and a role for the Surveyor. Because that is who she is, unless I discover otherwise.
And it's fools obsessed with certainty who're quickest to pull the trigger.
The factory door is open, its sigh blowing into my face. The hit is down there, ready for the taking but I push it shut, heave my armchair in front of it and head to my billet, passing Lucky Jonas on a camp bed staring at the ceiling.
-We're gonna have to take it down the stairwell, I say.
He blinks: -Apache style... Gun-rods up yo' skirts... Beautiful, man, dancin' like Rihanna...
I leave him to his screwy, open-eyed nightmares.

The door opposite mine is silent. So it should be. I enter my billet, dump my Bergen and see Sheena in the corner, wrapped in covers. Unsure if she's real, I lie down with my feet against the door to wait for dawn, while the old stuff floods in: a man rising in flames; a WMIK punched from underneath; a woman screaming at me; Kats on crack; ISIS with cameras; a Poet spitting in my face; Mum crying over my photo; the Caretaker slipping down a duct, beckoning.

I know my night visitors. I feel her hand on my body when it gets bad.

I wake up alone, wash, put dry socks on, boots and jacket, and take down the books I've lined the window with, reorder my Bergen with everything I own: notes, multi-tool, memory stick and spare clothes. I slip the Transformer toy into a pocket, swing my pack onto my shoulder and stand in the corridor, closing my door. I lay my hand on it. This is the first place to call my own and there's no-one to stay and share it, because I cannot rest; I dread what this day will bring.

I take my plan to Blackwood, and he nods, puffs his cheeks at the ambition, adds details of his own and we settle on it.

-Stay alive, I tell him. -Stay alive enough for both of us, will you..? And he smiles: -Deliver us from evil.

It's New Year's Day. The decorations are up, and it smells of coffee, mainly because Jonas is nowhere near it; he clambers on his machine with guys in overalls. Miss Morphine sighs over Chef's eggs, and Mo 13 buries himself in decent porridge alongside the two ex-jihadis and an Asian bloke in a beard I don't recognise, who grunts his disgust at the pair and Mo 13 reacts, claims to know what he's doing.

Zoë Palmer and Tyler are quiet. The boy glows when Sheena puts hot chocolate in front of him. She makes no acknowledgement of me, and I wonder if I did imagine her. I squeeze in beside the boy, and balance my Transformer next to his. They battle and mine is defeated. She, however, has their bags, packed. Maybe she would've preferred to have been on the other side of the door last night.

The Anarchists smash the stairwell into the factory wider until it gapes like a patient prepped, then stop for brews, wearing T-shirts despite the fact we can see our breath.

I explain the plan to Mo 13.

-No, Psycho, I'm not going back to that hell and I'm not leaving Kerry alone here, he says.

Work Experience ruffles the dog and tells me yes, okay, if I do something for him – have a word with the girl in the yellow dress? The one he's fancied since she came here...? I nod at his dog and say flea control is available. He's anxious beneath the bravado. We all are.

I take a coffee to Blackwood, his eyes shut and blanket up to his neck. I say his name, hold out the mug and his eyes click open. He watches the steam curling into question marks, leans forward and the blanket drops away, revealing black boots, black jeans and a black hunter's jerkin beneath his military greatcoat stripped of rank insignia. Gone is the park-bench-reject look and in its place is something stranger. He forces a smile across the side of his face, a mask since the drone struck him in Syria; since I murdered the Hidden One.

-You're right, P. We have the momentum.

Blood flows into my fingers. Maybe today I can fix it. Today, some will win what I can't have, and my peace has nothing to do with it.

I check my kit while the Parlour fills with men, women and children. More than last night, including ex-Thugs and ex-jihadis, and every nationality under the sun, if anyone can remember the sun. Some have seen what happened with Tyler, and others heard about it – the boy has celebrity status.

Blackwood explains my principle of simultaneity and who'll do what, the fittest and strongest remaining with the kids, because that upside-down way is how we'll do things, and he declares that New Year's Day will be remembered for this.

-If miracles happen, they make us responsible. We mustn't be the idiots of fate. Make peace with each other and your Maker and mean it. If we want peace, we need to be at peace.

And they get it. I can't believe they do, but easily a hundred come forward, others waiting in the passageway. They're not the ones I'd choose, but Blackwood is ecstatic. Punk Dayz says we need a flag. Rebel colours. There's a rapid discussion – a confederate flag, a pirate one, the black flag of anarchy, maybe a rainbow, or the green of paradise, or red of revolution..?

Gracya pipes up. -Make it a clear one? she says. -Like, transparent? It will let the light shine through, and... They cheer at her idea before she can finish it and Sheena knows where to find the material – it covers a dozen doorways down there, of course.

Chef steps in and shares out chocolate, wrapped and labelled, and he thanks a mechanic in overalls, who bows to more cheering. The ancient labels they've found, in red and blue declare: *Snow's Victory Cocoa.*

-Phase one, I tell Blackwood, -is complete.

-I hope it's for more than this, he says.

-Than what?

Chef pipes up: -Fatty acids and cannabinoids hitting the frontal cortex, affecting motor and memory. Phenyl ethylamine, the love drug generated before and during sex. Amphetamines.

Hallucinogens. Dopamine, serotonin and 1,3,7 trimethyl xanthine – popularly sold as caffeine – hitting the central nervous system in a volatile mix of sugars... Need any more ingredients..?

We laugh, good and deep: -Thanks Chef... Happy New Year to you, too.

And I remember the green hills and bully-boys who backed off because they saw my focus. The dragonfly settled on the nettles by the stream and I plunged my feet straight into it, trainers and all, feeling the water around my skin, with the hunter.

Blackwood puts Zoë Palmer and Tyler beside me.

I watch her, and ask her to open her tablet.

She's unsure. I ask if Blackwood has explained anything? She shrugs and says they've only discussed a few 'disposal methods'.

They sound pretty serious to me, I quip, and when she smiles, I sense the warm, soaped surface of her, and my own sorrow, like a loss. She wipes the screen and geometry spins. I point south of the map, into space. -We get out... that way.

She shakes her head.

But we have to stop the demolition, and she has influence. I explain that part of the plan.

-Think of yourself as Special Forces. When it's done, you disappear any way you want.

She gnaws a fingernail. I don't want her to be put at risk, but – and a feeling I can't name because if I do, it might sound too much creeps into my stomach and I will go out of control – if she stays here, she'll do something that will take us all down with her. Out there, she stands a chance of getting her freedom.

She'll do her best, she says. She glances at me and emotions clash like rocks.

And I need overwatch. Maybe Blackwood's paternosters have it covered. Deliver us. Deliver me. This time, I hope they do.

So Jonas' team dismantle his machine and carry it to the bottom of the stairs where they rebuild it and get it thundering the one that goes: Hi Ho, Hi Ho...

-Apache style, he winks. -Take your weapon to pieces and dance like Rihanna, yeah, Psycho...?

I smile. It's off to work he'll go. With his twisted history lesson and his perfect kind of Snow White.

Mo 13 is less sure, left guarding the Parlour. He looks nervy with a stick in his hand and an assistant beside him – a former Thug with a new permasmile.

-Just make sure nobody gets through, I say, -not without scuffing their Nikes.

The Terp swallows his reply as Jonas sparks up a headlight like an alien's eye, plus a flashing orange light from a rescue van on the tail of his beast, all powered by truck batteries.

We compare phones and watch them fill with the Anarchists' network, in touch and ready to move our separate ways.

Zoë Palmer fusses with Tyler's coat. He holds up his Transformer, bristling with unfeasible weapons. He asks if I've brought mine.

I pat my pocket and the boy declares: -Then let's go..!

Blackwood laughs and repeats the boy's order, adding: -Be careful, everyone. Stick together and Godspeed, all.

He hugs the Sapper, then joins me and Zoë Palmer. Jonas' section roll his crate into the passageway, the hundred residents following it with a tum te tum and a whatever, singing their way into the corridors.

Choosing a different route, I lead Zoë Palmer and Tyler,

Blackwood, Work Experience and his dog, spray-painting our way into the darkness.

Soon, we no longer hear the machine, just the spray can's rattle and hiss, and the building's sigh as we creep into its bones one final time, to claim them.

53: Day 62 Plus: 'Poppies Are Rags Ripped Out Of The Sky'

We stop an hour later for a rest and a drink. Tyler's enthusiasm has worn off. Work Experience tries to cheer him up with a playfight, but the boy is fed up and has a full blown tantrum. Anyone could hear us coming so I put him on my shoulders where he sits on my Bergen, warm and bony, his weight bringing agony into my lower back, but Zoë Palmer stays beside me, hand on her son's knee, on my shoulder. Like a family. We have a dog, a priest and a witness behind us, graffiti-ing our confetti.

Another hour later, we step onto a ledge, the usual glazed roof above us letting daylight soak into a chasm. On the other side is a row of archways, reached by a rusty bridge. But those arches are open to the elements, filled with sky, the cityscape, and the sound of straining engines. We are here.

I call time-out. The Teenager slumps with his DS and the dog sits panting. I put Tyler down and he goes to the Teenager's elbow, who tilts the screen toward the kid and pounds his thumbs even harder into the gadget.

Blackwood's as pale as limewash, but he pulls himself together and wants to press on. I tell Zoë Palmer to wait here with the lads while Blackwood and I cross the bridge to scout out the arches.

When we get there, the wind hits our faces with freedom, and diesel. The scene is spread below us. We're only five storeys high, and beyond us is a sea of mud and rubble looking like a tsunami has reached the walls and gone out again, leaving islands, some of wood, some of brick, and one of tangled wires like a vast nest. At the low tide mark, white-box houses sit in the sludge; the estate creeping even closer than before, the frayed flag with the company logo set back a little now, bearing the same brand that's printed on the beasts that shriek, below us, biting into the factory, making the brickwork shudder, working even today.

-Last week, I say, -up to a hundred metres out, that land was inside. There was a hall over there where some city hipsters had their art show. Now look at it…

Blackwood's face is stiff and drawn. -I'm not ready for them… I'm not…

Zoë Palmer is watching.

-I can defend this wall, I press him, -but you have to help her do her bit.

He says he hasn't studied enough, planned enough… His eyes are downcast. Zoë Palmer starts crossing toward us.

The bricks move.

And she's with us. Her face is raw with cold and maybe more. She hugs herself against the blast, looks from Blackwood to me and back again, and I'm saddened to my centre.

-Blackwood, I say, -they are stealing this place from underneath you.

He says nothing. I turn to Zoë Palmer. Everything in me is breaking. I draw out a paper that didn't make it back into her bag the night I searched for Tyler's medicine, and on the bottom is her name, and at the top is the same logo as on the flags and machines attacking us. -You are part of all that, I say, voice cracking. -Right from the start. That map of yours is so you can tell them what's in here. I want to believe in you. But if you double cross this man who saved me… you have no idea what we've been through. You wouldn't believe it if I told you, like you won't believe your boy got better.

Blackwood lays his claw on my arm, tells her: -I asked you to wait until I was ready.

Tears leap into her eyes: -But Whistler says you're dead! They think they own it!

I swear into the gale.

-I thought I was dead, cries Blackwood, -but we need this place as it is, for the life we're trying to make in here. We don't need houses we can't buy! We need more..!

-But development is good...! Growth is good!

-Why..?

Zoë Palmer waves at the builders below: -They're winning, James, she says, -and one day all this... factory crap... will be cleared away and then--

-It won't though, will it? he says. -It'll carry on in people's hearts. We built a school-house once... Remember that, P..? That village? All of it got destroyed a week later when someone decided it didn't fit their picture. Well it's the same human hearts. It's the same game. I can't go out there and tell them I'm alive. I broke some big rules in that game, and Whistler knows it.

-Then do the deal with me, she says.

And she shows us her phone with a number on its screen, and her business bank account framed all around it. I've not seen money like that my entire life.

-It's just an option. I'll raise the rest...

The wind howls. The engines whine. The city crouches. Defeated.

She snaps, wild with confession: -I won't sell out to Whistler, she cries, -I hate him more than you can know. Give it to me and I will make it work for you. Keep the mansions, let me have the rest – give me the rubbish you don't want.

-Why? Why do you want it so much..?

-Because it killed my family and I can't escape it and They won't let me prove myself and I will never get a break like this again –

people like me never do – and I have Tyler to think of and I know what to do with it and you don't. Isn't that enough?

The smell of diesel hits us. The rain begins, outside.

There's a call from Tyler, coming across the bridge, arms spread to hold the railings. Work Experience and his dog follow on.

Zoë Palmer rushes to gather her boy, kissing him, bringing him the rest of the way onto shuddering brick. He's terrified by the view and clings to her. It twists my heart so hard I can hardly stand it. Work Experience puts a hand on the boy's head, telling him good job, Monster Killer.

-Mum, I got to level three..!

Blackwood kneels and dips forward until his forehead touches the dirt, then sits back and yells at the clouds that boil above the glass roof.

A vibration in the structure makes me reach for balance.

He tells Zoë Palmer: -I don't want to sell up and I don't want to fight you.

I flash him a look.

-Please understand, he croaks. -Their system is vile in my eyes, destroying the poor and making consumers dull to truth. Why should I play by their rules..?

The floor shakes. Work Experience grabs the dog and Tyler grips his mum.

-Okay go, says Blackwood. -Tell them I'm alive. Say you've seen the owner. Tell them to stop. I am busy and I will come when I am ready.

-But what if–

-They don't believe you? Or Whistler lies? Then shake the dirt off your feet. You have two days. You know the plan.

-Then give me the deeds – temporarily – as proof!

He shakes his head. -They're in a safe place now...

Her face falls, despairing, and a hundred yards away to our

right, a wall tips out and folds into the air, separating toward the mud below, where men watch it arrive with a boom.

We need to move. I pull Blackwood's arm over my shoulder and urge us on while the chasm yawns on our left and the world gapes on our right. Glass shatters, high above, and I yell us into cover. Work Experience throws himself over the boy as knives explode around us.

When I've checked no-one is hurt, I haul us into motion. Winter bashes and rain falls, but we put ground between us and the demolition, reaching the last arch, where a second bridge leads back into the factory, and an iron stairway, partly bricked in and sheltered, spirals down to the ground outside. I release Blackwood, who crinkles like a packet, and I hold out my hand to Zoë Palmer.

Face washed in rain, she takes my slippery fingers and clutching Tyler, we start down the stairs, the crash of machinery making everything shudder as we circle, my knees aching, debris pouring from the factory, generations of brick, timber, plastic and steel, pulled off in wedges with a roar in the empty structure and in my fractured heart as we reach the ground, so cold now that I can't feel her hand in mine.

She unpicks her grip and we face each other. I'm blasted by ice and stripped of everything.

-Come with me, she says, sending a bullet into my soul.

-You can live in my house till you get on your feet...

Hope and desire race through me, questions pouring out...

-Blackwood... I stammer... -He...

She presses her cheek against mine, touching the scar on my neck with her fingers.

-I'm sorry... she pulls away, -I've offended you... I'll...

She gathers Tyler and doesn't look back, leaves the shelter of the bricks, heads out onto the building site with him, keeping low.

"Offended...?"

I call out. I remind her to lower the flag if they believe her. Or if she changes her mind. Wants to come back. To talk. Anything. I don't want these to be our final words.

But she's beyond hearing, reaching the trees by the fence, forced to trudge across the muck toward the houses and machines. The men in helmets seem astonished. There's a spirited exchange and she points up at the ledge where Blackwood is hidden – but not in my direction. She grabs a phone and makes a call, pulling Tyler into the house with the flag while the men return to their work. The flag stays up; the pounding doesn't stop. She has two days.

I begin the climb, fire in my chest, ice in my face, crashing, crawling.

"Sorry" for what..?

At the top, Work Experience is alone with his dog. He waves his DS at the bridge. -He's gone back in... You look a mess, Sarge...

It's raining glass and water in a post-industrial meltdown.

I need a drink.

> A greater fear
> suspends my soul until it slowly spins:
> I mean the grief below. Brought on by pride.
> That load is with me as this climb begins.
> - Dante, *Purgatorio*

Part 6: Heartland

54: Darks 62-63: 'Operate in Accordance with the Law'

We have good sight of the ground so I make a map out of bricks, allocate the houses numbers and nominate an RV. The house with the flag, where Zoë Palmer and her son are, becomes 'Compound Zero'. As night closes in, the flag stays up, with no let-up in hostile action.

So the enemy possesses standard, tracked and wheeled hardware, none armoured. There are twenty guys in helmets, plus a dozen Security at the gate. They have the potential to call down unknown numbers including Police, so their response time is our window of operation. Weather is damp, so mud will cling but the ground is rubble, compact if unstable. We are heavily outnumbered so we will rely on speed, surprise, and dissimulation. We do have a dog, however, which if Work Experience can handle it, is an advantage. We toss our empty bottles of hooch into the chasm.

On the morning of the second day, with half our hide-out destroyed, there's new movement in the field. A pale four-by-four emerges from the factory and bounces to Compound Zero. I shake Work Experience awake, to verify what I see.

Out steps a gorilla, followed by the white suit of Whistler – there is no mistaking him. Work Experience has the same expression of horror as me. I want to charge down there straight away but the mission is to wait out, observe.

Whistler is met at the door by Zoë Palmer. He enters, accompanied by a lackey in a business suit. Ten agonising minutes later he strides back out, glaring up at the factory, his sidekick recording and lawyer-like.

He pauses in the mud and scours the factory's open honeycomb, looking for something. He cups his hands around his mouth and yells – I can't make out the words – gets back into the vehicle and it lurches out of sight beneath the far end of the dereliction, heading in.

The machines shriek louder, energised, pressing harder. A dormant JCB joins the attack. A dump truck coughs a burst of soot and rolls forward.

In a window of Compound Zero, Zoë Palmer's face is as small as a pill. The flag remains. She has not succeeded.

I take four bottles out of my Bergen that I've filled with generator fuel at the Sanctuary, giving two to Work Experience.

We unscrew and re-pack the necks with rags, fight off the cold and wait out the daylight, the dog in the Teenager's lap. I watch the excavators butting the wall and check my phone. Still nothing.

As darkness falls, lights go on in Compound Zero, like Christmas compared to how we feel. We are stiff limbed, soggy and thirsty. Even Work Experience's thumbs are too numb to play. We eat a can of corned beef each, while the dog is restless and the demolition continues under floodlights; they want to bring this section down tonight. I feel pain for Zoë Palmer, but glad she did not compromise our location. That tells me something.

We hike down to a harbour position where Work Experience smirks: -Fix bayonets...?

I smile grimly. -Make sure the mutt does what you tell it.

He says it will and tightens his blades. The doctors told him to take no risks, but look at him now. I open a final hooch, and we empty it together, for warmth, while a section of wall comes bitten down.

On my count, we break cover, keeping out of the floodlights, and advance through valleys of rubble, collecting weaponry – steel rods and wire – while the dog sniffs about.

Masonry spins through the air and an excavator whines, swinging its jaws and farting smoke.

With a bottle each, we attack at state red, carrying a steel offcut between us. Going over the top into a blaze of light, we advance on the nearest JCB and jam our metal into its tracks. Work Experience ignites my bottle. Flames catch and smoke. With fog in my eyes I lob the cocktail at the engine just as the cockpit swerves and the bottle clatters against the bonnet. Fire blooms harmlessly on the ground but a shout goes up. Working fast, the Teenager lights his own Molotov, that invention of the Finnish Winter War for the Finns to battle with Soviet tanks and he aims it better, hitting a grille, sending fire deep into the motor. The driver yells over the roar of the engine and scrambles out as the JCB is engulfed. We dive away as half a dozen men in hard hats start shouting, reacting to the blaze and one of them calls out:

-Squatters..!

I hurl a brick at them to keep them thoughtful and we rush the second vehicle, stabbing rods, shards, rubble into the guts, until the Teenager bursts the radiator, making it hiss. I'm out of breath and so is he, and as the driver runs for it I'm happy for the dog to stand on a mound of wood and bay at the men. They have no idea how many of us we are, pouring out of the factory. It would've been nice to have some distractions on the ramparts but we have to work within our resources, and hey, I'm starting to enjoy myself.

We attack another excavator. This time my bottle penetrates with a satisfying wallop and we run at the men, howling and exploiting their confusion while they stagger back from the fire, us and the dog. They're not paid enough to fight 'fucking junkies' as we head for the houses. Then one of them screams behind me.

I turn and see Work Experience yanking the dog, its teeth

buried in a builder's leg. His colleagues are closing in, leaving their vehicles to burn like beacons until one of them lands a punch on the Teenager.

The mission or the lad. I admit it – I hesitate. Him and that bloody dog. But if he makes it out from under the builders, there's still a chance he'll get to the RV and complete the mission.

I take my last unlit Molotov and run at the men, yelling with the bottle in a throwing position. They scramble away and I crash beside the bitten one, hammer the bottle onto the dog's head. Work Experience flings himself at me, but the creature lets go so I drag the Teenager onto his feet, fuel leaking all over my hand, and he pulls the dog with us, away from the floodlights toward the houses.

I press my bottle into his grasp and send him on his way through the compounds while I enter the first block, kicking a door in, making sure that Security, who've arrived in numbers now, can easily see which one I've entered.

I advance house by house as sirens announce the arrival of firefighters and coppers, weaving my way through doors, swapping and ducking, keeping them on my tail.

Meantime, houses elsewhere begin to catch light, balling into flames and I lose my pursuers as they peel off to deal with it. So I go to Compound Zero, flag still flying and her face at an upper window, watching the reflected fires and pleading into her phone. She spots me, drops the handset, presses her palm against the glass and rests her forehead on it, eyes on mine. She has failed. We hold each other's gaze, before I cut the rope that holds the flag and pull it to the ground, roll it into my jacket.

She watches me turn away to the RV and break into it. Work Experience is there, huddled, smeared and staring out of a window at the swelling inferno, his dog beside him. He has the brochure for the house clutched to his chest and the bottom of the curtain is soaked from his bottle. A tear rolls down his cheek. It's hard for a homeless lad to burn what he has dreamt of. I know that.

I squeeze his shoulder and give the dog a ruffle. Chest aching, retinas etched with her face, I can barely speak, but we must assess our position and prepare to break out. The Teenager gazes at the brochure with the lighter in his other hand, brings them close together, pauses, pockets the brochure and puts away his Zippo, unsparked. I look the other way.

On my count, we drop out of a back window and move from shadow to shadow until we reach the factory and stagger up the remaining scrap of outer wall, leaving my heart in the mud. One last bridge spans the chasm where glass glitters in the depths. If we'd waited any longer, the demolition would've taken it and there would've been no way back. We collapse into cover and take stock of the scene below.

Zoë Palmer's village is boiling with flames, except for Compound Zero, where her face has vanished, and the house that Work Experience spared. Blue lights flash and workers rush through the smoke.

Enemy halted. Mission accomplished. Fuel and ash in my mouth.

The Teenager weeps on his knees.

His dog growls at two figures running this way, separate from the melee, and I yell her name. It's her, unmistakably pulling Tyler back toward the factory. A gang of Security see her too, and start running to intercept.

I clatter down the stairs and meet her, her face a mess and Tyler petrified. I hustle them up ahead of me, ready to take on whoever threatens our rear. Voices shout, boots clang, but a greater explosion swallows them as a fuel tank ignites in the mud. It illuminates the world like a comet.

When we reach the top, I drop to my knees and puke into the chasm, my regret falling into it like stars.

55: Dark 64: 'Avoiding Attrition'

We cross the remaining bridge and Zoë Palmer pounds her fists at my head, chest and shoulders, screaming until she cries into her sleeve.
 -Why? I ask her, sore from where she's whacked me. -If you can't stand us so much, why d'you come back?
 Because they fired her, she sobs. For a moment I think she'll hit me again but she holds Tyler's hand like he's her last anchor and it all comes out. She told them the Owner was alive and had the deeds and they didn't believe her. They brought out Whistler who sacked her. He said he paid her to make maps, not ghost stories. He told her she'd never work again, gave her an hour to get off site and sped the demolition up.
 Her eyes match the rain for tears, but my phone interrupts. It's Jonas with music in the background, panicking.
 I turn to Zoë Palmer because there's more to this than she's letting on, and I ask her, gently, what she ever thought Whistler would say, and she breaks my heart, snotty and rubbing her eyes: -I don't hate you, she says. -That's the truth. Sometimes I maybe even love you... guys – I don't know... But you've conned me... or you're the kindest people I know...
 And she cries, freely, and I feel every desperate scar of myself, the battered bones I am, thinking I'd rather face an ISIS butcher than hold her gaze. I know she would've sold us to Whistler if she could have, because she thinks it's the right thing to do, to give Blackwood money and get us out of here. She knows I've guessed that what Whistler asked her in that house was not if Blackwood was alive but

if she'd done the deal yet, and he would've taken the deeds from her because the money she showed us isn't hers, it's his.

-I can't say you're wrong, I tell her, -or that Blackwood's kind, or that any of us are, but do me one small favour? Please, Zoë Palmer? Just act as if we can get there. Blackwood's found his beliefs and they're better than they were before, and it's better than business-as-usual, so I'm gonna act like we can turn this world around – and I'm gonna do it for the ones this world threw away. Do we have a deal..?

And I take her hands in mine not because I'm good or right or proper for her but because I want my electric anger against this world and my part in it to pass down my fingers and into hers. But I guess she only sees the madness in my eyes, as she breaks off to explain to Tyler that mummy's not-really-crying, it's okay.

Remaining here is not an option, nor is going back to the houses, so we fix our torches and she looks at me like she did before, like a hillside after a storm. She takes a grip on Tyler and nods her readiness, and I understand without needing to hear it. We will walk into our fears again, side by side.

I can't ask for more.

So we move, tracking our graffiti, finding the impossible route that Jonas' machine took until finally, at the far end of a forest of pillars, a doorway pulses with music, crowd noise, and a flashing orange light, like breakdown recovery.

Work Experience tethers his dog, gives it biscuits, and with Zoë Palmer beside me gripping Tyler, we engage, striding into a pack of people dancing and sweeping the air with transparent flags. I recognise residents from Sanctuary, these people with nowhere they'd rather be: hipsters whose designs were never bought and builders the banks bled dry, junkies on the wagon and businessmen whose air-miles crashed, mums on respite and soldiers with blood on their hands, strippers breaking cover and all the homeless singing for their roots, waving their see-through Sanctuary flags, singing the song that creeps along: Eenie-meenie-minie-mo-pick-a petal...

Some sing as Jonas deejays anthems from his cockpit, others do personal shuffles. They welcome Zoë Palmer and Tyler with delight while music powers them like a common heartbeat, and I'm suddenly, strangely hungry.

I go to Jonas who pulls his headphones down and grabs my collar. There's too many of them, he yells. How can we push them back? I climb up beside him and survey the situation.

Blackwood is here. He moves through the residents crowded against a ledge where a stairway drops into the reason for Jonas' panic: a cavern filled with humanity. I had no idea this place could swallow so many. They move beside production lines, like the factory of old, but these are trestles loaded with food, the audience shouting, heaving in time to the music. We are the entertainment, face to face with the entire mob of Victory Cocoa and the machine can go no further. Down amongst them, Whistler's black-jackets are pushing activists this way.

I yell at Blackwood, who doesn't seem to want to stop them, but speaks to individuals, resting his hand on them. Some laugh, some sink out of sight; others wipe their eyes and raise their hands, but naturally, like coming home is natural.

Out in the production hall, partygoers grapple. Fires are lit and food gets thrown while the guys up here go hungry, and it does smell good, but hot-heads are on the stairs. A woman Blackwood has spoken to is bleeding from the head while a bully with a quiff is cheering because he threw the bottle at her, at someone who was soft enough to pray. Zoë Palmer watches with wide eyes so I climb down and lift Tyler into my place, protected by the machine, put ear defenders and a hard hat on him, tell Jonas' team to push the crate to the stair-top and block it off at top volume.

I tell Zoë Palmer to stay with Tyler and I weave my way to Blackwood just as the Quiff arrives. I fly at the guy but Blackwood jumps in and I catch his ear instead, see Quiff glaring down at me. I grab his bottle-hand and push, skull bouncing into his face and forcing his wrist to crack. Blackwood shouts "No!" so I drop the Quiff who rolls, crying while the Padre speaks to him like he does to all the others.

Jonas' team heave the machine across the stair-top entrance, sealing it, playing: This Little Light Of Mine at killer volume. Flags whip, including Sheena's, who spots Zoë Palmer and closes her eyes.

I whirl into Work Experience who points out a huddle who're nursing the woman hit on the scalp and fussing over the Quiff. I don't know who's supposed to be cared for, anymore.

Blackwood separates from greeting Zoë Palmer and swirls his arm around my shoulder. My head spins. All the agony in my chest lurches and I fall to my knees at the mezzanine's edge, beneath all my hate, my failure and sleeplessness. He waves away my okays, saying he's 'P.' now; he's got no fear left. I tell him I have fear enough to fill an army. I show him the flag from the house inside my coat and he grips me in shared guilt. I sway on my knees, exhausted. I want a drink, but the thirst seems wrong. -Get up, he says, -Rise up, Marine P.

I look and see he's bent to his right against huge pain, keeping himself stitched in, sweating, his greatcoat hiding a stain.

-When you get back to Sanctuary, he shouts, -look in the last chapter and do what it says. Please..?

I press my hands into the filth and push myself onto my feet. I do not wipe my hands. They're mine, with all their dirt.

-But you'll read that chapter yourself, I say, seeing Zoë Palmer torn between her boy and approaching Blackwood, so I speak loudly into his ear, making my sudden admission: -It's you she wants, Blackwood... It's you...

I'm shouting my sadness into Blackwood's face and he can't hear me.

He declares instead: -If all we want is what we think will make us happy, P., then evil blows around us. I was a weak man, P., and you've saved me.

I push him away.

He grabs me back: -That girl at the monastery lived, P.! It was a sign that we could've spread a new kind of hope. But the world calls it impossible. That's why they snuffed it out..!

I seize him by the collar of his coat.

-Blackwood, I'm the one who snuffed it out.

And even as the chaos intensifies, he speaks as if we're the only men left alive, and says: -I've done terrible things, P. Can you show me how to fix it?

-I can't save you, I tell him. -My dead don't rise.

And he grips me like a rope. -Do the impossible, P.! That's the mission! Remember the stories and the strength in prayers that make no sense! Do it, because evil does not want us to believe that we're here for a reason, it wants us just to consume things and other people and avoid our own pain...

We could argue, take sides, get others to do it, fight until we miss the point so I return his grasp with all my strength. I have no better plan than to crush my brother.

-Be delivered, P., he gasps.

We let go and face each other. My voice chokes:

-You too, Blackwood.

And his icy eyes hold mine. Whoever is first to say 'Thank you' will admit more guilt, when both of us are fighting for parity. We bow our heads and it's begun. I release him from all the pain and useless hope he's caused me, bringing me to hell and making me think impossible things… I brought myself here and I deserve it, that's the truth. I am Dante and he is my Guide who can't make the journey without me. We're thrown together by the ordinary world and we've tried to make a safe place in a corner of hell, and the whole damn thing is falling apart – but I don't care.

I release him from his debt to me and vow I will make this place break open. I will stop chasing every last hunger when I think it's the only thing I can do. I will not despair. I will not be Defeated.

Together, we lift Zoë Palmer onto Jonas' machine with Tyler, the safest place in this chaos, blaring happy songs. Blackwood climbs up beside them and the Sapper fades his noise to a single, vibrating note.

Zoë Palmer and Tyler cower.

All the music has come to this.

One note.

56: Oh Dark Thirty: 'No plan survives...'

We were fighting for Victory Cocoa. Let my notebook explain: If there are only laws of humans and nature, we must learn to live in the loopholes.

Consider.

Threat is the basis of money, and Debt comes riding on a pale horse. This is an Immanent Frame, and closed, like a box, like a building you cannot escape.

Victory Cocoa must be stronger than this.

If there's nothing higher than our desire, then we consume like an act of defeat. Our Defeat can be quiet, like chardonnay or abstinence, unhealth or fitness, self-pity or even the love we crave... We scapegoat whoever stands in our way, and put our own shame on them. We consume them, too.

Victory Cocoa must be stronger than this.

An older resident was crying at the table. The younger ones who'd come here clutching estate agent leaflets asked him what was up, and he said "Sorry". They asked him what for, and he said for charging the highest price he could get for his house. Because of what he'd wanted, they could not afford it; he had been advised by others, and he had things he wanted to do with the cash. If only, he said, he'd been asked what they could afford, they could've had what they needed: shelter. They told him it wasn't his fault but he insisted; he could've broken the chain, and they would not have died, in debt, in shoddy houses.

Victory Cocoa must be stronger than this.

Jonas cuts the sound and the mob look up, like a sea coming off the boil, hundreds of people breathing, coughing, clinking.

Blackwood's eyes close. We, the guilty, stand with him to be judged.

I've seen officers readying troops; leaders denying death. What I have not seen is a man smashed and bleeding, arm raised, holding the peace, gone to a different place.

A minute passes, maybe more.

The Finnish anarchist plants his arse down, followed by his Spanish mate, and others drop, too. Work Experience sinks, exhausted, and more follow; an army being thinned.

Even in the well, some kneel, faces dipping out of sight. Others topple as if their drug has risen. The majority are standing, unsure. Me, I lean on the machine, Bergen biting deep.

Shadows flit and a murmur spreads, sighing into a groan. Blackwood's arm stays high, face blank and battered. A darker presence seems to stretch out, angered at this interruption.

I exhale smoke, women, rocks and men, fire-cover, kids, dust, Zoë Palmer, Kats, a poet and his girl. It goes out in a cloud, not finished, not over, but out in front.

The factory quietly rolls, its ancient belly full of us and all our broken bits.

A slow clap begins, and a "Fuck You!"

Blackwood whispers. Jonas fits a microphone into his fingers: -Oh... my... God... Jesus.... For..., he sways. -For... give... us our debts as we forgive others their debt against us...

He finds the note where the machine left off, drawing his words from far away, -For-give... give.... give.

His lilt swells, he stamps his boot, bouncing the words around the air. I see Kats with her man, in the crowd, the dealer and agony rises because she was the one, once – she goes, swapped with a fighter I killed long ago and the terror of both grabs me just the same. I deserve this. But her..? I push my way to the edge.

Blackwood calls: -Whoever forgives...! We have room..! Give... live and stay...!

If she's down there...

-Forgive..! he sings: -In pain and in freedom... Give..!

Someone out there yells: "Deejay what the fuck", and Thugs with tears tattooed on their faces squeeze past the rig. I should be ready for action but they trip in front of Punk Dayz and Sheena, who give them water. A third invader, a woman who looks like she could be at the school gates, claws up at Blackwood's legs, mouth moving wordlessly.

I crane over the railing while the dead start mounting the stairs, weeping, and Jonas' engine is rolled back from the entrance by this uprising.

There's a laugh, loud and forceful, whipping up the crowd and a bonfire flares, revealing Whistler under a lamp, beckoning, but the mood thickens. Patchy curses are thrown against him and a Reindeer approaches him. There's a scuffle and Whistler's light goes out. A giant shadow dives to the floor, a presence falling.

I ask Blackwood if he saw it, but he doesn't hear me. He's climbed from the machine and is going down into the well. I tell Lucky Jonas to get Zoë Palmer and Tyler out of here and I follow Blackwood, against the stream of those coming up. At the bottom, he keeps moving out amongst people who divide, mocking, finding exits and pointing fingers in his face while Jonas, above us, begins a symphony that fills the air. Blackwood touches and sends people stairwards. Others say what a bag of shit, these tunes, and a missile clatters past him. I reach out but instead of Blackwood I pull a young guy towards me needing a fix. I tell him to go up and get sorted, manage to see Blackwood slip into the unrest, when a blow to my

Bergen topples me into the muck of an upturned table, rubberising the oxygen out of me. I get up, dripping with floor juice, and call Blackwood's name, straining to catch sight of his straw-top, pushing through the melee who either want to go up or want to get out of their heads and I see her, bug-eyed, in broken heels and miniskirt from a long night's clubbing, trailing after her new man. So it's true. Kats.

She tugs at her dealer in the expensive shirt he's clearly worn for weeks and space opens up between us, and I have nothing but the word in my head, asking or offering: -Give. Forgive. I...

She wobbles on her heels like I'm in a dream she has all the time, and she pulls at him, wanting to go. He's got a scar and a golden stamp on his head, and I fix him, too, and say yes. Give. For. The violence in my chest...

A group invades the space, and Kats and her dealer vanish.

I call out, crying my first tears since Mum plastered my knee by the swings, my throat strangled with sadness and relief. It is finished.

Crying like a baby I push on, looking for Blackwood. I reach a lamp on a tripod that three lads and a lass stagger off with. It blacks out and a generator dies. The crowd howls. Lights blare from Jonas' machine where orchestral music climbs above the glittering phones people wave between the bonfires, which are growing. I jog with a crowd away from the music toward a cold wind, the panic becoming a stampede with the Defeated drinking, shooting up or toking, teenagers staggering, dislocating, a woman fighting off arseholes at which I throw myself in desperation, take a whack to the face, black out and when I pick myself up, there's no weight on my shoulders. Horror courses through me.

I fight for focus. My loss is nothing compared to what I may never find. I call out Blackwood's name, turning over bodies, bumping into people heading for the cold while Lucky Jonas charges the air with hums and birds. Adrenaline pounding, Bergen gone,

Kats who got rid of my child, dissolved, Blackwood lost, Zoë Palmer hating me for burning her village, everything I valued seems gone. I dig into my combat pockets and thank God the memory stick is there, with my notebook and Transformer. I close my fist around the toy and surrender to the emotion, double tap to the heart.

The cold wind pulls me to broad stairs that lead up to a double entrance, open onto an area of tarmac, with fences in the distance, across which blue lights flash and dogs bark – and above it, a starry night. Scattered mob wander between the Police and moon, so I crawl towards my way out, when the presence I've known here since I arrived fills the walls around me, pinning me with its attention, its beard and weapon, striding, hissing: *Jussst busssinesssss...*

Lucky Jonas drops a beat, far behind me, and a choir rises. The shadow reacts, grows against the walls and flees out of the doors. It could easily have been someone running past a bonfire, but the night is what it is: an exit for shades, the abode of death. Cold. As usual. There's nothing out there, never has been and never will be. I see the fires behind me and a requiem, *dona nobis pacem*, the machine calling for Blackwood.

I tumble back to the well, rolling bodies over and searching, searching, searching until I'm forced to sit.

Blackwood isn't here.

I return to the mezzanine and the lights and voices, the sweet sound of home, the place you go after trauma. I find Gracya, Sheena and Punk Dayz, grab Jonas and Zoë Palmer with Tyler still on board, leaving the hall.

-Blackwood..? I beg them. -... here?

Lucky Jonas' face falls. -Not with you..?

Zoë Palmer jumps in panic so I order Jonas to take her and Tyler home, while Sheena puts an arm around them, and I'm thankful. Soaked and coughing, I collar the Teenager and his dog. He's exhausted but embraces me, across our ranks, our ages, our uprooted pasts, and: -I forgive you, P., he says, and it knocks me; even this kid..?

I say what comes into my head:

-Mate. If I had a son, I'd be proud if he turned out like you.

My words hit him more than I intended, and they sink into me, too.

-My name's Callum, he says. -By the way...

But I can't do this, not now. The flames and the stink of rubber are strong despite the height of the ceiling. I tell him to look sharp. I want to see initiative, not mere obedience. So we go back and search until he can no longer move, his dog is at a loss, and I trip over too often, stepping into holes that are filling with water. We're joined by a group led by Jonas, who kicks at the skirts of bonfires. It's getting too dangerous to stay, but we check anyone on the ground, urge them to walk out one way or another, and thank God no dead, yet.

Then we find the body.

57: Dark Plus: 'Zero Hour'

Face down, slashes in his back and a belt around his neck: it's Whistler.
    The guys fall silent. I put a finger into the mob leader's neck. A pulse skitters under the oily powder. Jonas sucks his teeth. If we leave this devil, he'll die. If we don't leave, we'll die. Enemy combatant. Break our backs hauling his flesh to safety, or finish the job. Slice a vein. Let him drain. Take a photo for Facebook and move on. What are the Rules of Engagement now?
    The dog has found no scent of Blackwood. The smoke and mess leaves nothing, and we need rest and food. With fires growing, water rising and torches failing, we're forced to withdraw.
    We form a sledge from trash, drag the Politician onto it and tie him down. Jonas and I take a handle each and pull.
    I check my phone, feeling it buzz.
    What I get is a message from Zoë Palmer:
    They're coming for you now.
    The Police, the Authorities, the lawyers, the military, all those who invested in Whistler... I bet they are.

At Sanctuary, news of Blackwood's disappearance spreads. I gulp water and beans, tell Work Experience to drink, eat, and to look after his dog. I throw the last of Blackwood's painkillers from my pocket down my throat and explain to the others how the gates have burst open to the outside world. Nobody moves, now that the option is there. Mo 13 wonders if Blackwood walked out, but I say no, no way, not into the arms of the Cops.

Miss Morphine's crew triage those we've rescued, including Whistler, and Mo 13 shakes his head. What a swap. Blackwood for this animal.

Zoë Palmer ushers Tyler to their room, stepping over rubble, getting away from Whistler as firmly as she can.

Three times we go in search, we the remnants of Two Section, beaten back by bonfires raging twenty feet high, water gushing from broken pipes creating a lake that hisses around the flames. We use a raft of junk that we lash together to get across the flood, but find no-one. Armed Police shine lamps in from the gates, calling for Whistler and Blackwood, seeking him as much as we do. That's when I see a shape wedged into a drain, sucked into its trench by water rolling in like molten chocolate.

I haul the lifeless, dripping shape on board. It's Blackwood's greatcoat.

The factory sighs.

The flood slaps at the walls.

Blackwood is gone.

58: Darks and Days: 'System Shock'

Police with guns are moving through the lower building. There's a map out there; Zoë Palmer's. She says does Whistler look like he has it? Okay but did he rip it from you? He's locked in a room where Miss Morphine feeds him antibiotics – more mercy than he gave his customers. I stand beside his mattress and watch him shiver; the man who made his Surveyor so scared that she preferred to run to me who burned her dreams to the ground; a man who treated his people like prey. He stinks. It gives me no comfort. I see a consumer of Blackwood's reckless mercy.

Through nights that follow, the community of Victory Cocoa gasps at the hole Blackwood leaves behind. I take his book from its shelf, tucked between The Brothers Karamazov and a book of white walls in a forest by an architect called Alvar Aalto and I read it, locked in my billet, feeling her silent door, unsafe, like before.

He's out there, under the waves or in a fissure. He never picked a room of his own, only the sofa by the stove, with clothes, a blister-pack, a Bible like a truck's run over it and a wedge of papers crammed into *Industry & Architecture*. Sheena brings me touches of time and healing, and I tell her there's so much I didn't say, so much I didn't understand, with his filthy coat stripped of rank insignia still damp on the back of a chair in my room. Even when I hang it in front of the burner, it refuses warmth. Zoë Palmer fingers it; others avoid it. I wrap it tight around me, the mould of it, read his papers and sleep where he slept, homeless again, waiting for the Police.

The residents are well fed but unsettled. No-one knows how long we've got, but work gives shape, and people are kind to one another, sharing what they have.

Jonas starts each day by reciting the verses until teardrops appear at the last Amen. He surprises me but makes the same point Blackwood made: if you want this, please stay; if not, then go. Many do. In Sanctuary, you have to see what isn't there yet, look past the antiquated stuff and recycled trash, the generators and cooking smoke, threat of failure and dodgy newcomers – although we were all mob once, truth be told. The mood is not as united without Blackwood, however, and although Tyler reminds everyone that he'd been fixed up; the whisper is, he'd have gotten better anyway – so say the ones who tend not to stay. Among those who do, though, living an impossible freedom, even for a short time, laughter creeps into the air, acts of sharing and honouring lift the mood, like making chocolates for no obvious reason, or a kid's birthday roaring in the school room, or the Anarchists and Chef creating a batch of hooch, or like Arun in his chariot getting The High Rises around the piano. There's no point to these things but they happen. They happen so that we honour and forgive each other. Because we are not in a box.

I thumb the final chapter: A New Heaven and a New Earth. It begins: 'Babylon is fallen; mystery the great.'

Folded into it, are two sheets of paper.

One is Zoë Palmer's spreadsheet with its question channelled into a number and I wonder how it's possible to love three people and be so wrong for them...

Is this The Happiness? To be released from love..?

Sometimes I wish I'd been content with what the world can offer, under its laws of materiality, natural selection and risk management. But I ache to be free.

The second paper makes me smile.

59: Dark Final: 'The Importance of Knowing When You Are the Insurgency'

Gracya hammers on my door. Armed Police have reached the stairs and sniffer dogs have broken our mazes. The factory has not shrugged them off. But I'm not ready. I don't understand everything yet. I could still learn.

I order an evacuation into the Mansions, to the last wall, where there's chairs and benches and rugs.

From the six of us who began with Blackwood, I reckon we are now three hundred souls, including kids. It's a shura of elders, youngers, plain and pretty, every shape and race that's tired of being the Defeated. They're fixers, cooks, artists, carers, workers, thinkers, defenders, builders, lost ones, criminals, watched-ones, refugees, seekers. They wear thick coats and blankets, and have to be convinced by whatever I propose. They've taken the risk to stay, and Investigators are coming. Even Whistler huddles in a corner, watched by ex-Thugs and Mo 13's ex-jihadis.

I stand at a wobbly café table and place Blackwood's coat on it, take a swig of hooch for warmth and call for attention. I hold up the second paper and I'm on a high, today, even greater than being under fire because I'm not going to kill, but set three hundred people free, if they agree:

-This is the last will and testament of James Blackwood, Chaplain to 42 Commando, Royal Marines, owner in title of Victory Cocoa, its lands and hereditaments, witnessed by Ms Zoë Palmer, Senior Surveyor at...

My chest explodes. I take another drink. I sense her looking at the floor.

-It states that Mr Blackwood has no cash, but sets out the disposal of his...

I fold the tongue-twisting words back into the book.

-He promised to make this factory vanish.

They gasp as I stuff his greatcoat into a rubbish sack.

-He never wanted relics. No new faith. He had an old one, lost it, found it. He wanted to share it but I'm no expert.

I open up to them, painfully knowing that I'm speaking to Zoë Palmer sitting there, and I reveal every tattoo, every scar, the dragonfly across my back, the welt on my neck biting as I make my declaration to people who may never understand, might only see their own rage and trampled hope or annoyance at this jumped-up soldier with blood on his hands. As much as I can, I confess the horrors I've committed; things I must be delivered from. I cannot fix them. My dead will stay dead. The Caretaker had the gift of fixing things and we remember him. But for the rest of us? A soldier told me once that there are no atheists in foxholes, and I agree, so here's a couple of lines that roll around my head when I need them: *With my God I can scale a wall; my arms can bend a bow of bronze...* I need that kind of strength when the mission is greater than we are.

I place the coat in its bag on the floor.

They will hear a plan in a moment, perhaps an impossible one, I tell them.

-I recommend it to you, every part of it.

I nod to Sapper Jonas, frayed from patrols, who brings Miss Morphine and Mo 13 with him. Full of nerves, he addresses the three hundred, who lean forward, and like a slap in the face, I realise these are all my true friends. We walk side by side.

-Hear me now, the Sapper raps, -and if you agree, let me have a witness!

He reads out Blackwood's plan and it's debated in our ramshackle shura, in groups with people giving summaries of what they're hearing. Sledge-hammers rest by the last wall, if anyone wants to try that way, and the door is open to anyone who wants to leave. Hands rise and are counted. The will is agreed: For those who want it, the factory is theirs, shared out piece by piece. And the cost of a share of Victory Cocoa is both cheap and priceless – it is everything you own.

They vote, and Jonas makes a declaration in the praying verses and as he does so, lips and mouths exhale, voices murmur, dream and interpret, speaking deliverance on the walls. Our breath steams into one cloud, one voice, one agreement... and the factory fades.

We share it between us, in all its grit and glory, in all its sprawl and bricks and burnt parts, its floods and unknown rooms and passages, halls and packing places, cut wires, pipes, graffiti, trash and tiles. Agreeing, we share it out and put it beyond a single owner, and beyond money.

When the Police arrive, they cannot touch us.

We are not squatters. We are the owners. All of us.

Arrest us in our hundreds, if you can.

60: Dawn: 'New Victory Cocoa'

At the end of things, with this notebook in your hand, you'll be the judge. Maybe you'll understand why we didn't hand ourselves in, or surrender to the game, and agree to exist inside a box. Not in this life, nor in the life to come.

Hell's gate is broken. Spring arrives. The flood dries up and we throw the Mansions open, letting the wind blow any foulness out.

Instead of hiding, we form up and move through walls, shouldering Lucky Jonas' machine, climbing the steps to the main gates, and the Police in their riot gear are in shock. There is nothing they can do as we pass them, their visors flipped open, leaning on their weapons as if they can't see us, pushing through their cordon like a ghost parade. I step through blue and white tape, singing like the others, into the terraced streets.

We scatter into the city. Some of us occupy empty buildings, watching out of windows. Others stick with the carnival, passing drivers and shoppers with unseeing eyes, some of whom think they can hear our songs, the shades from the old factory, and they smile at their own hills and dragonflies. Our songs invite the Defeated to depart the old life; all who have fallen foul of a world that cannot satisfy, that holds no victory over endless craving, all those who want to, may come to Victory Cocoa and forgive or wander, for we have many passageways.

So we haunt the mind of the city, and returning to the factory, we repair the generators, run them on chip-shop oil, take power from the sun. Partitions are removed to build new sections. Ancient fire-escapes and traps are changed and people walk on safe paths, day and night. Beds, chairs and bathrooms arrive and the place comes alive with power tools, paint and smell of baking. Fields are planted on the roofs and children play under the sky. We hum with communication and our currency is kindness, according to the New Rules, although we are still learning them. So we give, give, give.

Chef revives old recipes, and we run the restaurant now, and trade well. Sheena tracked down Auntie B's farms in Ghana and they supply us. By Easter, Bristol has Snow's Original Egg and The Caretaker's African Sunshine Selection, and our open days are packed with visitors who don't want to be Defeated any more. I send words to Mum, and have an apartment for her when she arrives, and when we meet, I hope I have not disappointed her in my death.

It's early days – disputes happen, tested in the margin we give each other. But we know our victory depends on this: Pain and freedom. So the Parlour is where we serve Airborne Stew. It reminds us all we're behind enemy lines and that this is the day we win or lose: a decision we make every time, and I go there, every morning.

Some arrive at Victory Cocoa who don't like the New Rules. They want to push back, making Even Newer Rules, but I see nothing new in that. They consume according to their appetites, becoming Defeated, wandering the corridors into stained glass palaces and some return, bloated and uneasy, others vanish, like Troy and Spooks, like Kats and her Dealer... I've never said there isn't heartbreak.

One day you will bang your head, be struck down by salts, get burnt up by sugars. We will be here to meet you. You'll shoot your enemies into open graves, and we will collect both them and you. On the day your drip stops, know us. When blowflies settle on your eyes, we are beside you...

One morning in the Parlour, I'm eating stew, dressed in a shirt with my tattoos hidden when a woman and her bloke stumble in from the factory, talking drunk. I eat on, watching a TV show on a tablet; a satirical review of the year, it's the News laughed at as if it's real, and total – expecting us to live inside it. Call for kindness and resurrection, and the Defeated will contain you with their News, and its satire.

The pair sit down and ask if they'll be moved on. I say by all means, take shelter. He asks if I can spare some change and I say: -Looks like you're sorted.

He asks again, saying they're hungry. I refuse him money and he tells me this is Sanctuary, innit? Ain't I supposed to help? His companion tells him to shut up, and I say she's right, money isn't going to work. He explodes. How would I know, with my fancy shirt, my iPad, big house and all these kids? How would I know what it's like? I tell him he needs to fix that, and they both swear at me. They tell me to fuck off. They have come in here, and they are telling me.

-Take shelter, I say, -and have some Airborne.

They call me wanker, leaving the way they came.

Maybe they're right. Mo 13 would've handled them better. But this place doesn't give you what you want. Did I obey the New Rules, with them?

Zoë Palmer stays in the village with Tyler, where Callum has a house, helping her rebuild it all in the ways she dreamt of, now she's free of Whistler and Tyler's father. It's her plan we follow when we sell what we don't need, to pay for what we do. But only to firms we choose. And never too much, and we calculate the happiness that she could not risk for herself. I love her, as you know, although it must be from a distance and in time that will become something else. Pain and freedom. It's what I've learnt since I broke in here. And as for the map she didn't give away, it isn't finished yet.

It would be nice to see Tyler, before I go. I sent a little something for his birthday. He would like Mo 13's school with its art on the walls. That crazy Terp's got a college-in-the-roof, with ex-enemies training for business, creating a fund that's managed by their former victims. They'll build a hospital in Habiballah this summer, and people won't have to run to the boats. I know, I know. But we will do it.

The mob has not gone. Each week, our residents sing in the belly of the building and rescue those who want it. And if too many of Victory Cocoa go back to Defeat, the remnant will move on; we will not sit still. We have come into the city, after all, and entered your derelict factories, homes, churches, your disused cinemas, your vacant government halls…

That's how They will find me. I walked out of Victory Cocoa with a mission in my soul, released like a verse from the Hidden One. So I bleed my way into the city, with a new name written for me. We are here, spreading outward.

My next move will be to London, into the roof of the House where They carve it up and chase after dragons, edging the poor and guilty into Defeat, vacant of any idea except Consumption. My God!

But you with these notes in your hand, see now: there's a void you pass each day, a building ruined by time and history. What would you do in it? Something kind? Something else? Think, because we are there, watching you. And we know you because we are you. And we are post-traumatic. We have unleashed the verses and there's nothing anyone can do about it.

Blackwood has not been found. He gathered his treasure and gave it away. Some say he's in his childhood room, some say he's closer, but I have my view: there are always parts of Victory Cocoa to discover, and souls who thought they were alone. Perhaps he's started a sanctuary where the job is even harder.

Sheena knows me in my darker hours, when she holds me in my unformed state. I'm learning not to hurt those who show me kindness. We learn together.

Are you the ones Zoë Palmer said were on their way? Or did you take a blow to the head? Fight disease for a year, then nothing? Her houses are as pretty as a blister pack, and I'm pleased for her, even if I have to move.

My heart is broken. But I broke it for the Cause.

So negotiate, because you cannot leave. With these notes in your hand, we could use your skills. You'd settle in. Even some former bosses have, like the Banker Politician, happy in his role in sanitation.

For we are the insurrection
and we are the life,
the Hidden Ones, air-kissed.
We burned your houses down
and for that you may arrest us but
others will replace us and resist you where they find you
with your clerics and your money-makers, liars, thieves and
jokers.

So do not mistake us for the State religion,
for we are being delivered, one debt at a time,
and we are not afraid of the darkness
because the dark itself belongs to us
with all its skin and birds and beasts
and all its freedom songs.
We occupy the heights
like a host, overwatching.
For we are the insurrection,
impossible, purposeful,
and we have many rooms,
oh so many rooms
for you.

Contact!

DRAGONFLY

Acknowledgements

Thanks without measure go to my dearly missed, late Äiti, and to my Father. To Alex for truly understanding the joy and toil of writing. To Kai and Leo for brightness. To Vesa, Jo, Lin, and Harry. To Chris Paling. To draft readers Rich Sayer, Mike Manson, Louise Gethin, big up. To the Bristol Festival of Literature volunteers and a pint for Pete Sutton. Ali Reynolds, early editorial. Richard Beard, wow. Fuad Mahamed, inspiring. To Suomi. To fellow art believers St Mark's Baptist Church & Café, Evan Hughes, American Joe, Robyn Boden, Geoff Hall, Resonance, LoveBristol, Chris Wood, Penny Woollard, Chris Wakling, Rich Harper (who frightened me), Lee Ford (who frightened Andy McNab). Paul Bullivant, photographer. Joe Burt, cover art. To Richard Jones at Tangent for belief and industry. To Bristol and Easton. To God where words begin and run out. To you, dear Reader, for choosing *Dragonfly*.

People to check out: Step Forward Homes & Invisible Wounds; ACH; Alabaré; Crisis Centre Ministries; Second Step; Meanwhile Space; New Economics Foundation; Resonance; The Community Land Trust Network; your nearest Anarchist Bookfair and Credit Union

I am indebted to the writers of many books but a few are: *Attack State Red*, Col. Richard Kemp & Chris Hughes; *Helmand Assault*, Ewen Southby-Tailyour; *Dead Men Risen*, Toby Harnden; *Standing Tall*, Corporal Andy Reid; *The Poetry of the Taliban*, Alex Strick van Linschoten & Felix Kuehn; *Pink Mist*, Owen Sheers; *Even The Dogs*, Jon Mc Gregor; *Walking with God through Pain and Suffering*, Timothy Keller; *Tuntematon Sotilas*, Väinö Linna. Poems by those who served and wrote on scraps of cardboard and T-shirts.

Dante quotations are from the masterful translation by Clive James.

jarimoate.com